LORD OF HEARTS

Lords of the Borders
Book One

Mary Gillgannon

ARE YOU SIGNED UP FOR DRAGONBLADE'S BLOG?

You'll get the latest news and information on exclusive giveaways, exclusive excerpts, coming releases, sales, free books, cover reveals and more.

Check out our complete list of authors, too!

No spam, no junk. That's a promise!

Sign Up Here

www.dragonbladepublishing.com

Dearest Reader;

Thank you for your support of a small press. At Dragonblade Publishing, we strive to bring you the highest quality Historical Romance from the some of the best authors in the business. Without your support, there is no 'us', so we sincerely hope you adore these stories and find some new favorite authors along the way.

Happy Reading!

CEO, Dragonblade Publishing

CHAPTER ONE

Caer Brynfawr, Wales, April 1204

OUTSIDE THE HILLTOP fortress of Caradoc ap Mabon, the wind moaned and the rain swirled in furious gusts. But within the chieftain's wooden keep, his English guests were warmed by steaming roast venison, the finest wine from Aquitaine, and the traditional music and revelry of Welsh hospitality.

Marared, Caradoc's daughter, watched the festivities from the edge of the room, her green eyes narrowed in fury, her body taut with outrage. She could not believe her father's betrayal. How could he have brought the enemy into their home? Everywhere she looked, English knights mingled with her father's warriors and flirted with the female servants.

She despised everything about the enemy, from their fine velvet and sarcanet tunics, to their cropped hair and shaven faces. They reminded her of fat, sleek predators, and she would not be more horrified than if her father had invited a bunch of weasels into the shed where their chickens and geese roosted.

For centuries the *Saeson* had oppressed her people, pushing them deeper and deeper into the mountainous lands of the west, where life was harsh and the weather harsher still. And now they wanted more. They built castles and towns in the traditional borderlands, then sent out troops of knights to guard their stolen domains. It seemed to Marared that the enemy's goal was to conquer and subjugate her people altogether.

"Sister, you look like a sour-faced scold." Her older brother Maelgwn brushed by her and interrupted her bitter thoughts. A drunken grin gleamed beneath his heavy black mustache. He thrust a cup into her hand. "Here, drink up and join the dancing. We've a shortage of women to make up the round."

"Never! I'd sooner cut off my feet than dance with a *Sais!*"

Maelgwn raised a dark brow. "Da wants to arrange a peace treaty with the English. He's tired of spending all our time raiding and fighting."

"Our father is a fool if he thinks he can trust those scheming wretches!" Marared strode off, her plain russet gown swishing as she walked. She'd refused to dress up for their guests and told her father she'd neither converse with the enemy knights, nor act as hostess. Even tolerance was beginning to strain her nerves. She longed to dash out into the furious weather. Anything to get away from her father's folly. But then the *Saeson* would have succeeded in driving her from her home, and she would not give them that victory.

She started toward the kitchen lean-to and on the way, met Aoife, her cousin from Ireland who also lived at Caer Brynfawr. "I can't bear this. I can't endure being in the same room with those conniving, lustful wretches!"

Aoife giggled. "Mayhap you should lower your voice. One of them just passed by seeking the garderobe. You wouldn't want him to hear you. Of course, he likely doesn't speak Cymraeg."

"One of the knights went to the garderobe? Is he in there now?"

Aoife nodded.

A plan formed in Marared's mind. A means of venting her resentment over their unwelcome guests. She smiled at her cousin. "Come."

Outside the garderobe, which was shielded from the hallway by a heavy curtain, Marared paused and winked at Aoife, then spoke in loud Norman French, "Stupid *Sais* bastards! One of them stepped on my gown during the dancing! What clumsy oafs."

"Aye," Aoife answered. "Not only are they clumsy, but ugly. With that short hair they look like shorn sheep and their mustaches are puny things."

"I wouldn't be surprised if other things about them were puny as well." Marared spoke even louder. "In fact, I've heard it said that English knights are hung like field mice."

Aoife made a sputtering noise. There was a sound from the garderobe. Marared and Aoife looked at each other in exhilarated dread.

"And I've heard their ballocks are solid wood," Aoife added. "Just like their heads!"

GERARD OF MALMSBURY, who was finishing his business in the privy, clenched his jaw. He had half a mind to thrust the curtain aside and show his tormentors exactly what sort of equipage *this* English knight possessed!

Perhaps they feared such a confrontation, for he heard more giggling, then the sound of footsteps. Rapidly fastening the drawstring of his braies, he shoved aside the curtain and glanced down the corridor leading to the hall. He saw two young women hurrying off, one with black hair, the other with red-gold tresses. The red-haired wench looked back at him and smiled coyly. His gut tightened. *The little bitch!*

Gerard sought to cool his temper. He would not allow a couple of ill-mannered Welsh wenches to provoke him. Gerard's overlord, Fawkes de Cressy, had charged him with making a treaty with the Welsh chieftain Caradoc, and he no intention of failing in his duty. So far, negotiations had progressed well. Caradoc had agreed not to attack Tangwyl Castle if de Cressy would pay him an annual fee of twenty silver marks and keep his men from raiding in Caradoc's territory.

All well and good. But there was another stipulation the Welsh chieftain proposed that Gerard found unsettling. Caradoc wanted the knight who held Tangwyl Castle to marry his only daughter, Marared. De Cressy had promised if Gerard arranged this treaty and was able to maintain it, he could have the honor of Tangwyl. Which meant he was the one who must wed the Welshwoman.

He had not met her yet, which seemed odd. But perhaps she was too young to join in the festivities. She likely looked like Caradoc, with hair so dark it was almost black, blue eyes, and a short, solid build. He was not averse to a stocky, capable sort of wife. Better than a flighty, saucy one, like the little minxes who had taunted him when he was in the garderobe. He recalled the brief glimpse he'd had of the red-haired wench.

The simplicity of her clothing suggested she was a servant. But no servant would dare such a thing. And how could a serving girl in a Welsh household have learned to speak Norman French? It was a puzzle. But one he didn't have time to solve at this moment.

Gerard made his way to the table where Caradoc was seated. The Welsh chieftain grinned rather drunkenly as Gerard joined him, and Gerard knew a moment of surprise. He'd thought the Welshman too canny to let down his guard. Caradoc shrugged sheepishly and said, "I needed to fortify myself before telling my daughter what I've agreed to."

Caradoc rose unsteadily and started across the crowded hall. Gerard watched his progress with interest, wondering again about the young woman who would soon be his betrothed. His curiosity turned to shock as Caradoc paused by a woman standing at the far end of the hall.

Even from a distance, Gerard could make out the distinctive gleam of her red-gold hair.

"YOU CAN'T DO this! You can't! I won't wed a filthy *Sais!*" Marared stared at her father in despair and outrage. When he'd asked her to meet with him in his private chambers, she'd been surprised. But nothing could have prepared her for his horrifying pronouncement: he'd arranged for her to wed the new lord of Tangwyl Castle. She felt like she'd been hit in the stomach. Nay, she felt like a trapped animal facing the final deadly spear thrust!

"Now, now, Marared, 'tis not such an awful fate. Gerard of Malmsbury is no monster. Indeed, I've been impressed by what I've seen of him. He appears to have fine manners and a steady disposition. He's ambitious, but not overly so. He also appears to be loyal. When I suggested that perhaps the two of us could come to some arrangement beyond the one I was making with de Cressy, he stiffly told me he was de Cressy's man and would do nothing without his approval. I liked that. I also liked—"

"But he's a *Sais*!" Marared interrupted. "How can you want me to marry our enemy?"

Her father shook his head sadly. "Things have changed since you were a little girl and the English burned us out. That's exactly what I'm trying to avoid, more bloodshed and destruction. More suffering for our people. If we ally ourselves with a strong and honorable Marcher lord, we can stop spending all our time fighting and finally prosper."

"There was a time when you'd never have invited the *Saeson* into our home, let alone make an agreement with one of them! You've grown old and cowardly! That's why you're doing this!" Marared dashed tears from her eyes. How could her father have changed so much? How could he betray her?

"Maelgwn agrees with my plan, and he's young enough. He's also the only son I have left. I want a longer, and better, life for him than what his brothers had."

With a sigh, Marared thought of Dewi and Padrig, who had both died as a result of the persistent struggle with the enemy. Dewi had been thrown from a horse during a raid, and Padrig had perished when he got lost in a sudden snowstorm while on patrol.

She drew a shuddering breath. "So, I'm to be the price you pay for peace. Bartered off like some prize horse."

"Nay. Nay." Her father's expression was pleading. "'Twill be better for you as well. You'll live in a fine, comfortable keep and have servants to wait upon you. 'Twill mean a life of ease and security."

"I don't want any of those things! I want to stay here and marry one of my own people. I want to live as Cymric women have since the days of Arthur and the other heroes."

Caradoc set his jaw. "'Tis not a woman's place to choose her own destiny. I'm your father, and that gives me the right to make decisions for you."

Marared stared at him in dismay. Perhaps if

she fell down weeping at his knees, he might reconsider. But it wasn't her nature to wheedle and beg. She squared her shoulders. "When? When am I to wed this English whoreson?"

Her father's mouth twitched at her crude language. "We've discussed late May, when the weather has improved enough for you to travel comfortably."

Marared smiled tightly. "By then, I could be a month gone with another man's babe. A cowherd or shepherd would do nicely."

Caradoc's face reddened and his blue eyes flashed. "You would not do that! You would not shame your blessed mother's memory that way!"

Marared felt her cheeks flush with embarrassment. Her father was right. She'd never be able to follow through on her threat. It would be a denial of everything her mother had taught her. Her beloved Mam had died five years ago of the lung fever and Marared still grieved. She thought now of Catriona's stern admonishments about duty to family and clan. 'Twas clear that defying her father would be terribly disrespectful. Honor demanded she abide by his decision.

Marared forced a tight smile to her lips. "Let us go back into the hall and you can introduce me to him."

GERARD HAD ONCE thought that possessing a castle and being a lord was worth any price. But gazing at his wife-to-be, he wondered if perhaps he had overreached himself. It wasn't merely that this young woman was one of the ill-mannered vixens who had taunted him in the garderobe. Or that she was far from his ideal of a placid, ordinary wife. Nor was it her spectacular beauty that made him wary: her creamy skin, delicate features and wide green eyes as clear as glass. It was the look of contempt and loathing in those green eyes that caused his gut to tighten with apprehension. This woman was not merely displeased with the match, she *hated* him.

"My daughter, Marared," Caradoc announced. Gerard bowed, wondering if he should try to kiss her hand in the manner of the court. Nay, she would snatch away her fingers and embarrass them both, he was certain of it.

"This is Gerard of Malmsbury." Caradoc gestured. "Lord of Tangwyl Castle." He turned to his daughter and grasped one of her hands. After placing her fingers in Gerard's, Caradoc stepped back and announced to the hall, "I've given my daughter to this man, to take to wife and seal the agreement between his liege lord, Fawkes de Cressy, and myself. Heretofore we will be allies, seeking to preserve each other's interests and united against our common enemies."

Gerard could see Marared struggle not to pull

away. As her chest heaved and the nostrils of her dainty nose flared, he was reminded of a terrified filly haltered for the first time. She would take careful handling.

Gerard's body reacted to the thought. She might be a wild hellion, but she also stirred his blood like no woman he'd ever met. She would stir any man's blood. That hair, like a glowing flame. Her supple, curvaceous form, enticing even in the plain gown. She had a face to inspire men to do battle. Although at this moment, it appeared she was ready to do battle with *him*. While Marared's full lips curved sweetly, her green eyes clashed with his like Greek fire exploding against a castle's ramparts.

The fury he saw there alarmed him, but Gerard reassured himself it would all be worth it. For the bastard son of a hired knight, having authority over a fine castle was a dream come true. He must rise to any challenge he faced in order to keep his hard-won prize.

MARARED REGARDED HER soon-to-be husband with narrowed eyes. Gerard of Malmsbury towered over her father by more than a handspan and his chest and shoulders were broad and muscular. He had wary, hooded eyes that gave nothing away and a chiseled jaw. An air of predatory danger clung to him, reminding her of a cat ready to spring.

Marared chewed her lower lip. She'd thought of English knights as loud, loutish and stupid, yet her husband-to-be did not appear to be any of those things. The air of intensity that surrounded Malmsbury unsettled her. He looked as if he would be a ferocious fighter in battle.

Well, she was a fighter, too. And May was weeks away. Much could happen before then. At least some of her father's clients and allies felt must feel as she did, that any bargain with the *Saeson* was a bargain with the devil.

She slipped her hand from Malmsbury's grasp and started to walk away. Her father caught her shoulder and forced her to remain beside him. Addressing the gathering, he said, "We discussed a May wedding, but I see no reason to wait that long." He glanced at Malmsbury. "The weather is such that you'll not want to leave for a day or two anyway. I was thinking of fetching a priest and holding the wedding tomorrow. What say you, Sir Gerard?"

Marared stood stunned. Her father had guessed her mutinous thoughts and intended to forestall them. How did she get out of this?

She looked at Malmsbury, hoping desperately he would refuse her father's suggestion. The knight met her gaze, his expression unreadable.

CHAPTER TWO

GERARD'S MIND RACED. Caradoc's proposal was unexpected. Yet it made sense. Why delay the wedding for weeks and leave part of the treaty unsettled? But despite the clear logic of the plan, he was apprehensive. He'd counted on a little time to get used to the idea of being married. Even so, there was no graceful way to reject Caradoc's suggestion.

He nodded to the chieftain, hoping his smile did not appear as forced and stiff as the rest of him felt.

"A wedding it is, then," Caradoc pronounced.

Gerard spent the rest of the evening in a near daze. There was more drinking and dancing, but he struggled to focus what was going on around him. He was very relieved when it came time to retire. Caradoc offered him the use of the guest bedchamber, but he told the chieftain he'd rather bed down with the rest of his men. He needed time to think. To get used to this startling turn of events.

It was late when he and his rather drunken companions made their way through the gusty, swirling sleet to the barracks. Gerard gradually fell back until he was walking beside Guy de Mortain. When they reached the long, low building, he pulled the knight aside. Guy was the only man accompanying him he could truly call a friend. They'd both served at Valmar Castle for years.

Guy's dark eyes immediately probed his. "You're to be wed to a beautiful Welsh princess. Yet you look as grim as a man planning his own funeral."

"She doesn't want to wed me. Indeed, she called me a filthy *Sais*. I'm not certain what the term means. Englishman. Foreigner. Something like that."

Guy's eyebrows shot up. Then he shrugged. "She's probably as shocked as you were. It appears her father gave no warning of what he intended. Not to mention, she probably expected her wedding to be much different. A grand, festive affair with all her kin in attendance."

"I don't think that's it. I truly believe she despises me."

"How can she despise you? She doesn't know

you. Give her time, she'll come around."

Guy clearly didn't understand why he was distressed. *He* wasn't a bastard. *He* hadn't spent his life being disparaged and ridiculed. Although no one mocked or dismissed Gerard these days. He'd risen high enough that his illegitimate birth didn't matter. Still, the memories of the early years lingered. When he was very young and growing up in the village, it hadn't been so bad. But when he went to serve as a page and then a squire at Valmar Castle, the jeers and jibes from the other boys had been relentless. It had taken years of hard work and dedication to prove himself and silence the taunts. He'd thought he'd moved beyond feeling shame over his heritage. But the sneering remarks he'd overheard in the garderobe had brought it all back.

"You think I should go through with it? Even knowing she's very displeased with the match?"

"Have you a choice? Caradoc made it clear he thinks this is an important part of the agreement with de Cressy. Must be some sort of barbaric Welsh tradition. Bind you to him with a blood bond so you'll think twice about betraying him."

Gerard felt a stab of anger. "De Cressy's offer is an honorable one. That Caradoc insists on this wedding shows a lack of faith in my overlord. We both know Fawkes is a man of his word."

Guy's mouth quirked. "But *Caradoc* doesn't know that. He's used to dealing with his traitorous countrymen, who turn on each other all the time. Not that our race is much better. King John would have happily paid someone to murder his brother so he could claim the throne. You'd think he'd be happy now that's he's got what he wanted. But, nay, he'll never be content until he's gotten revenge on everyone who's ever disparaged him." Guy's expression turned grim.

Gerard didn't want to talk politics. His focus was on his impending marriage. Guy was right. He should be content. Marared ferch Caradoc was beautiful. He'd never dreamed of having a wife so lovely. Yet, if she never unthawed, the marriage would be miserable.

What a foolish thought. Few marriages were love matches. He'd come so far and fulfilled so many of his dreams, he should not let such silly fancies poison his success.

"You're right. 'Tis nothing to worry over." He motioned toward the barracks doorway. "We should get some sleep. 'Twill be another long day tomorrow."

MARARED DUCKED INTO the hall. The sleet on her cloak immediately began to melt. She hung the garment on a pole near the hearth before hurrying past the guests and servants sleeping on benches. Down the corridor, she entered the women's bower. Aoife got up from the bed they shared. Although her brown eyes gleaned with intensity, she spoke quietly, in deference to the other women sleeping in the room. "I'm so glad you're back. I feared you'd done something utterly foolish."

"Such as running away?" Marared also spoke softly. She pulled her clammy gown over her head and smoothed down her shift. "I certainly thought of doing so."

"What stopped you?"

Marared sat down on a stool to remove her boots. "The weather. The fact that there is nowhere I can go without taking my horse and alerting the guards at the gate. And there is the matter that if I run off now, my father would be humiliated."

"So, you're going through with the wedding?"

"I have no choice. I can't defy Da. Not in front of all his clients and allies. I'm trapped, like a coney in a snare." She straightened and then turned so Aoife could brush out her hair. "I'm certain I'll find a way to wriggle free, but it may take a while. In the meantime, I'll be yoked to that wretched *Sais*."

"At least Gerard of Malmsbury is fairly young and not ill-favored."

Marared let out a huff of exasperation. "I

don't care what he looks like. He's the *enemy*."

GERARD STOOD NEXT to his wife-to-be, feeling even more uncomfortable in his blue velvet tunic than he had the night before. Despite breaking his fast with a hearty meal of bread and cold venison, his stomach felt hollow and sour. He'd been glad there had been more meetings with Caradoc and his allies to fill up the day. It had given him something to focus on besides the upcoming wedding.

But now the moment was here. His bride stood rigidly beside him. As the priest prompted her, she repeated her vows in a clear, strong voice, promising to love, obey and honor him. He did the same. Caradoc motioned that it was time for Gerard to give Marared the ring, the family heirloom the chieftain insisted should be part of their vows.

As soon as she saw it, Marared's pale face flushed with color and she jerked back. Caradoc was immediately beside her. "*Cariad bach*, your mother would have wanted you to have it this day."

Gerard held his breath. Marared gradually recovered her composure and held out her hand. Gerard sought to place the ring on her middle finger.

Again, Caradoc intervened. "Nay. It goes on the third finger, the one from which the blood flows directly to the heart."

Gerard did as Caradoc asked, although it seemed absurd. The chieftain might have been in love with his dead wife when he gave her the ring, but there were clearly no such tender feelings binding Gerard with this woman.

The priest pronounced them wed and Gerard leaned to kiss Marared. After a dry, passionless touching of mouths, they drew apart. The icy hostility in her eyes made all his doubts come rushing back. *Blessed Jesu, what had he gotten himself into?*

The rest of the evening passed in a blur. Another extravagant meal. There was more wine as well as mead, the cloyingly sweet drink the Welsh seemed to favor. Caradoc and his allies all toasted them. Then Gerard's men drunkenly took up the duty of honoring the couple.

Gerard pretended to imbibe from the beautiful, enameled cup that Maelgwn, Marared's brother and Caradoc's heir, had forced into his hand, but he actually drank very little. His whole body was tight with tension. He didn't feel like a man who had taken a wife, but a man about to engage in warfare. He must keep his wits about him.

It wasn't long until Caradoc suggested it was

time for the couple to retire. He led them to the back portion of the keep where the guest bedchamber was located. When they reached the door, he looked at Marared. "Do you need one of the women to help you undress?"

"I can manage quite well on my own." She shot Gerard a hostile glance, then opened the heavy oaken door and went in.

Caradoc cleared his throat. "Despite my eagerness for this wedding, I want you to know my daughter is precious to me. If you hurt her in any way, the treaty we've agreed upon will be voided." He glanced up at Gerard, his expression grim in the flickering cresset lights. "If you do any wrong to her, I'll find a way to make you pay. You can be certain of that."

Gerard didn't know whether to be insulted or exasperated. He wanted to tell Caradoc that as far as he was concerned, he was more in need of protection than the man's daughter. For all he knew, his bride might attempt to kill him while he slept. But years of service had taught him diplomacy. He bowed to Caradoc. "I will deal with your daughter as if she is the finest, most valuable gift I've ever received. Indeed, she is certainly the most beautiful one."

Caradoc continued to watch him, blue eyes assessing. Then his host regained his hearty, blustering nature and slapped Gerard hard on the back. "You needn't cosset her too much. Marared is half-Welsh and half-Irish. You won't find a hardier, more resilient bloodline than that."

Gerard did not find this information comforting in the least. The Welsh and Irish races were both famed for their tenacity and bravery in battle.

AS MALMSBURY ENTERED the room, Marared regarded him warily. It was all very well to swear she would never share this man's bed, but now she must defy him face-to-face. He had a legal right to her body. What would he do when she refused to disrobe or let him touch her? Would he strike her? Lay hands on her and force her?

She couldn't help glancing at the tiny white scar that slashed across one of his cheekbones. The mark reminded her that this was a knight, a battle-tested warrior. For all her bold words, there was no way she could best him physically. But if he took her maidenhead by force, she would have reason to hate him all the more. She would never accept this marriage.

After staring at her for long seconds, he finally spoke. "You obviously had no desire for this marriage. I am sorry for that."

Marared felt her eyes widen in surprise. She hadn't expected him to begin this way. "Desire this marriage? Nay, I did not. I had hoped to marry a man of my own people. I certainly did not want to wed a—"

"Stupid *Sais*…whom you believe to be hung like a fieldmouse?"

Despite herself, Marared flushed. It was one thing to taunt an unknown enemy. Another to hear her insults repeated by the man who was now her legal husband.

He smiled, although she doubted he was amused. "I can assure you that I am neither stupid nor poorly endowed. I would be happy to prove it, in fact."

Marared took a step back. "'Twas only a silly jest."

He took two steps nearer, looking very serious and determined. Marared could feel her heart jumping in her chest like a panicked deer. Her mouth went dry.

"Or do you dislike me because I have no mustache and my hair is cropped?" He drew a hand through his short, wavy brown hair. "My hair will grow. I could also stop shaving if I thought such trivial matters were the true source of your animosity."

She didn't know how to respond. Was he suggesting he was willing to change his appearance to please her?

"What else do you despise about me? Did I not hear you also disparage the manners of my countrymen, suggesting we are clumsy, graceless dancers? That may be true. I don't know. I've never learned to dance."

The thought came to Marared that if he did learn, she doubted very much he would be clumsy at it. He struck her as a man who did everything well.

"The fact is, you don't know anything about me. Nor do I know you. Your father took me by surprise. I thought we'd marry a few weeks hence. I expected to have some opportunity to converse with you before..." His gaze raked her body. "...Before we would be intimate."

The bedchamber seemed to have shrunk down to nothing. She was acutely aware of him. Of his maleness. Of the power in his big body. Of the implacable will in his hazel eyes. She took a step back, preparing for the worst.

He watched her, the tension between them building moment by moment. Then his fierce mien softened. "I never expected to take to wife a woman I've scarce said two words to, except for our vows. I could use a little time to get used to the idea of this marriage. I'm willing to propose a truce. For tonight at least."

"A truce?" Her voice was a croak.

"Aye, a truce in this battle you wage with me. I'm willing to put off the bedding...for tonight." He smiled again, faintly. "You'll have to remain in doubt as to my sexual attributes a while longer."

She could not believe what she was hearing. Was it a trick?

"If your father expects us to produce a bloody sheet on the morrow, there are ways to arrange that. We'll keep our agreement a secret. Between you and I alone."

His words suggested an intimate pact between them. Ridiculous. He was her enemy. All they were doing was putting off the inevitable confrontation. In some strange way she was disappointed. She'd geared up for this battle and now it was delayed. "For how long?" she demanded. "How long until you deem it time to consummate the marriage?"

Ten heartbeats passed. "We can't put it off forever. You are clearly old enough for bedding. And there are the legal issues to consider. No matter what we pretend with your father, the marriage is not valid until I...come into your body."

Come into your body. The words evoked a strange, shivery feeling inside her. But that was absurd. She despised this man, for all that he was pleasant to look upon. And not nearly as disagreeable as she'd anticipated. What *was* behind his offer? Was he genuinely trying to be courteous? Or, was it some sort of ruse? Maybe he wanted to ensure the marriage remained invalid so he could escape the agreement with her father. But that made no sense.

She repressed a sigh. Her head ached, and she truly was exhausted. Maintaining her furious rancor took a great deal of effort. "A truce. I'll agree for now, with the final terms to be discussed later." She narrowed her eyes at him, wanting to make certain he knew this was only a temporary lull in the battle. "I'll sleep in the bed, and you may have the floor." She went to the bed, jerked off the thick wool coverlet and threw it at him.

After taking off her slippers, she climbed in bed. A pity she was wearing her best gown; the velvet would probably be ruined by sleeping in it. But she refused to strip down to her linen shift. The thought of sharing a bedchamber with this big, virile stranger was unnerving enough without being half-naked as well. She snuggled down into the remaining blankets and allowed herself to let out a weary breath.

BY THE SAINTS, his wife was a shrew, Gerard thought, as regarded his wife lying in the bed with her face turned away from him. He'd attempted to be gracious and considerate and she'd flung his courtesy in his face, much as she'd tossed him the coverlet. Did she really expect him to sleep on the scratchy, rush-covered floor? He'd endured much worse. But her haughty manner riled him, pricking his pride as the stiff floor rushes would prick his body. He'd given her his word he would not touch her and the bed was more than large enough for two.

Was it that she did not trust him? Or that she loathed him so much she didn't want him near? The thought stung. The few women he'd bedded had seemed to find no fault with his appearance. He could not believe she considered him repulsive. Indeed, she should be pleased she was not married to some balding, fat-bellied old man.

The wench didn't know how good she had it. Not every man would be so understanding. Most would have taken it as their due to bed her. They would not have been put off, even temporarily.

Considering it that way, his decision seemed foolish. The marriage must be consummated to be valid, so why was he taking this risk? Was it because he felt sorry for her? Or did his decision to call a truce stem from the vague fear that if she let loose with her viper tongue, he would find himself provoked into doing something he would regret later? Although he didn't have an especially quick temper, a man could endure only so much.

And how did she perceive his forbearance? Did she scorn him for being weak? A hellcat like her might expect to be forced, and only respect a man who compelled her to do his will. Had he given her cause to think him malleable and weak?

This woman seemed to have gotten the upper hand already, putting him on the defensive. And he had backed down, telling himself he was being kind and courteous.

He went to the bed. "Move over." She turned to look at him, her eyes wary and watchful. "I said we would have a truce. That doesn't mean you can dictate all the terms. The bed can easily accommodate both of us."

She heaved a huge sigh and made a great show of moving to the other side of the bed. Gerard tried to decide how much to disrobe. She was still fully clothed. If he stripped down to his braies, it might make her think he meant renege on their bargain and force himself on her in the night.

He removed his boots, but left on his remaining garments. His court tunic was heavy and the braid adorning it thick and scratchy, but with only the wool coverlet she'd allowed him, he might well get cold in the night if he took it off. The way she'd gathered all the other bedding around her made it clear she didn't mean to share. He picked up the coverlet, climbed into bed and spread the blanket over him.

As soon as he closed his eyes, he saw Marared as she'd appeared the day before. The enticing curves the thin wool of her gown had revealed. The grace with which she moved. He thought of her wavy, red-gold hair, like a gleaming sunset reflected in a turbulent river. How her creamy skin would feel like the finest silk beneath his fingers. He thought of her taunting rosy mouth, which seemed to demand to be silenced with deep, probing kisses.

A shudder of pure lust swept through him, and he wondered why he was obsessing over a woman. Normally, he thought little of the charms of the fairer sex. He always had more important things to focus on. Acquitting himself well as a squire and then as a knight. Doing his duty and impressing his overlord.

Why did this woman entice him so strongly? Was it because he knew she was *his*, and he had every right to bed her? Or was it because she was so fiery, so fierce, so like an enemy to be conquered? There would be an undeniable thrill in making such a woman sigh and moan with pleasure.

He reminded himself that so far, she'd shown no sign of letting him get close enough to indulge such fancies. Did she hate him simply because he was English? Or did she have something else against him? He wondered if she'd discovered he was a bastard. The lack of a more formal name than *Gerard of Malmsbury* might reveal the embarrassing circumstances of his birth.

The thought made him angry. Then melancholy. But neither emotion did anything to tamp down his arousal. He must find some way to distract himself. To get the beguiling woman beside him completely off his mind.

He took a deep breath and began to consider the improvements he planned for Tangwyl Castle.

HE WAS ASLEEP—THE wretch! Marared shifted on the bed, her body tight with resentment. As tired as she was, slumber eluded her. But her husband had no difficulty. She could hear his slow, even breathing.

Prick! Dolt! Lackwit! She mentally threw at him the slurs she'd heard her father's knights use when angry. Hatred rose up inside her like the incoming tide. He slept on, unaware.

She had to stop thinking about him. Forget his presence in the room altogether. Otherwise, she'd never sleep.

But sleeping was the least of her worries. Her life was changed forever. The ring on her finger was a reminder of how she was bound to him. She twisted it around, feeling the smooth shape of the large cabochon emerald. Her mother's ring. Now hers.

She recalled the feel of his hands as he placed the ring on her finger. Hard, callused hands, the hands of a fighting man. Yet, he had been gentle enough. Indeed, she'd been surprised by his graceful, courteous manner. He was not the crude beast she'd anticipated.

If she allowed herself to admit it, he was actually quite attractive. Brown hair, but not as dark as a Cymro's, cropped in the English style. Unusual eyes. At first she'd thought them light brown, but there was a touch of amber and perhaps even green in them as well. She recalled how the skin around them crinkled when he smiled.

Not a young man. He was thirty if he was a day. Perhaps that's what lended him an air of quiet authority. That was her sense of him, like a still, deep pool. She was used to her boastful, merry, hot-tempered countrymen, and his subdued demeanor unsettled her. What would it take to provoke him? Some part of her would be compelled to find out.

A faint smile crossed her lips. Aye, she meant to test her husband, drive him to his wit's end. They would see how calm and unruffled he was when she told him that she *never* meant to allow him to share her bed.

Savoring the thought, she settled back against the soft sheepskins padding the straw mattress.

CHAPTER THREE

TWO DAYS LATER the weather cleared, and they left Caer Brynfawr. As they set off down the trackway, a lump rose in Marared's throat. She glanced around at the steep hills, dark with pine and gorse. How she loved this place. She would miss every rock, every little rill and runlet of water trickling musically down the slopes. Every tree and bush. The graceful gyrfalcons and merlins soaring on the air currents above them. The *Saeson* might scorn this place as desolate wasteland, but it was her home, the place where her heart lay. Glancing up at the silvery overcast sky, she made a silent vow. *I will return. My children will be born here, I swear it.*

As if sensing her defiant thoughts, Malmsbury guided his chestnut destrier slightly closer to her pale gray palfrey. At least she was riding her beloved Gwenevere. The mare was not only beautiful, but swift and responsive. Traveling into enemy territory, it would be good to have a quick means of escape.

"Have you ever been away from your home before?" Malmsbury's question, spoken in his deep, quiet voice, aroused Marared's ire. He was trying to make conversation, to put her at ease and make her forget they were enemies. Well, it would not work.

"Aye. I've been to Ireland several times."

"Do you have family there?"

"My mother's kin."

"Is that where you learned to speak Norman French?"

She looked at him coldly. "You needn't try to make conversation. I'm not a child who requires entertaining."

He raised his brows. "While I'll admit I was committing the grievous sin of trying to distract you from the pain of leaving your family, I was also thinking of myself. It's a long day's ride to Tangwyl. I thought it might be pleasant to converse along the way."

She shot him an incredulous look. Did he not understand? She had no desire to share anything of herself with him.

He glanced at the landscape around them. "I know many men who dislike Wales. But I've always thought this land has a kind of fierce beauty. It's so wild and untamed." He looked at her pointedly. "So exhilarating."

Was he implying he enjoyed the challenge of their marriage? The fool!

But despite her resentment, she kept silent. She must not reveal herself too openly. If she was going to win this war, she must be clever and not give in to her temper and speak imprudently.

"This place tests a man. Forces him to dig deep inside himself and discover how badly he wants to prevail." Again, he looked at her. His message could hardly be clearer.

"Are you telling me the truce is over?"

"I was speaking about the land. Besides, I now think that comparing things between us to a battle was a poor decision. I should have chosen my words with more care. In fact, we don't know each other well enough to be enemies."

"Is that so?"

He nodded. "You may think we're on opposite sides of some sort of conflict, but that's not enough to make us foes. True adversaries feel a passionate hatred for each other. Such extremes of emotion take time to develop. We've only just met."

He was wrong. She *was* capable of hating him, even if she didn't know him. He was a *Sais*. Nothing else was required to make her loathe him.

"Besides, your father and I are allies, so that

should make us allies as well." He smiled. "I'm sure we want the same thing—peace between our peoples. Perhaps you and I simply need to start over. If you will try to overlook the coercive aspects of our marriage, I will overlook your rash insults of me and the rest of my countrymen. We could pretend we're meeting for the first time."

She found his suggestion preposterous, but she dare not say so. Let him think she was willing to give him a chance. Aye, that would be the best course. Lull him into complacency. "Very well. We've only met. Now what?"

"You should tell me about yourself, and I'll do the same. I believe that's the way it's done in a normal courtship."

She felt her smile sour. This was not what she had in mind, this subtle game of wits. "What shall we talk about?"

"You mentioned Ireland. I've never been there. Perhaps you could tell me a bit about it."

Ireland. It seemed a safe subject. "I've visited there several times. My mother's family holds land in the southwest." She took a breath, remembering. "'Tis a gentle place compared to Wales. The colors of the landscape are mellow and soft. The contours of the land flowing and graceful. There the mist kisses your skin instead of flailing it with dampness and cold."

"What are the people like?"

"Not so different than the people here, the

Cymry." She used the word pointedly. Welsh was the English term for her race, and Wales their name for her country. To her, the name for her people would always be Cymry, and the term for her country, Cymru. "Like us, the Irish are independent and proud. Brave and loyal. And yet, if they suffer insult or injury, they never forget it. They will have vengeance, no matter how long it takes." She looked at him as she said this. It was foolish to let him know the depths of her animosity, but she could not help herself.

His face wore a slight smile. She knew that lustful, hungry expression. How many men had looked at her that way when her father's attention was diverted? But there was a difference, a cold flutter in her stomach reminded her. This man had her father's blessing to do what he wished with her.

How could Da have agreed to this? Selling her off to buy a season or two of peace? Did he not know that no matter what alliances he made with the English, they wouldn't last? Her father might accept a truce, but other men would not. She considered the few large landowners and important clients who had not been at the meeting with Malmsbury. Men like her cousin Rhys. His father, Cynan, her Da's brother, had never stopped fighting the English until the day he died. Neither would Rhys.

But that did her no good now. She was wed

to this man, bound to him by law. How was she to endure it? And how did she remain true to her people and survive in the meantime? Her husband was currently acting the role of gracious courtier. But over time he would tire of trying to win her over with fine manners and consideration. Then, what would he do? For all her bold words, she was afraid of Gerard of Malmsbury. She sensed ruthless ambition in those cool, wary eyes. An implacable will driving his lean, powerful body. He was not an enemy to take lightly.

She wished she'd had Aoife come along. Her cousin had offered, but she'd told her there was no point dragging someone else into this mess. Besides she knew Aoife didn't want to leave Caer Brynfawr. Aoife still yearned after Rory, an Irish warrior who had been sent to serve at Caer Brynfawr as part of the long ago agreement between Marared's mother's family and her father's. Marared had her doubts that Rory would ever show any interest in Aoife. Even if he did, it would probably not last. Rory always struck her as the sort of man who was only interested in the pursuit.

At the time, it had been easy to refuse Aoife's offer. But now Marared realized how alone she was. As part of the agreement, several of her father's men were traveling with them to join the garrison at Tangwyl, while several of Malmbury's knights remained at Caer Brynfawr. But her father's men would not intervene in matters between her and her husband unless they thought he was mistreating her. And this man was too clever to ever appear anything but courteous and honorable. He hid his scheming, devious nature very well. And yet, it must be there. He was a *Sais*.

At least he'd given up trying to converse. There was a kind of victory in that, but a very shallow one. He might well ignore her until they reached Tangwyl, but at some point, it would be time to retire. Then they would have to negotiate their arrangement once more. Alone with him in a bedchamber in his own castle, she would not be in a position of power.

The hills grew less steep, the budding bushes and underbrush more profuse. They were leaving the highlands. Soon they would be in enemy territory. A sense of foreboding tightened like a band around her chest. She'd visited the lands to the east of her father's when she was a little girl. Her memories were of thick forests giving way to rolling pastureland and rivers that flowed lazily through gold-green meadows. A gentler world, much as she'd described Ireland. But even Ireland had the influence of the sea with its restless, unpredictable nature. Here everything seemed peaceful and mellow. It already felt warmer.

She used one hand to loosen the hood of the

heavy, fur-lined mantle she wore. In the lower lands of the English, she would feel oppressed and trapped. Which she was. She was bound to the straight-backed, enigmatic knight riding next to her. Most men would have taken her maidenhead, or at least tried to do so. This man had appeared willing to wait, at least for a time.

But how much longer would he forgo the bedding? As he'd said, there was the validity of the marriage to consider. Not to mention the way he looked at her. Nay, he would not wait forever. Only until he got her alone in *his* stronghold, surrounded by *his* people. Then, when she was helpless and alone, he would force her to give in to him.

Little arrowpoints of fear pricked her belly. At the same time, part of her wanted to get the confrontation over with. The waiting was tying her in knots.

WHAT A CONTRARY woman his wife was, Gerard thought as he rode beside her. She was doing her best to make it clear she did not accept this marriage and never would. Well, he was more than a little stubborn himself. She implied he would never win her regard. Perhaps not. But he would not stop trying. So far, he had defied all predictions and expectations for his life. He had reached his goals by working steadily and relentlessly, outlasting all his enemies and detractors.

He glanced again at Marared. She had proclaimed herself his adversary, but by the saints, what a stirring, compelling one she was. His body was tantalized with the thought of what it would be like to make this conquest. She was all fire and ice. Hair aflame and cool white skin. Eyes like a cat's. That mouth. Jesu!

Perhaps he should try talking to her again. But so far that had yielded little, except proof of her continued animosity. Perhaps it would be better to leave her alone and see if her anger cooled. With that thought in mind, he urged his destrier ahead of her mount.

His mood improved as they rode down a slope and gazed at the gleaming gray stone of Tangwyl Castle in the distance. This was a prize worth nearly any price. Even being wed to a woman who loathed him.

But he would change that. After all, it was not *him* she hated, but who she *thought* he was. He would prove to her that he was different than the English knights she had known before. Not some ill-mannered, contemptible brute, but a man who respected women and treated them with courtesy and consideration. In addition, he would make it clear what he was offering her—a comfortable and luxurious life, and the kind of security most women could only dream of. He let his mount drop back beside Marared's. "What think you?"

She shrugged, her lovely face set in a contemptuous frown. "I've seen several castles in my lifetime."

"Tangwyl has many advantages. The river guards it on two sides, and the steep defile behind makes it difficult for a large force to launch an offensive."

She shrugged again, obviously uninterested. He reminded himself that she was a woman, so it was normal for her to be unconcerned with battle logistics. "The castle also has many amenities. I recently put glass windows in the solar, so you will have good light for sewing without shivering in the winter air. And all the walls were lime-washed and the rushes replaced last fall. I think you will find it quite comfortable."

He observed no spark of interest in her eyes, but he pressed on. "We've had a good harvest and there's plenty of food in the cellars and storage sheds. Also an excellent sheep clip. This area is renowned for the fine woolen cloth our weaving women produce. We can't compete with the Flemish imports yet, but we sell a great deal in London. Perhaps I could take you with me sometime when I visit the court."

She gazed at him with an incredulous expression. He wondered if she felt overawed at the idea of visiting John's court. "If we went to London, I would make certain you had clothing that would show off your beauty. Although I know little of women's fashions, I'm sure my overlord's wife, Nicola de Cressy, could assist you in selecting fabrics and designs."

"You're jesting, aren't you?" She looked like a cat about to spit. "You really think I'd go to London? I'd rather enter a wild beast's den than that wretched *Saeson* cesspool!"

Gerard was taken aback. Every woman he'd ever known would have been delighted to be offered a new wardrobe and the chance to visit London. What sort of untamed hoyden had he wed? Clearly the way to this woman's heart was not with luxury items and extravagant gifts. What the devil *would* tempt her?

The familiar sense of frustration crept back, and he cursed Caradoc for his haste in seeing them wed. Because of the Welsh chieftain's impatience, he'd had no opportunity to get to know his bride. He considered that the reason Caradoc rushed the wedding was he hadn't wanted him to discover Marared's true nature. Perhaps the Welshman feared Gerard would back out of the treaty at the thought of spending the rest of his life wed to such a shrew.

But even if he had known about his new wife's waspish temperament, he would have still gone through with the marriage. If it came down to it, he would give up his life for the sake of Tangwyl. The satisfaction of holding such an impressive castle was worth any price.

His jaw tightened with determination. He'd come so far and endured so much. Even after all these years, he could still hear the taunts and insults: *Bastard! Worthless whore's son!* His father's legitimate children had hated him and never missed an opportunity to ridicule him and make him aware of his inferior status. Thankfully, his father had seen fit to place him as a page at Mordeaux, far away from his half-siblings in the east.

But even there he'd struggled with the handicap of his birth, because he trained alongside boys who were surer of their position in society. Once they found out he was his father's by-blow and not his heir, they had teased him relentlessly and made him the butt of their jests. He'd had to wait until he was big enough and fierce enough to defend himself to finally silence his tormentors.

But that was only the beginning. The next step was to earn his spurs as a knight and prove himself worthy of a position in Mortimer's garrison. Then Fawkes de Cressy had killed Mortimer and seized Mordeaux, and he felt like he was starting all over again. It had taken another seven years to gain his commander's notice and convince de Cressy he deserved more responsibility. But he had done it, working tirelessly to perform his duties with discretion and efficiency, until it became natural for de Cressy to entrust him with more and more until putting him in charge of this strategic keep.

He'd finally reached this pinnacle of his ambition, and Tangwyl was his to rule. But to keep it, he had to find a way to deal with this maddening woman.

He wished he'd had more experience with the fairer sex. There'd never been time for dalliances. Like most men, he'd satisfied his needs with whores, but this woman was not some wench who serviced rough soldiers. She was a noblewoman, and one who'd clearly been indulged all her life.

He thought of the only other *lady* he'd really known. Nicola de Cressy was nothing like Marared. Rather than being fiery, she was the epitome of cool elegance. Even when she was wroth, her manners were impeccable. He could not imagine her ever insulting a guest in her home or openly displaying animosity to anyone. His overlord's wife and Marared were very different. This woman seemed passionate and impulsive, rather than composed and regal.

The heedlessness of Marared's nature probably came from her upbringing. She'd never had any reason to learn to guard her tongue and dissemble. She'd grown up protected and cosseted, with the assurance of a safe, comfortable future. She had no idea how cruel and harsh life was for most people.

It startled him to think how little they had in common. He thought constantly of the consequences of his actions, always focusing on the future, rather than what was happening at the moment. To be wed to this impetuous woman felt like being tied to a whirlwind. Somehow, they must reach some sort of agreement. He didn't want to have to be on his guard in his own home. He must get her to accept him and this marriage.

He turned to look at her. Marared had thrown back the hood of her mantle, revealing hair as bright as polished bronze. The rich color of her tresses set off her pale face and made her green eyes gleam like jewels. Combined with her pert nose and full rosy mouth, the effect was breathtaking. Heat immediately filled his groin at the thought of finally sharing a bed with her and possessing her beautiful body. He had every reason in the world to consummate the marriage. Every reason.

But how to go about it? How should he initiate lovemaking with a woman who was as prickly as hedgehog? He'd never had a virgin before, but he knew they must be readied. Unless great care was taken, she might experience pain during penetration. Then she would really hate him.

A band of apprehension tightened around his chest. Nothing in his life had prepared him for this. It was like meeting his deadliest enemy, but instead of seeking to defeat them in battle, he had to charm and cajole his foe to agree to terms. What weapons were appropriate in this situation? He'd tried pleasant words and expressing concern for her welfare. But she appeared angered by his every attempt to please her.

Maybe he should fight fire with fire. Perhaps she only understood coercion. That must be how Caradoc dealt with her. He should have asked the Welsh chieftain's advice for dealing with his daughter when he'd the chance.

As they started down the trackway to the drawbridge, Gerard made his decision. They were entering his realm and it was time he enforced his will upon his wife. He would not be cruel, but he would be firm. He was her husband; she must accept that.

CHAPTER FOUR

MARARED SUPPRESSED A shiver of foreboding as they neared Tangwyl. She'd lied to Malmsbury. The castle *was* impressive. Formidable walls of gray stonework, crested with the jagged teeth of the towers, loomed up from the river valley. Compared to Caer Brynfawr's low, wooden walls and sprawl of dwellings and storage buildings, this place seemed overwhelming. She wanted to turn her horse around and gallop back to the mountains.

But there was a whole troop of knights behind her, blocking her way. She could only go forward, into the menacing maw of the castle entrance, the portcullis gate like huge jaws ready to snap shut behind her.

Malmsbury glanced back at her. She told herself to breathe deeply and steadily so he would not guess her fear. If she maintained a defiant façade, he might decide she was too much trouble and leave her alone.

Either that, or he might demand his rights with brutal force. She felt both dread and relief at the thought of being raped. Dread for the pain and humiliation. Relief at the thought it would make her hatred of him even fiercer and more unquenchable. As it was, although she despised him for being a *Sais*, she couldn't quite hate him as a man. He'd done nothing to arouse her personal animosity. Perhaps he was right and true enemies had to have something personal between them. Mayhaps being from different races wasn't enough.

They clattered across the drawbridge and entered the bailey of the castle. Ostlers and squires came forward to take their mounts. A boyish, fair-haired youth helped Marared off her mare. She wondered if he had Saxon blood. Their race had also been terribly oppressed, yet they had learned to live with their conquerors. Perhaps that was because the Saxons were not that different from the men of William the Bastard, the brutal knight who had led his army across Britain near two centuries ago.

The Saxons were farmers and lived in lowland settlements, while the Cymry primarily grazed livestock and hunted. And the Saxons were obviously not as bold and proud as her people either. Otherwise they would never have given in.

Malmsbury approached. "Aubrey, take milady to the solar." He motioned to the young man who had helped her off the horse. "Then fetch Hilda and tell her to make certain my wife has whatever she requires."

At the word *wife*, the youth jerked around to stare at Marared. His expression of surprise made it clear the household hadn't known their lord was to be wed. Young Aubrey quickly recovered himself and bowed. "Milady, if you would follow me."

He led her into the castle, and Marared had a glimpse of a vast hall filled with trestle tables as she followed Aubrey to a stairwell. They climbed and climbed, finally reaching the level where the solar was. Once there, Marared had to suppress a gasp of pleasure. This place was nothing like the drafty living quarters of her uncle's keep in Ireland. It was almost cozy, with sheepskin coverings on the floor, bright tapestries on the walls and a variety of cushioned stools and benches for sitting.

And light, glorious light. Four windows along one side let in the pale daylight, while their greenish glass glazing kept the cold and damp out.

"Lady." Aubrey bowed again. "I'll fetch Hilda to serve you."

As soon as the young servant left, Marared began to explore. On one end of the large room, there was a heavy damask curtain. Pulling it aside, she beheld a great bed. She swallowed hard. This was obviously where the lord of the castle slept. And where she would be expected to yield her body to his. The size of the bed intimidated her, reminding her of the tall knight she would share it with.

She jerked the curtain back in place and paced around the rest of the room.

"YEA, MY LORD. She's settling in. I helped her wash and change her clothing, then had food sent up." A smile brightened Hilda's lined face. "'Twill be good to have a new mistress here, and a young and lively one as well."

"Was she…did she seem content?" He worried Marared had already revealed her animosity. It would be embarrassing to have the whole castle know his wife had been forced to wed him.

"She was very quiet, as if caught up in her own thoughts. No doubt she is homesick." Hilda clucked sympathetically. "Must be hard for her to leave her home to live among strangers. At least she speaks our language. 'Twould be miserable for her if she did not."

Gerard silently breathed a sigh of relief. Marared could not have behaved too badly or Hilda would not be so sympathetic. Perhaps now that Marared was here and faced with the reality of her circumstances, she would come to terms with the marriage.

He asked Hilda to have bread, cheese and pottage brought to him in the hall. After eating, he went to the bathing shed and removed his garments, including the heavy hauberk he'd worn on the journey. He washed quickly in the tub of water servants had heated for him. Lady de Cressy set great store by bathing, so it seemed like a good idea to be scrupulously clean when he went to his bride. He didn't want to give her any reason to shun him. That she thought he was a *filthy Sais* was bad enough.

He dressed in a loose tunic and braies climbed the stairs to the solar. He'd thought she might be in bed. It was well past vespers and they'd made a long journey. But when he entered, she was seated on the window seat, staring out at the twilight sky. She rose as she heard his footsteps and turned to face him.

She was clad in her shift, with a heavy woolen shawl wrapped around her upper body. Gerard guessed she was not so much cold as she was trying to keep the thin linen garment from being too revealing. Well, he'd have it off her soon enough. She could not hide her body from him. She was his wife.

Her stance was wary, like an animal poised for flight. Her face, nearly expressionless. He remembered his resolve to be firm. She would not refuse him this night.

"Milady. I think it's time for bed." He nodded toward the curtained area.

She raised her chin. "I'll not sleep with you. Find me another chamber or fetch a pallet so I can bed down on the floor." She glanced around the room. "Or, even a blanket. I could curl up on one of the benches."

"We are man and wife. 'Tis right and proper that we share a bed. At Caer Brynfawr, I offered you reprieve because we had scarce met. But you've rebuffed all my attempts at conversation, so we will have to proceed even though we are as yet still strangers. I promise I'll be patient and gentle. There is nothing to fear."

"You think I'm afraid!" In the candlelight, her eyes seemed to throw off green sparks. "'Tis not fear that makes me refuse you. I'm simply not willing to offer my body to my enemy."

Gerard went rigid. This was not going to be as easy as he'd hoped. "You made vows before a priest and dozens of witnesses. One of those vows was to obey me."

"What else could I have done under the circumstances? I had no choice."

Gerard forced his voice to calmness. "It

doesn't matter why you wed me. The thing is done. You can't change your mind now."

"Truly?" Her tone was dangerous. "What will you do? Force me?"

He took a step nearer, trying to intimidate her. "'Tis my right."

She raised her chin. "Seize me, then. Throw me on the floor, or the bed, or wherever it pleases you. I'll fight you." She smiled. "I grew up with three brothers. I know a trick or two."

Dear God, what had he gotten into? The idea of grappling with a woman was utterly foreign. All he could think of was how easy it would be to hurt her, and his mind recoiled. "Why are you doing this? You know you can't prevail. Even with a weapon, you're no match for me."

"It doesn't matter if I win. My goal is to keep my pride intact. I'll not willingly surrender my maidenhead to my enemy."

"We're not enemies. Your father and I have an agreement. You can't hate me simply because I'm English. Such reasoning is childish. Witless." He was losing patience. What did she hope to accomplish? Did she mean to provoke him into raping her so she could justify her dislike of him?

"Ah, so now you insult me. How typical of your kind."

"I've also complimented you, treated you with courtesy, afforded you every comfort." He gestured to the cozy, well-appointed room.

"I'll not change my mind. You can't tempt me with gifts and empty flattery."

He closed his eyes for a moment, seeking to tamp down his burgeoning frustration. What did he do now? He'd vowed not to back down.

He opened his eyes and lunged. Her response was quick, but not quick enough. He grabbed her by the arms. She flailed and jerked, but could not break free. He held her tightly, thinking he'd never been this close to her before, except for the brief kiss that sealed their marriage ceremony. With her face mere inches away, he was acutely aware of the flush of blood beneath her milky skin, the throb of the pulse in her throat, the tempting softness of her lips, parted to reveal white, even teeth. Jesu, he'd never had a woman half this lovely!

He leaned forward to kiss her. As his mouth brushed hers, he felt her teeth and reared back. "By the Cross! You b—" He stopped before the insult escaped his lips.

"Go on. Call me names. As if they could hurt me."

"I don't want to hurt you."

"Then leave me be!"

"I can't do that. You know as well as I this marriage must be consummated."

"Then, force me. 'Tis the only way you'll get what you wish."

She's right. And that's what she wants. He

vaguely remembered overhearing some knight talking about his lover and how she liked it rough. Maybe Marared was the same. Although how could she know what sort of lovemaking she preferred? Unless she wasn't a virgin. What if she'd lost her maidenhead previously and hoped that if he raped her, he would be too caught up in the struggle to notice her lack of a maidenhead?

Something inside went him dark and cold at the thought. She was his! And he would have her!

He tightened his grip and dragged her toward the bed. She flailed and fought. Once past the curtain, he dumped her on the silk coverlet, then immediately climbed up to straddle her. Forcing her wrists over her head, he glared down at his bride. The shawl was long gone and the thin fabric of her shift stretched taut against her body, revealing the soft contours of her breasts. His shaft was rock hard beneath his braies. Her scent was sweet, provocatively female. That, and the potent eroticism of her nearness, threatened to undo him.

But there were awkward details to overcome. He'd have to release one of her wrists to pull down his braies and pull up her shift. And he really wanted to have the garment all the way off of her, so he could see her naked. He desired no quick, thoughtless tumble, but to love her at his leisure. To caress her soft skin and explore the graceful curves that so intrigued him. To kiss not only that bedeviling mouth, but the rest of her body. To taste the honeyed essence of her skin. Suckle her breasts…

Abruptly, she began to thrash. All his heated imaginings were futile. This first time he would have to enter her quickly and get it over with. Later, when she was resigned to her circumstances, perhaps he could attempt seduction.

He finally forced her to stillness by using his weight to stop her desperate movements. Now he could feel the full length of her soft, supple body pressed against his, and it was nearly unbearable. His heated flesh screamed for release. "Please stop struggling. I don't want to hurt you."

"Of course you do, you puling whoreson! You're an animal like the rest of them! A crude beast!"

She was striking out this way because it was the only weapon she had left. He'd overpowered her, and now she was desperate. Why wouldn't she give in? What sort of unholy determination drove her? If she were a man, he would admire her for being so tenacious. But under the circumstances, her behavior seemed absurd. She couldn't win, so why wouldn't she give up?

Maybe it was a matter of pride. She might think giving in was shameful and cowardly. "Marared. I want you to know, if you surrender to me, I won't think less of you. You've fought a good fight. Behaved as fiercely and valiantly as any warrior. No one can fault you for being weak."

"As if I cared what you think! As if I *desire* your regard!" The pupils of her eyes were huge. Her nostrils flared. Her fair skin flushed. Despite her fury, he'd never seen a woman so beautiful, so enticing. All that fire. To bed her would be like riding a river of flame.

But there was still the problem of getting their clothing out of the way. And even then, he couldn't simply thrust into her. That would be too brutal. He would have to ready her. Coax her body into yielding, even if her stubborn spirit would not. But how could he do that when he needed both hands to hold her down?

He considered tying her to the bed. But that reminded him of trussing up an animal. He could not subject her to that.

MARARED COULD FEEL her muscles growing fatigued from resisting. Why didn't he get on with it?

She could feel the hard weight of his body. The sensation of having him on top of her actually felt quite good. It made her want to squirm and rub up against him. He would think she was struggling, but actually she would be enjoying the pressure of his body against hers.

She could not want that. She hated this man.

It was only that he was so very near. She'd never observed a man this closely before. She could see the individual hairs of his whiskers. Rough dark stubble against the tanned skin of his jaw. Although she would never admit it, she liked that he did not have a beard or mustache. She could see his mouth and its shape intrigued her. It appeared both hard and soft at the same time.

And his eyes. In some lights they seemed amber. In others, gray. Right now they were a light shade of green, with a wheel of smoky gold in the center. His eyelashes were surprisingly long. His brows had an elegant arch. It was the narrowness of his face and the hard look of his jaw that made his features seem so harsh and formidable.

If he tried again to kiss her, she would only fight a little. And she would not bite this time…at least not very hard. Oh, how she wished he would get on with it! This was torture.

Slowly, he raised himself, although he still gripped her wrists. He would have to let go to pull up her shift. Then she would struggle…but only enough to make him think she was still fighting him.

He released her and rolled on his back. Marared was startled. Was he giving up? Had she truly won? He blew out the lamp on a table by the bed, then lay back and closed his eyes. "Climb under the covers."

When she didn't move, he got out of bed, drew off his tunic and dropped it to the floor, He blew out the night candle on the table and climbed in bed. "Get under the covers. It grows cold."

She considered saying she would sleep on the floor rather than share a bed with him. But the stone floor, even with sheepskin rugs, would not be very comfortable. She wriggled her way under the coverlet, keeping a good distance from him. Staring up at the ceiling, she wondered how she would ever sleep.

He turned on his side, facing away. "'Tis is only a continuation of our truce. The battle resumes tomorrow."

CHAPTER FIVE

AS HE PRETENDED to sleep, Gerard wondered
if he was a coward. But what else could he
have done? They'd reached a stalemate. Under
such circumstances, a wise commander retreated.
He didn't want to force her. If he raped her, she
would have won. He would have shown himself
to be exactly what she accused him of being—
crude and cruel. There had to be another way.
Mayhaps he could slowly wear her down. Give
her time to grow used to him and to her new
circumstances, then try again.

But how was he to endure in the meantime?
He was unbearably aroused. His lawful wife lay
beside him, clad only in a thin linen shift, and he
could not touch her. She was so beautiful, so
passionate and fiery. When she did finally allow
him to take her maidenhead, their coupling

would likely set the bed linens ablaze.

That is, if she ever gave in to him.

But of course she would. He'd endured much worse tests of his resolve. This situation, frustrating though it might be, was only temporary. He would prevail. All his instincts told him his wife was actually quite innocent. He would use her naivete to his advantage. He would be subtle and cunning. And patient. Patience—he'd always had plenty of that.

He took a deep breath, trying to relax and free himself from the maddening tension wracking his body. 'Twas only a matter of time, and then he would possess everything he desired. Not only Tangwyl, but the enticing woman who came with it.

MARARED GAZED UNSEEINGLY into the darkness. Was it simply a matter of standing her ground and he would give up? Nay, her adversary's retreat was only temporary. He'd already prevailed in one way. She was sharing a bed with him, something she'd vowed earlier she would not do.

But there was nowhere else she could sleep. If she got up and tried to take one of the blankets to bed down on the floor, he might grab her and start tussling. Her wrists already ached from resisting his iron-like grip.

Although he'd won that battle, it didn't matter. He would never have the victory he sought; she would never lie willingly beneath him.

The thought aroused strange feelings inside her. Having his body pressed against hers had been…interesting. She could not truthfully say she had disliked it. But it was a far cry from being deflowered. She knew the first time was supposed to hurt. That was another motivation to fight him.

But there were other things men and women did together that intrigued her. Kissing, for example. What would it feel like to have her husband's well-shaped lips pressed against hers? Not in a dry ceremonial kiss like the one at their wedding, but a real one?

Stop it! You can't have thoughts like that! He's your enemy! It bothered her that she had to keep reminding herself how much she hated him. She was already growing used to this man. Here she was, lying inches away from him, as if they had not grappled violently earlier. She'd meant to bite him or knee him in the groin or hurt him in some fashion. But she hadn't managed to do so. He was stronger—and cleverer—than she'd expected.

Of course, she hadn't engaged in physical conflict for years. Not since she was a young girl wrestling with her brothers. They'd stopped before she reached womanhood, saying they didn't want to hurt her. She'd scoffed at them, but it was probably true; they could have injured her. And this man possessed even greater strength and experience than her youthful brothers. He could easily force her against her will.

But he hadn't. And she had the uneasy sense it was because he didn't *want* to hurt her. Could it be possible he wasn't a crude brute like the English were supposed to be? Nay, she could not accept that. It made everything too difficult and confusing. More likely he had some other scheme in mind.

Or, it could be he didn't think bedding her was worth the trouble. He was obviously a practical man. And he had what he really wanted—Tangwyl. The challenge of conquering his wife was clearly secondary. He'd said the marriage must be consummated to be valid, but who would protest if it was not? Certainly not her father.

Raising her head, Marared risked a quick glance at the man in bed beside her. He lay facing the wall and had not moved in a long while. She felt a twinge of anger at the thought he was asleep. A part of her wanted him to keep struggling with her. It had been exhilarating to match her strength against his. To feel his hard, muscular form pressing her down on the bed.

What if he never touched her again?

The thought didn't inspire the sense of relief she expected. Indeed, she felt almost disappointed. A part of her wanted him to persist in fighting her. Such a man she could admire, even if she also hated him.

THIS WAS MISERABLE. Lying beside Marared, he felt tormented by arousal and longing. If he wasn't going to get satisfaction, he must find somewhere else to take his rest. There was another bedchamber, but it was on the other side of the keep. And if he slept there, the whole castle would learn of it. He must think of another plan.

He thought of the two chairs in the solar. If he pushed them together, maybe he could bed down across the seats. Nay, he was too tall. It would have to be the floor. But he would need at least one of the blankets. The room was definitely chilly. He should have had someone light the brazier before they came to bed, for her comfort if nothing else. But he wasn't used to having a wife.

He repressed a sigh. Was she asleep yet? He shifted on the bed, moving slightly closer to her. After waiting to see if she moved away, he decided there was a good chance she had drifted off. He climbed out of bed and retrieved his tunic. After donning it, he lay down on the sheepskin rug.

He wished he had his cloak, but he'd left it in the stables with his saddlebags and tack. Maybe if he turned on his side, he'd stay warmer. Even with the rug, the stone floor was uncomfortably hard, and he could feel the chill from it seeping into his body. He rubbed his arms with his hands and flexed his shoulders, trying to generate some warmth. It was going to be a miserable night. He wasn't certain he would sleep at all.

Then he thought of Marared's cloak hanging from the clothing pole. It was made of soft, finely-woven wool and lined with fur. He would feel awkward if she woke and found him using her garment for a blanket. But it was her fault he was reduced to this circumstance.

After shivering a few more minutes, he got up and fetched the cloak, then lay down again. This was much better. There was hope he could actually sleep. On the morrow he'd come up with something else. Maybe he could have extra bedding brought up. Hilda could be trusted to be discreet. She wouldn't put it about the whole castle that his new wife had apparently banished him from the bed. He was less certain of Edith, the girl Hilda had chosen to act as Marared's bodyservant. But there wasn't much else he could do. It didn't seem likely things with Marared would go any better the next night. Or the one after that. If she was ever going to let him bed her, he was going to have to find a way to thaw her attitude toward him. How was he to do that?

He sighed and turned on his back. Take one step at a time. Go slow. If only his body would cooperate. It was one thing to tell himself to be patient. Quite another to get his over-eager body to agree. Despite the hard floor and his earlier struggle to stay warm, he was still aroused.

Abruptly, he realized why. The cloak smelled of her. Some sort of flower scent, probably from the herbs used to freshen the garment when it was stored away. And some other fragrance that was uniquely Marared. The effect on his body was potent. Almost as bad as lying next to her. He sighed again. It was going to be a long night.

WHEN HE WOKE it was still full dark. His body was stiff and cold. He rose, intending to stretch, then decided he might as well start his day. The first thing was to arrange a proper bed. A straw-stuffed mattress, something that could be rolled up and stored out of the way. Marared had brought her own storage chest, so that meant he could use one of the two already in the room to store some blankets.

He grimaced as he realized what he would be signaling to Marared by making these arrangements. If he didn't insist on sharing a bed with her, she would know he wasn't going to take her maidenhead by force and think he'd given up.

He hadn't, of course. Merely decided on a different approach. He meant to gradually win her over. Get her used to him and to the idea of being married. Once she didn't see him as such an ogre, he would try again.

There was a part of him that worried she would never relent. She seemed so determined. Like a wild animal that would rather starve than be tamed. But she wasn't a wild creature. More like a skittish filly that needed careful handling. Some men thought you needed to dominate a horse and break its will in order to control it. He'd always believed slow, gentle coaxing and earning the trust of the animal was a better method. Certainly, it seemed a more appropriate approach with a woman. He didn't want Marared to merely acquiesce to letting him bed him. He wanted her to enjoy the experience and want to do it again. And again.

Simply thinking about coupling with his wife aroused him. He'd better get on with his day. Get busy and stop thinking about her. He glanced at the bed, compelled to seek out another look at the bedeviling woman he had wed. The curtains, although not drawn all the way, blocked his view.

With a sense of relief mingled with regret, he left the room.

MARARED SAT UP and stretched. She could see sunshine streaming into the room.

Pushing the curtains all the way open, she got out of bed. Malmsbury was gone. She smiled at the thought of him sleeping on the floor. It was a sweet victory. But she knew it was temporary. The next night he would probably try again. She found herself looking forward to it.

By day, the bedchamber was beautiful. She admired the play of light on the elegant objects in the room—the ivory and onyx chess set on the table by the cushioned window seat, the bronze brazier, the crimson and gold fabric hanging on the wall. Then she reminded herself that she was in an English castle, the lair of her enemy. Her stay here would be only temporary. Best not to get used to the luxuries of the place.

From the storage coffer she'd brought, she fetched her clothes. Once dressed, she found her hairbrush, sat down on a stool and began to untangle her hair. She'd made some progress when a tentative voice called from the doorway, "Milady, would you like me to do that?"

Marared looked up to see a skinny girl of

about twelve years standing just inside the solar. She had straight, mouse brown hair, blue eyes and a snub nose. The girl curtsied awkwardly. "I'm Edith. I'm supposed to help you dress and wait upon you."

"Who ordered you to do so?"

"Hilda. She said you were to be the new lady of the castle and I should do your bidding in all things."

Hilda. That was the older woman with the calm gray eyes and thin face who had assisted Marared the night before.

Marared nodded to the girl. "You may start by helping me get the snarls out of my hair."

Edith took the brush began and began her work. She had a gentle, deft touch, which was helpful. Marared's hair was thick and obstinate.

"Tell me," Marared said. "Are you Saxon?"

Edith shook her head. "My family have always lived in this valley."

"Then you must be Cymreig, that is, Welsh."

Edith shook her head again. "I don't speak Welsh, or the old English either. But my family has always served here at Tangwyl, even before it was a castle."

"That's because a long time ago, a brute named William the Bastard conquered your people and made your family slaves and servants."

"William the Bastard." Edith's deft fingers

stilled for a moment. "I haven't heard of him."

"He was from Normandy. He came and killed the Saxon king, Edward, and seized control of nearly all the island. But he couldn't conquer my people. They were too fierce and cunning."

"How do you know all this? If it took place so many years ago?"

"The Cymry have long memories. Our bards tell us tales about kings and heroes who lived hundreds of years in the past. We are the only ones who belong here, everyone else came later."

"Not my family. I told you, they've lived in this valley as long as there have been people here."

"Then they must have been Cymreig. But since they are now English lackeys, it doesn't matter."

Edith stopped combing her hair. "If you hate the English so much, why did you wed one of them?"

Marared turned to look at the serving girl. Edith's clear blue eyes focused on her with curiosity. "I had no choice. If your father chose a husband for you who you despised, what would you do?"

Edith took a sharp breath. "You despise Lord Gerard?"

"I do."

"But, why? He's fair and reasonable in the way he deals with everyone. I've never seen him lose his temper. And he's handsome as well. If I were a lady, I'd be pleased to wed him. And he is the lord of the castle." Edith gestured. "All this is yours, this beautiful room and the leisure to enjoy it." She looked at Marared again. "What sort of man did you think to marry who could offer you more than this?"

"A Cymro, a Welshman. I care nothing for these fine things. I'd rather live in the mountains in a cave or a lean-to, as long as I was wed to a man of my own people."

Edith shook her head. It was clear the serving girl thought she was utterly witless. That was because Edith's people had no pride. They had been ground down by the English for so long, they simply accepted their lot. But Marared would never do that.

Where was Malmsbury? If he chose to ignore her, she would really hate him.

"YOU'VE GIVEN HER a tour of the castle?" Gerard asked. "Tried to help her settle in and be comfortable here?"

"Of course, milord," Hilda answered. "We did exactly as you ordered. I took her everywhere. The kitchen, buttery and brewhouse. The weaving shed, stables, smithy, beehives, grainery and storage buildings, the chapel and the garden."

They were in the hall, not the most private place for a conversation. But since there were few servants around, Gerard dared to ask the question that had gnawed at him all day. "Did she say anything as you were showing her around?"

"Milord?"

"Did she express any opinion of her new home?"

"Not to me, but…" Gerard braced himself as Hilda pursed her lips, as if tasting something unpleasant. "I sent Edith to help her dress and braid her hair. The girl was quite distressed when she returned. Said that milady had spoken openly of not wanting to wed you. Said you were her enemy."

Gerard exhaled a sigh. He might have known Marared would not keep her hostile attitude to herself.

He glanced at the servant. Hilda had never been anything but dutiful and helpful since he'd come to Tangwyl. And he truly needed a woman's advice. "I'm afraid my wife has not accepted her new circumstances. She's a headstrong sort, and rather spoiled. Her father sprang this marriage on her with no warning. She nurses a bitter animosity toward me simply because I'm a *filthy Sais,* as she refers to me."

Hilda raised her brows, but said nothing.

"I'm certain she'll come around, although it

might take time. Regardless what she says about me, I want her treated with all the courtesy and regard due my wife and the lady of the household. If she desires to supervise any aspect of the castle's affairs, I will expect her orders to be obeyed without question."

The servant nodded. "That is as it should be, milord." Hilda started to leave.

"Hilda." Gerard considered asking her advice about more intimate issues. Hilda was a widow. But even though he was certain she had been wed for some years, Gerard suspected she would not be able to give him the counsel he needed. Her lot in life was much different than Marared's.

He inclined his head to her. "Thank you."

MARARED DUMPED THE belt she was embroidering on the bench beside her. She stood and began to pace. This morning, Hilda had shown her around the castle. Afterwards, the servant had escorted her back here to the solar, obviously expecting she'd spend the rest of the day sewing like a proper lady. Ugh! She'd lose her mind if she had to stay up here and sew all day!

She went to the windows and stared out at the nearly cloudless sky. What she really wanted to do was to go riding. The weather had warmed, and it felt like spring was truly here. If she were home, she would not miss this chance to get away from the stuffy confines of the holding. The wind would still be brisk, but once she dismounted and made her way down into the little hidden valley that was one of her favorite places, she would be sheltered enough. There would be wood violets and snowdrops, and daffodils spreading their golden beauty across the land.

She sighed, thinking longingly of her days roaming the highlands. Until she was free of this wretched marriage, she would no longer be able to do such things. If she got her horse and left the castle, Malmsbury would think she was running away. Not altogether a bad idea. Although where would she go? If she returned to Caer Brynfawr, her father would simply have some of his men escort her back.

She sighed again. Unless Malmsbury decided to repudiate the marriage, she was stuck here. Repudiate the marriage—now that was a thought. What if she was so disagreeable that he grew tired of her lack of manners, and decided to send her back to her father? Another reason not to let him take her maidenhead. An annulment of the marriage would be much easier to obtain if she were still a virgin.

But what would it take to get a man like Malmsbury to give up? He was clearly almost as stubborn as she was. If he tired of her tart tongue and waspish behavior, he could simply avoid her or leave the keep altogether. She was the one who was trapped, not him.

Indeed, she thought miserably, if she was Malmsbury, that's exactly what she would do. Ignore her. Perhaps even lock her away if she became too difficult. Old King Henry had kept his wife confined to a convent for twelve years.

A spasm of fear went through her. She'd die if she had to stay in this room forever. Hilda wouldn't have shown her every nook and cranny of the place if she expected her to remain in the solar all day. She might not be able to venture outside the castle walls, but at least she could move freely within them.

She went to the clothing pole by the bed and took down her shawl. Wrapping it around herself, she started toward the door. At that moment, her husband entered.

"I thought I would go walking around the keep." She met his gaze stonily. "If I meant to try and escape, I would have taken my mantle."

"Escape?" He looked startled. "You feel like a prisoner here?"

"What else am I? Forced to live in the lair of my enemy?" She saw a muscle twitch in his jaw. Remembering her earlier fears that he might lock her away, she decided she must guard her tongue better. "I'm restless, and 'tis a pleasant day. I thought I would go to the garden and sit in the sunshine."

"I'll go with you."

Marared followed him down the stairway. Surely he could not desire to spend time in her company. He must have some other motivation for accompanying her. What was it?

This man baffled her. He wasn't anything like what she expected. It unsettled her that he was so subtle and mysterious. Such qualities made him a dangerous opponent.

WHEN WOULD SHE *ever stop treating him like a predator about to pounce on her?* Gerard tried to relax as he made his way down the stairs. His wife's behavior was exasperating.

But despite her hostility, he'd thought about her all morning. In fact, he'd gone to the solar to tell her he wanted her to sit beside him at the evening meal in the hall. If he forced her to share his company, maybe she would gradually thaw toward him. Besides, even if he could not possess her body, he wanted the pleasure of looking upon her beauty and having her near. In some ways it was torture, but there was still satisfaction in knowing she was his.

As they left the castle and crossed the bailey, he said, "Now that you've seen more of it, what think you of Tangwyl?"

She shrugged. "It appears to take a great many people to run the place. There's so much work to be done. Like those poor women in the weaving shed who must toil all day long on the looms."

He heard the resentment in her voice. She pitied the people of Tangwyl, viewing them as little better than slaves. "They would toil just as hard, and have much harsher lives, if I did not provide them with food for their families in exchange for producing cloth for me. Tangwyl offers them a way to earn a livelihood. It also provides them with protection when the Welsh come raiding."

"Was that not the point of this marriage—to stop the raids?"

"Even so, who knows how long the agreement will last?"

"You doubt my father's word?"

"There are other Welsh chieftains besides your father, and they may not accept the truce simply because he does." He paused before adding, "Besides, there are certain aspects of the agreement that have not yet been fulfilled."

"If you have a complaint, take it to my father!"

"I'd rather not. I'd much prefer to come to some sort of agreement with you."

She stopped walking and faced him, her

hands on her hips. "Did you come along to browbeat and coerce me?"

"Of course not." He spoke through gritted teeth. Damn this difficult woman!

She started walking again and he followed. She might be the most vexing woman in Christendom, but she was also one of the most entrancing. Her anger only heightened her allure, making her eyes glow, her fair skin flush, her whole countenance take on a dangerous, intoxicating beauty.

She reached the garden gate and went in. Gerard was right behind her.

CURSE THE MAN! Could he not leave her alone! Marared halted at the edge of a patch of herbs. Although most of the ground was still bare, she could see mint and chives poking through the soil. Malmsbury came up beside her. As always, his good looks and brooding, thoughtful manner unnerved her. He was like some deep, quiet mountain pool, potent with the promise of things unknown and magic lurking at the bottom of its ancient depths. Like the tarn near Caer Brynfawr, where she used to gaze down into the dark water and imagine King Arthur's sword was hidden there, its bright blade and jewel encrusted hilt obscured by the murk.

"Not much to see this time of year."

She faced him. "Many of the plants are dormant, but they're still there."

"Do you know much about gardening?"

"Some. My mother used to have a beautiful one when she lived in Ireland."

"What about at Caer Brynfawr?"

"The mountain climate is too harsh to grow more than a few vegetables and herbs. Indeed, we get most of our grain from along the coast and the isle of Mona."

"When did your mother die?"

She frowned at him. This discussion was becoming far too intimate. "Five years ago, of the lung fever."

"At least you had her that long."

There was a hint of sadness in his tone. Nay, she would not ask him about *his* mother. He was her enemy. She did not care what grief he might have known.

"Why did your mother, an Irishwoman, wed a Welshman?"

"Their families had been connected for generations. Perhaps they were even kin. Not close of course, but enough that it was logical for them to wed."

"So, their marriage was arranged because it represented a useful alliance?"

She glared at him. "There is a difference. My

parents were not enemies."

She wondered if her stubbornness made him angry. He took a step closer. She stood her ground. He seized her arm and pulled her toward him. Before she could react, he brought his mouth down on hers. The sensation of his lips on hers was so shocking, for a second, she forgot to fight him. Then she recovered herself and jerked away.

She stared at his lean, hard face. His enigmatic hazel eyes bored into her. Moisture glistened on his lips, and she remembered how they had felt against hers. Firm and enticing. She could feel a tingling heat spread through her body. God help her, she wanted him to kiss her again.

His mouth quirked with bitterness. "I suppose you are right, that this is not the time nor the place. I can hardly lay you down on the bare ground. And it's a bit too cold to remove our clothing."

She flushed at the images his words evoked. Of their half-naked bodies entwined on the earth. She knew how people coupled. She had once surprised her brother Maelgwn with one of the kitchen girls. The memory suddenly altered, and became her and Malmsbury. His lean hips thrusting, while she was the woman shuddering and moaning beneath him.

An involuntary tremor of longing seized her. She wrapped the shawl more tightly around herself and raised her gaze to Malmbury's, trying to regain her hostility. But inside, she felt weak and quivering. There was a burning ache in her lower belly and her legs felt as if they would not hold her up. His gaze aroused even stranger sensations. In some helpless, traitorous part of her being, she desired him. Longed for him to kiss her. To feel his body against hers. For the hard lance of his phallus to penetrate the throbbing place between her legs, and soothe the ungodly ache he had incited.

He bowed formally. "Good day, madam. I will see you in the hall tonight for the evening meal." He turned, his body as straight and stiff as a new blade. As he strode off, Marared exhaled a silent moan of regret.

Sweet heaven, she would be the death of him! Gerard clenched his hands into fists as he started toward the keep. It was maddening to be so close to his wife and know he had the right to possess her, yet be forced to walk away. Worst of all, he had no idea if he was making any progress. He was beginning to wonder if she would ever soften.

Stubborn, difficult, infuriating wench! If she were a child, he'd turn her over his knee and take a switch to her behind!

Now, there was a provocative thought. He could imagine her naked bottom, creamy white and as softly rounded as a ripe apricot.

The mental image brought a wave of sexual need so intense, he paused to recover himself. Had any man had ever died from unrelieved lust? Probably not. Unless he completely lost his wits and stumbled off the castle ramparts while obsessing over his untouchable wife's incredible allure.

Jesu, how had this happened? He'd always been so controlled and disciplined. Never before had he allowed anything to distract him from his objectives. Here he was, on the verge of having everything he'd fought so hard for, and he became a besotted halfwit!

Not besotted. It was simply a matter of wanting what he could not have. Once he bedded Marared, things would settle down between them and he'd be able to deal with her better.

With effort, he forced his thoughts away from his provoking wife and continued across the bailey.

CHAPTER SIX

GERARD TOOK A deep breath before stepping into the barracks. Three days had passed since they'd arrived at Tangwyl, and the stalemate between him and Marared continued. She spoke to him only when spoken to. Slept in the same chamber, although with her in the bed and him on a pallet on the floor. Sat beside him at the evening meal, but ate in silence. It was wearing on his nerves. As he went about his duties around the castle, the frustration over his lack of progress with his new wife followed him like a nagging shadow. It didn't help the weather had been cool and rainy, cooping everyone up inside.

When he reached the barracks, he found the men gathered around a brazier meant to take the chill off the spring air. They were polishing armor and repairing harnesses. A pair in the corner were playing draughts. They looked up a bit guiltily as they saw him.

Gerard nodded to Llew ap Hywel, one of the knights who had accompanied them from Caer Brynfawr. "If I could speak to you."

Llew got up and followed Gerard out, his weathered face impassive. Gerard walked to the cistern where the horses watered. The rain had stopped briefly, but it was clear from the dark, heavy sky that it would be only a short reprieve. He faced the Welshman. "Sir Llew, I need some advice."

The man nodded, his dark blue eyes respectful, but also watchful and wary.

"I'm certain you've known Marared a long time."

"All her life."

"Can you give me any insight into her nature? Suggest any way for me to get her to accept me as her husband?" There, he'd done it. Revealed the bald, bitter truth. If Llew was so inclined, he could share the sad details of Gerard's marriage with every knight and servant at the castle. But Gerard felt certain he would not. Even if he didn't know Llew ap Hywel, he knew his sort. They were tip-lipped even with their closest companions.

Llew was silent for a long while, his expression distant. "Since her mother died, Marared has been allowed to run wild. Her father indulges her, as does everyone at Caer Brynfawr. Carodac mourned his wife deeply, and Marared is the very image of her. But Catriona—his wife—she would never have approved. While Catriona was alive, she made certain to keep Marared busy and to involve her in all the tasks of running the household."

A blunt speech, in answer to Gerard's blunt question. Gerard felt a new respect for Llew ap Hywel. Clearly, the man wanted this alliance to work as much as Gerard did.

"I appreciate your honesty. But it gets me no closer to a solution."

"You must find a way to engage Marared's interest and help her find a place here. She is capable and intelligent. She needs to have some responsibility, to spend her days doing something meaningful. That's what will help her become part of this place and learn to care about the castle and its people."

It was good advice, although Gerard was still at loss as to exactly how to accomplish it.

Llew looked up at the sky. "When the weather clears, take her out riding. Perhaps that will ease her homesickness a bit."

"When the weather clears." Gerard grimaced. It would help all their moods if the rain would stop.

He thanked Llew and sought out Hilda. He

found her in the kitchen, supervising the preparation of the evening meal. Fine lines creased her forehead and bracketed her mouth. She turned when he called to her. A smile softened her sharp features. "Milord?"

"Is something wrong?" he asked. "You look distressed."

"I fear some of the hams in the cellar have gone bad. They were probably not smoked properly last fall. 'Twill mean the pottage the next few months will be very bland."

"Is there anything else that can be used instead?"

"Mutton, of course. But it doesn't add the same flavor."

"Perhaps we can have some of the squires set snares and catch some hares."

Hilda gave him that quick smile again. "Fresh meat is always welcome. I'm surprised you know about such things, milord."

"When I was a boy, we often ate hare stew." Perhaps she would guess from his words that he hadn't grown up in a castle, but in a simple village croft. Normally, he avoided drawing attention to his background. But he didn't think it would make Hilda look upon him unfavorably. She was a kindly woman.

"I suspect you should be the one to arrange that, milord. I know little about snares or hunting."

"I'll talk to the squires. This time of year, they don't have much else to do."

"Was there a reason you sought me out, milord?"

Gerard glanced at the kitchen staff. They all seemed busy at work: sorting dried peas, chopping leeks, kneading bread and the like. But Gerard suspected they were all listening intently. Since he'd arrived at Tangwyl, everyone had treated him with deference, but he knew the castle inhabitants were very curious about him. Although he tried to behave as a lord should, he was still a bit overawed to find himself in a position of such power. He knew he often behaved too familiarly with his underlings. Like the conversation he was about to have with Hilda.

"Come. Walk with me a moment."

He had intended to take her out into the yard, but when they reached the doorway he realized it was raining heavily. Not wanting to go into the hall where they could be overheard, he said, "Why don't you take me down to the cellars and show me the hams you're talking about."

"Of course, milord. But we'll need a candle or torch to see where we're going."

Gerard took an unlit torch from a bracket on the wall and they went back into the kitchen to light it.

Once the torch was lit, Hilda reached for it.

"If you will allow me, milord. I know the way far better than you." She was clearly baffled by his desire to see the hams, but she led the way down the stairs to the storage cellars under the kitchen. A dozen hams hung from the ceiling supports. Hilda motioned. "I can show you the ones that are starting to rot. They start to turn a greenish hue and smell rank."

"There's no need. Indeed…that's not the real reason I wanted to come down here. I wanted to talk you about my wife. In private."

Hilda hesitated before speaking. "I'm not certain I can help you, milord. She's not like any gentlewoman I've ever encountered. Not that I've known that many. Lord FitzAdam didn't often entertain company, and both his wives died young."

"What I wondered was…have you become aware of any aspect of the castle that interests Marared? That is, was there any time when you were giving her the tour of the keep and yard that you felt she had…engaged with what you were telling her?"

"I'm afraid not, milord. She seemed disdainful of everything I showed her. That is…she wasn't rude. She didn't say anything untoward. But I could tell she found fault with almost everything."

Gerard knew a rising sense of gloom. How was he to act on Llew's advice when there was *nothing* that pleased Marared? She seemed determined to hate every aspect of her new life.

"Milord?"

He could see pity in Hilda's eyes. *Curse it! He didn't want to be pitied!* "Thank you, Hilda. I…I will think some more on the matter of the hams."

"MARARED?"

She turned, not only at the sound of her name, but at the familiar cadence with which it was said. Llew, one of her father's men, stood on the garden pathway. "Isn't it a bit cool to be sewing here?" He spoke in Welsh. "Would you not be more comfortable inside?"

"I have my cloak."

The weathered skin around Llew's blue eyes crinkled as he smiled. "Your lips are near blue, child."

Marared bit back the sharp retort that came to mind. Llew had always been nothing but kind to her. She let out a sigh, then turned away, not wanting him to see the tears glistening in her eyes.

He sat down on the bench beside her. "'Tis all right, *blodyn bach.* It only stands to reason you would be homesick. Tell me, what do you miss the most?"

She turned toward him, letting the tears fall. "'Tis hard to say. My mam, I suppose. I know she's been dead for years, but I've never felt the loss of her so greatly."

"You feel you need the advice of a woman?"

Marared nodded. "'Tis all so new. So overwhelming." She motioned to indicate the keep behind them.

"Have you told Lord Gerard this?"

Marared stiffened. "He's my enemy! Why would I confide in him?"

Llew's expression was gentle. "He's concerned you are unhappy."

Concerned that I will not let him bed me, is more like! Concerned that I hate him!

"He wants you to be…if not happy, then at least content with your lot here."

"That will never happen. Never!"

Llew didn't speak for a time. Then his gaze met hers. "Do you not think it was hard for your mother? To give up her life in Ireland and move to a remote mountain fortress so far away from her family?"

"But she loved Da! She *wanted* to marry him!"

"Did she?" Llew shook his head. "She didn't love him in the beginning. Indeed, she was dreadfully unhappy. Like you are now."

"I don't believe you."

"It's true. I was there. And you can ask your

da. Indeed, I'm surprised he didn't tell you these things. Perhaps he was afraid to."

"Afraid? Why?" Now Marared was truly puzzled.

"I suspect he didn't bother speaking to you on the matter of marriage because he'd decided it was hopeless. He knew that once you learned the man you were to wed wasn't one of your countrymen, you would be so angry, you wouldn't listen to anything he said. That's why he arranged this marriage without telling you and rushed through the ceremony. The truth is, as much as you were coerced, so was Malmsbury."

"That's ridiculous! He got what he wanted. All he really cares about is Tangwyl."

"Is it? Don't you think he hoped to have a wife who had some fondness for him? One he could get along with, at the very least?"

Marared clenched her jaw. "Then he should have married some *Saeson* bitch."

"What does that mean to you—*Saeson* bitch?"

"Someone like him!"

"But what is he? Is he English? Norman?"

Marared shrugged. "It doesn't matter. Either way, he's a foreigner. He doesn't belong here."

"Do you know why they call him Gerard of Malmsbury?"

"Never thought about it."

"It's because he's a bastard. He can't use his father's name."

Marared was startled. "He was born on the wrong side of the blanket? I thought among the English that meant the child had no rights, no inheritance."

"Aye. That's exactly what it means."

Marared was curious now. Among her people, legitimacy at birth wasn't terribly important. If a man recognized a child as his son, that was all what mattered. But she knew being born within wedlock was extremely important to the English. Even if you were the king's bastard, you were still a bastard. You could never inherit or claim any of the rights given to the man's legitimate children.

"If that's true, how did he ever end up as a lord?"

"He worked his way up. And got lucky in that his own overlord is also a self-made man. Fawkes de Cressy earned his position and wealth by serving beside King Richard at Acre. Before that, de Cressy was also a landless knight, like thousands of other men."

"And because of de Cressy's relationship with Richard, he gained control over Tangwyl Castle?"

"Actually, it was King John who gave de Cressy the honor of Tangwyl. When the last lord of Tangwyl died without an heir, John chose de Cressy—who has a formidable reputation as a warrior—to take control of the demesne. I think he thought de Cressy would be a good man to keep the Cymry in line."

Marared made a face of contempt.

"But de Cressy didn't want to leave his family. Not to mention, he's already wed. So he chose Malmsbury from among his knights as the man to rule Tangwyl."

Learning these things about Malmsbury made Marared uncomfortable. She liked to think of her unwanted bridegroom as privileged. A man who'd had everything in his life handed to him. Clearly, that was not the case.

Even as she felt a stirring of sympathy for Malmsbury, she quickly brushed it aside. He'd been sent here for the express purpose of subduing and controlling her people.

She faced Llew defiantly. "Do you hope by telling me these things, you can soften my outlook and get me to accept him?"

"'Twould be better for everyone if you accepted this marriage."

She narrowed her eyes at Llew. "You're a knight and used to following orders. But I was brought up to be proud of my heritage. I would never betray it."

"I'm not asking you to betray your heritage. Only to see your husband as a man, rather than your enemy."

"I can't change what he is!" Marared felt the familiar, reassuring anger rush through her. "He *is* the enemy, and naught can change that!"

Llew shook his head, his eyes sorrowful.

Then he inclined his head to Marared and left the garden.

Marared remained on the bench. She could feel the cold of the stone seeping through her heavy cloak. It seemed to penetrate her body all the way to her heart. She'd never felt so alone, so miserable. Why had she refused to have Aoife come along? It would have helped so much to have her here, so she had someone with whom she could share her anger and grief, without feeling like she was being weak and childish.

Of course, maybe she *was* weak and childish. All she'd done since arriving at Tangwyl was mope. That's what a child did. She was a woman and a Cymraes. She had more pride than that. Nay, the thing to do was take action. Find a way to change her circumstances.

But what? She couldn't fight the whole castle. Everyone here, even Llew, one of her countrymen, was on Malmsbury's side. What she needed was an ally. Someone from outside the castle who understood that her husband was her enemy.

She thought of her cousin, Rhys. He'd once told her he'd rather die than give in to the evil *Saeson*. Unlike her father, Rhys didn't want peace. He wanted to make the enemy's life so miserable they finally left the Cymry in peace.

But how was she to contact Rhys? He was probably at his father's farm, or with his small band of warriors up in the hills. How could she possibly get word to him? If she'd had a proper wedding, with all her father's client farmers in attendance, she would have had a chance to speak to Rhys. But everything had been so rushed. She'd been caught completely unaware.

She could send Rhys a message. But there was no one at Tangwyl she could trust to carry it to her cousin. Not to mention, 'twas unlikely Rhys could read. Although she'd chafed at her mother's insistence she learn to read and write, she could certainly see the usefulness of the skill now. She wondered if Malmsbury had ever learned to read. Not likely, given his humble beginnings.

Another advantage she had over him. The thought eased some of her sense of helplessness. But only for a moment. Then she again faced how trapped she was. A pawn in this game of power and strategy waged by her father and Malmsbury.

So much of her life, she'd been able to do whatever she wished. She'd never truly appreciated how much freedom she'd had. Because of that freedom, she'd always felt in control of her life. But the harsh truth was she had always subject to the will of her father, exactly as her mother had been. They'd both been married off to men not of their choosing.

Llew's revelation about her parents' marriage unnerved her. She'd always thought of her parents' relationship as a love match. But clearly it hadn't been one in the beginning. Leaving the gentle climate of Ireland to come to the wild highlands of Cymru must have been a serious shock for her mother. In that sense, things were worse for her mother than they were for her. Although she loved Caer Brynfawr, it had few of the amenities of Tangwyl Castle. The keep here was spacious and beautifully furnished, and the whole castle amazingly organized and efficient. Everyone seemed to know exactly what they needed to do. Hilda was a marvel, rivaling Marared's mother in her ability to anticipate what needed to be done and make certain it happened.

Clean linen? Why, of course. The weavers had woven it months ago, and it had been washed and put away in a storage chest. Fine beeswax candles? Dozens had been made last summer. The honey from the honeycomb had been stored away as well, to use to sweeten fruit, cakes and other treats, such as they'd had at the fancy meal when she first arrived.

Hearty food for the lean spring months? There was a whole storage cellar full of baskets of dried beans, peas, and apples, as well as sacks of ground wheat and barley, and dozens of hams hanging from the ceiling. Bunches of dried herbs were arranged on hooks on the walls, and there was a huge sack of salt from the coast. The amount of work and planning involved in setting in all those foodstores boggled Marared's mind. She'd dealt with many of the domestic details at Caer Brynfawr. But the thought of being in charge of a household as large and complex as Tangwyl made her stomach tie in knots.

Although Malmsbury hadn't given her any indication he expected to her to take over running the keep. He seemed to expect her to live like some pampered, useless pet. Like a captive bird kept in a cage for the sake of its lovely song and pretty feathers.

At the thought, Marared's gloom deepened. There was no place for her here, other than as a broodmare for Malmsbury. A role she was determined she would never fill. She had to find some means of escape. Come up with a plan to thwart Malmsbury. If only Aoife was here. Between the two of them, they would surely be able to devise a way to end this marriage.

That was it! She would write to Aoife. Although Aoife couldn't read, she could get Father Idwal to tell her what was in the message. But she could hardly write to her cousin for advice on how to thwart Malmsbury. If she mentioned anything regarding that, Father Idwal would immediately tell her father. But if she could arrange to meet with Aoife, they'd be able to talk freely.

The weather was gradually warming. By the time Aoife got the message, it would be well into spring and traveling would be much easier. They could meet at Abergavenny. The village was about a half day's journey from both Caer Brynfawr and Tangwyl.

Excitement flooded Marared as her plan came together. At last she was doing something. At last she had a plan of attack.

CHAPTER SEVEN

GERARD GLANCED UP at the clear blue sky and let out a sigh of satisfaction. Finally the weather had cleared and he could pursue his plan. Since the moment they'd wed, Marared had reminded him of a wild creature in a cage. Today he meant to set her free. With luck, once she got away from Tangwyl and all the reminders of her circumstances, she would start to relax. Then he could try again to convince her he truly cared for her happiness. He must make her realize he was a friend and not a foe. That was the only way her attitude toward him would ever thaw.

He strode across the castle yard, feeling more optimistic than he had in days. At the garden gate, he paused and took a deep breath. He must be very careful in what he said and how he said it. If he let Marared see how much he wanted to spend time with her, she might refuse to go riding with him out of simple obstinacy and spite. He must bring up the subject casually, as if it made no difference to him whether she accompanied him or not.

Proceeding into the garden, Gerard found Marared in her usual spot. The garden and the stables seemed to be the only places she felt at ease. Both Llew and the ostler, William, had mentioned her spending time with the horses, especially Gwenevere, her lovely pale gray palfrey. Although she ostensibly went there to groom the animal and feed it dried apples, both men had overheard her talking to the mare. It appeared the mute beast was the only creature at the castle with whom she felt comfortable confiding her thoughts.

As he approached her, Marared turned. For once, her beautiful green eyes were bright and her expression cheerful.

"Good day, Marared. And it is a good day, isn't it?" He motioned to the clear sky above them. "Finally, the weather has cleared."

She nodded agreeably. "Aye. The sunshine is very welcome."

Her attitude encouraged him. Maybe this wouldn't be so tricky after all. "It seems a waste to stay inside on a day like this. I've decided to go riding. I wondered if you would like to accompany me."

"Riding? Where?"

"No place special. I heard there was a water-fall up the valley. I thought I might try to find it."

She nodded again. "Aye. That sounds pleasant."

His mood lifted even more. "I'll have William get our horses ready and meet you outside the stables." He started to leave and then turned back. "I would advise you to take your warm cloak. Although the weather is balmy now, it could change at any moment."

She immediately bristled. "I grew up in the mountains. I know all about changeable weather."

"Of course. I didn't think." How easy it was to set this woman off. She seemed to look for insults in everything he said. He would have to weigh every word before he spoke. A daunting thought, but the potential prize of making his beautiful wife smile seemed worth it.

SHE SHOULDN'T HAVE been so sharp with him. Not when her plan was to gain his favor so he would agree to this meeting with Aoife. She would have to remember her goal and be on her best behavior.

Besides, even if she was forced to share his

company, the thought of getting away from the castle and going riding thrilled her. Being trapped here inside this last sennight had made her feel as if she was suffocating.

She hurried up to the bedchamber to fetch her cloak and pattens. Although the wooden-soled shoes weren't comfortable, they were essential for walking on muddy ground.

By the time she reached the castle yard, Malmsbury was waiting for her. Gwenevere nickered as soon as she saw Marared. She patted the mare's neck. "I'm sorry, girl. I don't have any apples today." She risked a quick glance at Gerard and saw he was amused. She was prepared to defend wasting food on a horse, but it seemed Malmsbury didn't care.

Once again, Marared found doubts nibbling away at her resolve. Malmsbury was always so easy-going and indulgent. He must think if he remained patient and pandered to her every whim, she would relent in her hatred of him. He was treating her like a child. But she wasn't a child, and she wouldn't give in so easily.

He helped her onto the mare and mounted his own fine chestnut gelding, called Hearthfire. Whatever else you might say about the *Saeson*, they had splendid horses.

They rode through the castle gate. Marared felt as if she was seeing the area for the first time. When they'd arrived a sennight ago, it had been late in the day and she'd been too resentful and anxious to pay much attention to her surroundings. Now, she saw how pretty the valley was. The grass and budding leaves of the trees seemed to glisten in the sunshine. The gorse on the far hills was in full bloom, creating patches of blazing yellow against the velvety green.

Near the river, she noted strips of newly-tilled fields alternating with fallow land. Several black cows grazed on the tall, thick grass of the commons. Clustered nearby were more than a dozen thatched houses with gardens behind them. As they neared the river, she saw the mill. Behind it, the surface of the millpond shone silver, like a newly polished blade. They followed the trackway along the river. Beneath the budding trees, bluebells spread out in a haze of purple, broken only by flashes of yellow from primroses peeking out here and there in the bracken.

On the river, white anemone and yellow irises glistened among the reeds, and purple vetch brightened the dappled shadows along the pathway. In the willow and alder, robins and wrens trilled and chattered. A wild pear tree was in bloom, its white blossoms filling the air with fragrance.

They crossed a meadow where a flock of sheep grazed. Several lambs frolicked in the thick grass as their mothers grazed contentedly.

Marared drew her horse to a halt to watch the lambs' antics. The sight of them reminded her keenly of home. She often helped with the lambing, holding the ewe if a lamb got stuck in the birth passage and had to be pulled, then briskly rubbing the newborn creatures with a cloth to get them breathing.

"They're quite appealing at that age aren't they?" Ahead of her, Malmsbury had halted his mount and was also watching the lambs.

"Aye, they are." A pang of loss swept through Marared. Helping with lambing was something she would likely never do again, at least not while she was wed to Malmsbury. *Ladies* did not muck about in the lambing shed or have anything to do with livestock. The familiar resentment returned, followed by determination. She would find a way out of this marriage. She would.

WHAT A MERCURIAL creature his wife was. One moment she was smiling, her expression soft and tender as she watched the lambs. The next, she was back to scowling. Gerard's determination wavered. How was he to ever break through Marared's armor of resentment? How was he to ever get close to her?

But she had smiled briefly, so taking her on

this ride was definitely a move in the right direction. She clearly loved being outdoors and found delight in nature. He urged his mount forward, focusing on the landmarks that the castle steward, Alden, said would lead to the waterfall. If he blundered around and they didn't find it, she would truly think him useless. She probably knew the way around her homelands as well as any of her father's men.

He pulled his horse to a halt and concentrated. Alden had told him to stay close to the river until they reached a great oak, the top of which had been struck by lightning. Where was the oak? Had they somehow passed it?

She pulled up beside him. "What's wrong? Why are we stopping?"

He turned and smiled at her. "Trying to find my way. I've never been to this waterfall before."

Her auburn brows drew together in thought. "We might as well keep going. The waterfall must be off the main river, and we haven't encountered any tributaries yet." She motioned with her head. "Maybe over that next hill."

It almost seemed like she was trying to be helpful. Perhaps being outside the castle boosted her mood so much that she was willing to be civil to him.

The trail was steep, through thick bracken. They crested the hill and saw a stand of oak. Among them was a large tree with a blackened top. Relief flooded him. He might not look the fool after all. He turned his horse. "This way. The waterfall is supposed to be down in this valley."

They descended into the narrow ravine. Oak and ash grew thick, and the ground was laced with curling fronds of fern and tendrils of ivy. They found the little stream and followed it to a place where the foaming water tumbled over the rocks to form a small glistening waterfall.

"I'm certain it can't compare to waterfalls in your father's territory."

"Even so, 'tis very pretty. I love the sound of it."

They both dismounted and let the horses drink. Marared made her way to the little pool that formed below the falls. Gerard followed, stepping carefully on the slippery rocks. She turned to look at him, her mouth quirking with mischief. "Be careful. This is a place of the Fair Folk, which means things aren't always what they seem."

"Fair Folk?"

"You know, fairies. The fey. They love water, especially swiftly moving water." She gestured to the mossy bank on the other side, a spot that looked as if it could only be reached by swimming through the falls or flying down from the sky.

"They probably come to dance there on a summer's eve. Can you not see them, all dressed in their finery? The ladies with tiny bells on their wrists and ankles and woven into their long hair, the tinkling sound mingling with the voice of the water to make the music they dance to? They would all be wearing bright colors and gold and silver adornments and look as splendid as the ladies and gentlemen of the London court. Or even more so, since the Fair Folk possess a rare beauty not of this world."

"I thought fairies were supposed to be drab and nondescript and blend into the landscape." When she gave him a surprised look, Gerard added, "I've heard a few tales of them from a knight I served with who grew up in Ireland."

"Ah. That's the Little People. Brownies and leprechauns. They're different from the Fair Folk. The Fair Folk are human-sized. They could pass for one of us, if not for their exceptional beauty." She turned back to the waterfall. "And then there's the nixes. There's likely a water sprite living beneath the falling water. If you look hard enough, you may see her face and her long hair streaming down. She might beckon you closer, but you must not heed her. The fey are cold-hearted and wicked. They love to lure mortals to their doom."

She turned to look at him again. The soft silvery light made her fair skin look translucent. Against the milky hue, her coppery hair and moss green eyes were more striking than ever. Perhaps *she* was one of the Fair Folk, he thought fancifully. Surely no mortal woman could be so lovely and beguiling.

He moved next to her, locking gazes. "You could be one of the fey. You are beautiful enough."

SHE'D NEVER HAD a man look at her like this. Malmsbury's hazel eyes were so intent. So yearning and hungry. As if he was a wolf and she a young, tender coney he longed to devour. But she didn't fear him. At least not like that. What she feared was the way her body seemed eager for the touch of his. The way her skin thrilled at the thought of contact with his. Other parts of her had come to life and were experiencing a strange craving. As if her body was a flower, unfurling, opening, beckoning him to be joined with her.

She reminded herself he was her enemy who she hated and despised. But the thought had no effect. Her mind might believe such things, but her body refused to do so. Her fingers still longed to touch his thick wavy hair. To trace the hard line of his jaw, darkened faintly with stubble. To stroke his muscular neck. And lower, to the broad expanse of his chest, where his flesh would be both firm and soft, the perfect cushion to rest her head against. She wanted to feel his arms around her and have his lips press against hers.

He must sense her thoughts, for his hazel eyes turned smoky and dark. Then he was next to her and all her yearnings came to life as he pulled her against him. Her arms went around his neck. He bent his head and their lips met and everything flowed together. The world shimmered around them until they were not two beings but one. One wild, desperate creature that clutched and shuddered and kissed and moaned.

She was drowning in sensation, sinking deeper and deeper into the swirling, shimmering magic. The scent of him, sunshine and sweat and maleness. His taste, sweet, yet edged with something dangerous and keen. His calloused hands stroked her back and then lower, cupping her buttocks and pressing her against him. She felt his arousal, firm and insistent against her belly.

She wanted it. Her whole body ached for it. Her flesh was hot and fevered. She kissed him more desperately than ever, as if the greedy nuzzling, licking, sucking contact of their mouths would satisfy her need. It did not. That required bare flesh against bare flesh. A true joining.

But their clothing was in the way. And the air was cool, and the ground was wet, and the only way to for them to mate would be standing up, like a stallion and a mare. And yet horses did not kiss and fondle and rub themselves against each other like they were doing now. And so, there was nothing for it but to keep clutching and kissing until they both went mad.

Her reason was utterly gone. He must have still retained some, because he finally drew away and held her at arm's length. His eyes were dazed-looking and stormy with regret. "Marared, we cannot…this is not the place…the way…"

He swallowed, his mouth working. "I want you desperately, but I can't think how we could do this." He glanced around, as if he could force their surroundings to alter in some way.

Freed of the savage, breathtaking pleasure his lips and body aroused, her wits began to reassemble. She realized what she was doing, and what she had very nearly allowed to happen, and went stiff with shock and horror. She'd been on the verge of surrendering to the enemy. And not merely surrendering, but yielding utterly, then reveling in her helpless submission. She'd been willing to not only let him take her maidenhead, but also to allow herself to enjoy every second of his absolute triumph.

She glanced around frantically. "'Tis this place. I've been bewitched. Beguiled." She set her jaw and fixed him with a steely gaze. "Naught has changed between us. I will not let fairy mischief take control of me. We're leaving. Now."

She went to fetch Gwenevere, who had wandered away and was trying to graze. She hurried to the mare, desperate to hide her shame and mortification. Bad enough he'd seen what a lustful, sluttish whore she was. She would not also allow him to see her crying like a pathetic child.

He came up beside her. "Here. Let me help you mount."

"Nay!" Her voice was a shriek. "I can manage! I can manage quite well without you! I don't need the aid of a wretched *Sais!*" She jerked the reins and dragged the horse off. The tears nearly blinded her, but she finally found a rock and clambered ungracefully onto her mount. The path was narrow, and there was no way she could race off like she desperately wanted to do. But as soon as they were out of this wretched valley, she would be clear of him.

HE'D WED A whirlwind. A fierce, elemental force of nature. His body felt raw and aching from the abrupt loss of contact with hers, and he was overwhelmed with a terrible sense of disappointment. *Was* it fairy magic that had turned her yielding and pliant in his arms? Some sorcery that changed his cold, distant wife into a woman yearning and eager?

Gerard surveyed the tranquil setting. Although he felt nothing odd or supernatural here, that didn't mean there wasn't truly some enchantment in this place. If only it had lasted. If only the passion that burst between them for a few short moments had not evaporated like mist in a sudden ray of bright sunlight.

But that was foolish. He was the one who had broken things off. And with good reason. He could not have bedded her here. There was nowhere soft enough nor dry enough to possibly allow consummation. And by the time they left the little glade and reached a place where they could continue their tryst, her mood would have shifted. After all, how long did any of her moods last? She was furious at him now, but by the time they got back to Tangwyl her rage might well turn to pensive silence.

That is, *if* she went back to Tangwyl. In her reckless state she might ride off in the other direction. She could get lost or hurt herself. He'd better go after her. Although he knew better than to attempt to speak to her, he must at least keep her in sight. He fetched his own horse and mounted. His erection made riding unpleasant. He ignored it.

CHAPTER EIGHT

HE LEFT THE valley, climbed to a nearby outlook and surveyed the landscape. Most of the hilly area was open, but there were a few hedgerows and stands of oak blocking his view. After a few moments of anxiety, he finally spotted the russet color of her cloak. She was headed away from Tangwyl.

He hesitated. Following her might make her even angrier. But he had no choice. She might be used to her father's territory, but she didn't know this place. There were many hazards lurking in rough, hilly terrain. She was his responsibility. He had to follow her. Of course, the truth was that he *wanted* to be as near to her as possible. Her body drew his like a lodestone.

For a time, her route took her away from Tangwyl. Then she turned back. When he realized she'd spotted him, he slowed Hearthfire. There was no reason to get close enough to give her an opportunity to lash him with her sharp tongue. Although, even her anger was strangely arousing. He enjoyed watching her green eyes flash and her face flush with rosy color. The passion of her fury reminded him of the passion of her kisses.

A foolish thought, but then, this woman had that effect on him. Her fiery temperament not only drew him, but made his own grounded, reasonable outlook on life seem very dull.

He followed her at a leisurely pace and wondered how long he it would take for her to cool down. Not long, he hoped. He didn't want her to go back to avoiding him. Even if nothing could come of it, being near her fired his blood and made him feel more alive than anything he'd ever experienced.

HE WAS FOLLOWING *her*. At first, Marared was irritated. Then gradually her anger cooled, and she experienced a vague pleasure. Let him dangle, she thought. Let him brood, thinking how close he'd been to taking her maidenhead, only to have her pull away at the last moment. It had been a near thing, but she'd escaped.

Unfortunately, her body seemed to get no satisfaction from her triumph. Her lower abdomen felt heavy and throbbing. Her nipples still tingled. And her mouth almost hurt, as if her lips were bereft at the loss of contact with his. She hoped Malmsbury was feeling the same miserable sense of loss she was.

Was her response normal? She had no way of knowing. No one to ask. Her sudden sense of loneliness reminded her of her plan to ask Malmsbury to let her meet Aoife at Abergavenny. She'd obviously ruined that. After the way she'd rejected him, her husband would be in no mood to grant her any favors.

Her wretched temper was always getting her into trouble. Now she'd have to bide her time before she dared broach the subject of meeting Aoife. Meanwhile, she'd have to endure the awful torture of being near him at meals, and at night in the bedchamber they shared.

It had been difficult before this. To have him so close, knowing he was nearly naked. He wore only his braies when he slept. They concealed his private parts, but she felt certain he was well-equipped to satisfy a woman.

Having observed animals mating, she had some notion of what sex involved. Although, unlike a dog or a stallion, men did not mount women from behind, make a few brief thrusts, and then go off as if nothing had happened. At least she did not think well-born men did that. If they had any manners, they surely took some time to flatter their partner and whisper a few fond endearments.

But married people might not necessarily engage in such pleasantries. Her parents had been affectionate, but that was because they truly cared for each other. Her marriage was an altogether different matter. After all, if she had her way, her marriage would soon be dissolved, and she would never have to see Gerard of Malmsbury again.

Which made it utterly absurd that she gave any thought to his attractiveness. She should be thinking of how to convince him to do this favor for her so she could escape this marriage for good. Somehow, she had to make up for her rude, insulting outburst earlier and get on Malmsbury's good side.

Should she ride back now and apologize? He might still be angry. Better to give him time to cool off. Then she would go to him and appear contrite and regretful.

As she rode into the castle yard, she held her head high, buoyed by her plan.

WHEN HE REACHED the castle yard, Gerard

dismounted and handed his horse off to the ostler. He'd given Marared plenty of time to get back to the castle. By now she'd probably hid away in the garden. Or maybe she was still in the stables grooming Gwenevere. It didn't matter. He had no desire to confront her. At the evening meal he'd have to sit beside her and attempt cordial conversation, but until then, he could be free of her and the intoxicating spell she wove.

He could not help wondering if she was right and there truly had been some sort of enchantment in the little glen by the waterfall. When he thought back to those brief moments—the feel of her lithe body in his arms, melding against his, her mouth eagerly returning his kisses. It did not seem real. Surely his prickly, hostile wife would never behave like that. After all, she hated him.

He sought to regain his sense of resignation. Although he believed Marared would eventually let him consummate the marriage, he'd told himself it would likely be a grudging, awkward encounter. Nothing like the thrilling, ecstatic embrace they'd shared by the waterfall.

He sought to banish his lingering arousal and regret for what might have been. Fairies and enchantments were silly nonsense, and the idea that his wife might come to desire him was about likely to come to pass as seeing one of the Fair Folk. He must stop thinking about Marared. The best way to do that was keep busy. He'd have something to eat, then ride out again. Lambing was past and had apparently gone well, to judge by all the lambs they'd seen. But he could always ride down by the river again and stop at the mill, or visit with some of the villagers. At least they'd be cordial to him.

He went to the kitchen where he ate a quick bowl of pottage. Leaving the kitchen, he nearly walked into Marared. She halted, looking startled. Then she composed herself and said, "Milord, I have been looking for you. I wanted to speak to you about something."

Was she going to apologize? Surely not. And he truly did not want to hear her reiterate her determination to never let him have his marital rights. "I'm certain it can wait until I get back." He felt a stab of guilt at being so short, but pushed it aside and moved past her.

"Milord." Her voice rose in obvious irritation. Then he sensed her fight for calm. "I wish to speak to you now. Mayhaps we could go to the—our—bedchamber."

He tried not to grit his teeth. Or to lash out at her. Did she think she had the right to command him? Did she truly think him that spineless and weak?

"I...that is...I have a favor to ask of you."

He was surprised by how uncertain she looked. Was her discomfort feigned or real? How did she alter her demeanor so quickly, at a snap of the fingers?

He almost refused, thinking it might be good for her to find out what it felt like to face rejection. But something in her face stopped him. There was no doubt she was conflicted. Perhaps her upbringing prompted her to apologize, even though her independent, contrary nature rebelled. An apology would salve his wounds a bit. At least it meant she recognized she owed him civility. "Very well." He inclined his head to show she should lead the way.

HOW THE DEVIL had she gotten into this predicament? Marared wondered, as she climbed the stairs to the upper part of the castle. A voice that sounded very much like her mother's answered: *If you hadn't seen fit to insult him, you wouldn't have to apologize.*

True enough. But that didn't make it any easier.

She moved briskly, fighting anger. And something else: fear. She was afraid of being alone with this man. Not because she worried he would do something to her. His strict code of chivalry bound him too tightly. Even if she struck him, she doubted he would raise a hand against her. He might not even raise his voice.

She felt deflated that she did not have a more worthy opponent. And yet, he *was* worthy. Somehow, with his calm and reasonableness, he had won all the battles between them. She was left with naught but bitter words on her tongue, taut nerves, and a disappointed body.

A body that even now was reminding her that no matter how vehemently she protested, she had actually enjoyed his kisses and caresses.

The discomforting thought made her want to swear aloud. Nay, she would not think about what had transpired in the glen. Her goal of meeting Aoife was what mattered. And her greater goal of getting free of this marriage.

She paused when they reached the solar, still feeling a sense of awe that she had access to this room and all its comforts: the carpet on the floor. The comfortable, padded chairs. The ornate brazier that warmed the room on cold nights. And most of all, the glorious light. Even on an overcast day like this, the glass windows along one side of the tower let in enough daylight that she could do fine needlework without benefit of a candle or lamp.

Not that she took advantage of the well-lit chamber. It was enemy territory and she tried to spend as little time here as possible. Malmsbury was her adversary; she must not forget that.

She turned and faced him. His expression was impassive, but his hazel eyes were wary. He feared she'd lured him into a trap. Which she had. She was going to lull him into thinking she'd accepted this marriage, even as she used his generous nature to plot against him. Guilt tweaked her. What she was doing was dishonorable. Her father might understand…eventually. But her mother would be appalled.

The muscles in her neck and shoulders tightened, and shame added to the potent brew of emotions making her stomach roil. She tried to smile, although she was certain it looked more like a grimace. "I'm sorry for what I said earlier. I should not have been so rude…and unkind."

He watched her with that watchful stillness she found so unsettling. As if he was a deep, mysterious pool. Monsters might lurk at the bottom. Or great treasure.

"You asked me here to apologize? Are you so embarrassed to be seen talking civilly to me you sought out privacy for that?"

The warm heat of a blush crept up her neck. "Nay, I…the truth is, I have something to ask you."

"What is it?"

She took a steadying breath. Things were moving too quickly. If she asked him for a favor now, he would know her apology was false. He would clearly see she was trying to manipulate him and be suspicious. She had to lull him into complacency. Make him think she truly had softened toward him. She could think of only one way to do that. The thought of it terrified her.

He was not stupid. Despite her vehement denial, he must sense she desired him. That her body—in complete defiance of everything she thought and felt—yearned for his. How did she admit to her attraction and yet stave off actual consummation?

A plan came to her like an arrowshot.

GERARD STARED AT his wife. It was obvious she felt no contrition for brutally spurning him. She spoke the words by rote, thinking he was so malleable and desperate her false apology would pacify him, and he would agree to whatever she asked.

"What is the favor you seek?" His words came out sharp and angry. He didn't care.

She gave him a quick, nervous smile. A dead giveaway of the falseness of her words. She knew he saw through her. That's why she moved away and went to stand by the windows with her back facing him. She wanted to hide her expression.

He braced himself. Whatever he did, he must not let her guess how much he wanted her. She must not know the utter helplessness he felt when he held her in his arms. In those moments, he would do anything to please her. Anything to make her want him. *He* was not stupid, but his body was. His foolish body would do anything to earn her compliance.

She turned and came back to where he stood. "The truth is…I want to consummate our marriage."

He stared at her, stunned. Then suspicion kicked in. She was still toying with him. He raised his brows. "Your behavior says otherwise."

She batted her eyes and shot him a winsome smile. "I do."

The utter falsity of her manner almost made him snort in disgust. Then he decided to play along. He jerked his tunic over his head and sat in one of the chairs to remove his boots.

"Nay, I…I didn't mean…"

He looked up, feigning bafflement. "'Tis an act easier performed naked." He motioned. "If you need assistance with the lacing on your gown, I'll help you as soon as I've finished."

She made a breathy, panicked sound. "But I…the thing is, I'm afraid."

This time he did snort. "You don't strike me as a woman who is afraid of anything."

"But it's true. I've heard there is pain. And blood."

He met her gaze, staring hard into her exquisite green eyes. "There are ways to minimize your discomfort. To make it pleasurable for you."

At the mention of pleasure, the atmosphere between them instantly altered. Gone was his bitterness at her deception. All he could think about was touching her cool, milky skin. Holding her slender form in his arms. Kissing those delicate, rosebud lips.

Her mood also altered. Her false anxiety transformed to genuine fear. But he didn't think she was alarmed about the physical discomfort of consummation. What panicked her was the thought she might enjoy it.

He got up and approached her. She didn't move away, but stood frozen like a hare as a predator approached. Well, he could be as ruthless as any predator. He took her in his arms and brought his mouth to hers.

CHAPTER NINE

NAY, *I DIDN'T mean*...the desperate, unspoken thought fluttered away, and all her clever plans vanished. She could think of nothing but the taste of his mouth. The firm, insistent pressure of his lips against hers. The feel of his bare chest, with its coarse hair and taut skin. His body, warm and hard. She could feel the power of him. His strength. She wanted to melt into that strength. Her arms reached up to encircle his neck.

She clung to him as his kisses made her knees weak, and her body limp and boneless. He was an ocean and she drifted along on his power, giving herself up to his rhythms. The rise and fall of his chest. The tantalizing dance of his tongue in her mouth. The glorious life and heat of his body.

Shimmering pleasure rippled along her spine.

It curled tendrils around her breasts and belly. Aroused a fire deep within her. Made her mouth water and her whole being yearning and hungry.

Still kissing her, he explored her body with his strong, calloused hands. He caressed her back. Stroked her buttocks. Gently squeezing. Pressing her against him. She could feel his arousal through his braies. A hard lance against her belly. She wriggled and felt his phallus come alive. Her body knew where that lance should be sheathed. What it was meant to do. Knew its purpose was to soothe the growing, desperate ache between her legs.

He pulled at her skirts, dragging them up. His hands found bare skin. She moaned into his mouth and her body grew frantic. Need awakened her from her pleasurable, drifting trance. She wanted more. More contact, skin against skin. For their bodies to be joined. She would die if it did not happen.

EVEN IN THE mindless haze of pleasure, Gerard was aware of the decision looming. Did he bed her like this, half-clothed, her skirts rucked up? If he drew away so they could undress properly, he might rouse her from her wild trance of passion. Cause her to think about what she was doing and reconsider. Her ardor would turn to anger, and she would reject him as fervently as she now embraced him.

He eased her toward the bed and disengaged to lift her onto it. Then he immediately climbed on top of her and began kissing her again. Between kisses, he managed to undo the drawstring of his braies and pull them down. He worked at the top of her gown and bared one creamy, silken breast. He nuzzled her nipple and then drew it into his mouth. Her answering moan of rapture almost undid him, but somehow, he maintained control. Even as he mouthed and kissed her lush, silken skin, he eased up her skirts and ripped off her loincloth.

Free to explore her lower body, he gently slid her thighs apart and pulled back to gaze at her coppery curls and rosy, shimmering petal-like folds. The sight made him even more impatient. With a gasp, he dipped his head to taste paradise. Her body seemed to explode. He gripped her hips tightly as he lathed and licked and tongued. She tasted of salt and heat and sweet, yeasty femininity, and he drowned in her essence.

When her moans became frantic, he sat up and moved his body over hers, his cock poised like an arrow over its target. But some vestige of reason recalled that she was a virgin. Instead of thrusting into her, he guided his cock to her opening and rubbed himself against her wetness, then pushed into her a bare inch. Enough to tantalize her but not breach her maidenhead. She cried out and writhed. He repeated the gentle assault, pushing deeper this time.

"Please, please! Do it!" she screamed.

Freed from the agony of holding back, he thrust deep. She screamed again and this time not from pleasure. He went still, giving her body time to adjust. Looking down at her face, he saw her eyes were closed and she was panting.

"It gets better," he murmured. "It does." Then he brought his mouth to hers.

INTENSE PRESSURE. HER body torn asunder. She didn't want him to kiss her, but somehow his mouth, gentle on hers, eased her pain. He reached down between them, fondling near where his body impaled hers. Her body responded. Relaxing. Opening. His shaft pressed deeper and still deeper. Something inside her yielded and broke free. Something else tightened and rippled. Whirled and danced. Then he was moving inside her, and she was arching her back and giving into the roaring fire that rose up between them.

A few moments later, it was over. He withdrew and his fierce lance turned back to normal flesh. Her own body felt weak and spent and yet trembled with delicious quivers of pleasure. She wanted him to kiss and hold her. Then she remembered he was her enemy. Her enemy, and she had surrendered to him. Completely. Utterly.

The thought banished the lazy warmth seeping through her, and she felt empty and lost. How had he done it? How had he so suborned her will? There was no enchanted spring or mischievous water sprite she could blame. Her body had betrayed her. Not to mention, he was good at this. Very good. He'd known exactly how to make her yield.

The thought made her furious. Not only at his cleverness, but also the idea he'd done this many times before. It enraged her to think of him with other women. Kissing. Coaxing. Teasing them until they gave him exactly what he wished.

She opened her eyes and glared at him. "How many women had you done this with? How many other maids have you despoiled?"

His eyes widened. He had obviously expected her to be subdued and meek. To purr and sigh and melt in his arms. To act like all his other lovers had. Well, not her. She would not do that.

Stiff with outrage, she sat up and fought to rearrange her gown, bunched and tangled around her midsection. She scooted to the edge of the bed and got up. But her wretched garment continued to thwart her.

"Here, let me help you."

She flashed him a look of fury and he froze. How compelling he looked, his dark hair mussed and his hazel eyes turned a dark, smoky hue. She drew her gaze away, determined not to seek out the beguiling lance of flesh that had taken her to paradise. He would be flaccid now, but that didn't matter. Her body remembered what he had done to her and wanted to do it again. She hated him even more for making her feel like this.

"Stay away from me, you....you..." If he were a woman, she'd call him a shameless whore. But what insult did you hurl at a man who was a spectacular lover?

She focused on taming her wretched gown, finally getting her bodice in place and her skirts untangled. Moisture seeped down her thighs. His seed mingling with her own secretions. She wanted desperately to wash, but there was no water in the bedchamber. And she wasn't about to raise her skirts and give him any ideas of tumbling her a second time. Although her body quite liked the idea.

Her miserable, stupid body. And him—the smooth, practiced lover. She wanted to glare at him and let him see her fury. But she feared her anger would weaken if she looked at him. Instead, she muttered the worst epithet she could think of: "Bastard!" and stalked from the room.

GERARD STARED AFTER his wife, feeling as if she'd slapped him. Even after all these years, the word still stung. And coming from her, a chieftain's daughter, a princess, it hurt all the more.

How could she possibly be so angry? What had he done...besides deflowering her with tenderness and skill and giving her pleasure in the bargain? Her changes in mood defied reason. She was the most infuriating, stubborn person he'd ever encountered. No one could please someone so prickly and defiant. So nonsensical.

Why could he not have wed a normal woman? She could have been old or ugly. With rank breath. Half-bald. Missing a limb. He could have dealt with any of that. But this...to be bound to this whirlwind, this wild, untamed force of nature. He constantly had to be on guard. To weigh his every word and action. Even when he was as careful as he could possibly be, it didn't matter.

He rose from the bed and snatched up his clothing. He wanted to go after her and give her a piece of his mind. Remind her that he was her husband and she had no right to treat him like this.

Nay, he didn't want to do that. What he wanted to do was quiet her tart-tongued mouth with kisses, hold her in his arms and have her again. She might insult him and rage at him, but it didn't matter. Nothing altered his yearning for her.

He dressed, breathing slowly and evenly, forcing himself to think. He should be pleased to have consummated the marriage and secured the alliance with Caradoc. He was lord of a fine castle. He'd never dreamed of reaching such heights. His father would be so proud of him.

The thoughts restored his equilibrium. By the time he left the room he was calm again. The only thing gnawing at him was the knowledge his wife couldn't avoid him forever. Eventually, they would be alone in the bedchamber again. And then, God help him, he would end up as powerless and vulnerable as ever.

MARARED PACED IN the garden. By the saints, she'd done it again. Failed to secure her husband's permission to meet Aoife. Given him what he wished and gotten nothing in return.

Not quite true. No matter what happened, she'd have the memory of their coupling. The feel of his body inside hers. Nearly unbearable. But also wonderful. She was still surrounded by the miasma of his scent, the reminder of his potent maleness. The tingling delight it aroused made her pause before a bed of gillyflowers. A tremor of remembered bliss passed through her body.

She squared her shoulders to shake off the mood. Life wasn't about pleasure. It was about duty and survival and prevailing against your enemies. She must not forget that. She'd missed her chance, but there would be another. Although she hated to delay setting her plan in motion, she had no choice.

But how did she deal with him until them? Having exerted his marital rights, Malmsbury would expect her to share her bed from now on. She would have to make it very clear she'd done her duty and they were back to being enemies. But if she was stubborn and cold and refused to let him near, he might not agree to let her meet with Aoife. She'd have to think of something else.

Perhaps for tonight she could avoid him by pretending to still be angry. Of course, it wasn't really pretending. She *was* angry with him. She was furious he was such a skilled and tender lover. Outraged that he had taken what could have been an unpleasant and painful experience and made it so enjoyable. It was madness, but that was what she most held against him. She despised him for making her unable to despise him. It would almost be laughable if it didn't reveal how pathetic she was.

The scriptures proclaimed females as the weaker sex, and said males were superior in every sense. But most of the women she knew were every bit as strong as a man. They might not be able to overcome a male in a physical combat, but in terms of reasoning and strategizing, they were certainly the equal of any male. Or mayhaps they were even stronger. How else did they survive the travail of childbirth?

But *she* was craven and worthless. An embarrassment to her line. All it took was a few kisses and caresses and she was at the mercy of her enemy. She found herself longing to see Malmsbury, to be near him. The thought made her queasy with shame. She needed to stay far, far away from him. But first, she must get what she wished, and do so without giving in to her shameful cravings.

How would she ever manage it?

IT TOOK A while, but she finally felt she'd regained enough control to leave the garden. She walked to the castle, her body stiff with trepidation. She would have to sit beside Malmsbury at the evening meal. It would be torture. But it also presented her with another opportunity to ask him about going to Abergavenny. In the hall, surrounded by people, he would not able to suborn her will with kisses and caresses.

First, she must tidy her appearance. She'd used the privy and washed after leaving the bedchamber, but not bothered to brush her hair or put on a headcovering. If she was going to pretend to be the meek, dutiful wife, she must look the part. She needed help.

She found Edith in the weaving room. As soon as she saw Marared, she rose from the loom she was working on. Her eyes were wide with surprise. "Milady?"

"I need your help with my hair."

Edith nodded and followed Marared to the bedchamber. Marared took a seat on the stool, staring straight ahead as Edith fetched her hairbrush from the coffer. She would not look at the bed, that potent reminder of what she and Malmsbury had done in this room only a short while before. Everything around her aroused memories that make her skin tingle and her heart beat faster. She could almost imagine the warm, musky scent of Malmsbury's skin and the sweetness of his seed lingering in the air. Could Edith tell? Had she seen the mussed bedcovers and guessed what they'd done?

Surely not. An innocent girl like Edith had no idea of the magic men and women could conjure between them. The potent, heady brew of lust and the way it could muddle your wits so completely.

"Milady, are you well?"

"Why would I not be?"

"You are trembling."

Not trembling. Quivering at the memory of their passion. Her cursed body. The priests warned the temptations of the flesh were a powerful evil. They were right. "Perhaps I was outside in the sun too long."

"You do seem flushed. Your skin is so fair. Even this time of year, the sun can burn it."

"I should have worn a headcovering. Indeed, tonight I think I will wear a circlet and veil to the evening meal."

"Are we expecting guests?"

"Nay. Why would you think that?"

"Why else would you wear a veil?"

How did she explain her sudden desire to appear modest and meek? She certainly wasn't going to wear a headcovering to dinner every night. "I feel like it, 'tis all. Can I not dress as I wish now that I am Lady Malmsbury?"

"Of course, milady."

Marared instantly regretted her sharp words. "I'm sorry to be so ill-humored. I do think I got too much sun."

"Do you worry milord will be displeased you've burned your fair skin? I don't think he is like that."

"Like what?"

Edith's hands stilled in brushing Marared's hair. "He isn't the sort to worry much about appearances or make much of being a lord. When he first came here, he let it be known he'd come from humble beginnings himself and that he intended to judge everyone on their work, rather than their rank or whatever history they might have at the castle. So he won't care if you don't always appear the refined and dainty lady."

Edith's words reminded her how clever Malmsbury was. By allowing the castle staff to start fresh with him, as well as pointing out his own modest background, he'd sought to win the people's loyalty. It looked like he had succeeded. He'd made them feel comfortable with him by pointing out he wasn't a rich lord's heir, but a bastard.

Had she hurt him when she'd called him that? No matter. She would not worry about his feelings. He was the enemy.

Edith finished brushing Marared's hair, then went to the coffer and removed the clothing on top to uncover the smaller chest containing Marared's jewelry and head coverings.

"You seem to know where everything is."

Edith's small hands rigid went on the carved applewood chest. "When you first arrived, I sorted through your things. To see what might need airing or to be hung on the clothing pole. I'm sorry, milady, if I did something wrong. I only wanted to serve you."

Marared shrugged. "The truth is, I know very little about dressing like a proper English lady. Perhaps you can advise me."

Edith opened the small coffer and began to sort through it. "Few gentlewomen visited here. But whenever one of them did, I took careful note of how they dressed and wore their hair."

"So, what do you think I should wear to dinner?"

"The green veil." Edith removed the length of shimmering silk and shook it out. "'Twill contrast pleasingly with your bright hair and rosy skin."

"You mean my *sunburned* skin." Marared shot the maid a rueful smile. Edith gave a tentative smile back. The expression made her almost pretty.

"With the gold circlet," Edith added.

It seemed very excessive for an ordinary evening meal. But Marared hoped it would help Malmsbury forget her harsh words and grant her request. Once she'd gotten what she wanted, she could go back to dressing however she liked.

CHAPTER TEN

G ERARD HALTED AT the entrance to the hall. *By the saints, who was that woman at the high table? His wife? But why was she wearing a veil?* Marared turned and smiled, completely befuddling him. The last time he'd seen her, she'd been furious and calling him names.

He went to his place and sat down. "Good even, madam."

"Good even, milord."

A servant came by with wine. Gerard motioned to his cup. He took a drink before hazarding a glance at his wife. With her exuberant red-gold curls tamed and covered, she looked young and vulnerable. Nothing like the flushed, wild-eyed woman who'd responded so passionately to his lovemaking only a few hours go.

He almost wondered if he'd imagined the events in the bedchamber. But his body had no doubts. Every inch of him still hummed with pleasure deeply satisfied.

He tried to think of some polite and mindless topic of conversation. But he had no idea what might set her off. His jaw clenched as he remembered her calling him a bastard. Did she know the truth about his past? Or was it simply a random insult?

He still had no idea why she'd been so angry. She'd *wanted* him to make love with her. Her ardent response proved it. Sweet Jesu, he could not understand this woman. Somehow, he must figure her out...before she destroyed his sanity entirely.

"Milord, I have a favor to ask."

Her meek tone jarred. He looked at her. Her expression remained bland and innocent. "Go on."

She gave him a nervous smile. "I'm certain you know that I've been...ah...lonely here. I thought perhaps if I met with someone from my home, it would lighten my mood."

"That's why I suggested you bring a maid or companion."

Her eyes narrowed. Only for a second, but enough to reveal that underneath the veneer of ladylike tranquility she was still wroth.

He spoke crisply. "If you've changed your

mind and now wish to have someone from your homeland visit, or even reside here, I have no objection. Tomorrow we can send an escort for them."

"I don't...that isn't what I wish. I merely wanted to see a friendly face for a brief time. I thought I could arrange to meet my cousin Aoife at Abergavenny. If you take the valley route, it lies halfway between Tangwyl and Caer Brynfawr."

"I don't see why Aoife can't come here. 'Tis not that much farther. Then you could have more time with her. She could go riding with you. With a proper escort, of course."

"That's not necessary." Her voice rose in pitch. "I only need to see her and...find out how things are at home. That is, at Caer Brynfawr."

She sought to pretend she was getting used to living at Tangwyl and coming to accept her circumstances. It was obvious she was lying. At least about that. The part about being lonely was likely true. She spent hours by herself, showing no inclination to share the company of her maid, or any of the other women in the household. Which made it even odder she would be satisfied with such a brief visit with her cousin.

A servant brought bowls of mutton stew. Gerard took a couple of bites, "I don't understand. Why can't Aoife come here?"

Marared pushed her bowl of stew away, as if

she was too agitated to eat. "She *could*. But I don't think it would be right to ask it of her. She's enamored of a man who lives at Caer Brynfawr. I don't want to insist she leave him."

"What about you going to back to Caer Brynfawr for a brief visit?"

"I don't think that would be a good idea. It might make me more homesick."

Probably true. But still…he couldn't overcome his suspicion she was manipulating him. That this request was part of some scheme to escape from the marriage.

He met her gaze with a steady, assessing look. "When do you propose to make this journey to Abergavenny?"

"'Twill have to be arranged. A message sent to Caer Brynfawr. If someone left tomorrow, Aoife could meet me the day after."

"I doubt the priory has overnight accommodations for female guests. You would only have an hour or two with Aoife before you would have to make the journey back. Are you certain you will be satisfied with such a short time with her?"

"'Twill be enough simply to see her face. And an hour or so to catch up on the news." A hard tone came into her voice. "Naught has happened here that is worth mentioning. I doubt it's much different at Caer Brynfawr."

Her dismissal of their lovemaking turned his growing wariness to anger. He took a drink of his wine. *Obviously, naught worth mentioning has happened here. Except that I loved you well and made you scream with pleasure.*

She seemed to sense his irritation. Her voice softened. "Aoife and I are close, but I don't confide *everything* to her. I'm certain we will speak mostly of trivial things, gossip about the household and news about how the lambing went. Things like that. One of the dogs, Taffy, was expecting puppies when I left. I want to know how many she had and what sex they are."

Gerard recalled the huge, hairy dogs he'd seen prowling around Caer Brynfawr. Wolfhounds from Ireland, he was told they were. "Your father's dogs are fine beasts. 'Twould be good to have one of them at Tangwyl. Perhaps later this summer Caradoc could be convinced to part with one of the puppies. The dog could be a companion for you, as well as protection when hunting." He met her gaze, wondering how she would react.

Her forehead creased. "I had not thought that far ahead."

'Tis clear you hope to be free of this place by then. He went back to his stew and ate steadily. She fidgeted beside him, then finally pulled her bowl closer and began to eat.

Why did she want to see Aoife so badly, and yet not desire her to visit? Did she need Aoife's help with something, and that something required Aoife to return to Caer Brynfawr? But what could that something be? What was she plotting?

Marared pushed her bowl away again and sighed. "So, will you do it? Send a messenger?"

"I will. On the morrow."

That seemed to satisfy her, and she resumed eating. Gerard finished his stew and ate some bread. Marared remained quiet. He was not surprised when a short while later, she again pushed the bowl away and rose. "Milord, if I could beg leave of you."

"Of course."

He watched her rise from table and proceed gracefully across the hall. All at once, his appetite deserted him. The intimacy they'd shared should have brought them closer. But he had no more idea what went on in his wife's head than he ever had.

It seemed incredible she could seem so unmoved by their lovemaking. The Church taught that women were the weaker sex, and more susceptible to temptations of the flesh. In that regard, as in many other ways, his wife was not like most women. The blissful joining of their bodies had not affected her.

Unfortunately, their lovemaking *had* affected him. He'd already been half in love with Marared. Making love to her had sealed his fate.

He frowned at the remnants of his meal.

When he was very young, he'd learned to keep a tight rein on his emotions. He was careful not to allow anything to interfere with his goal of being a successful and respected knight. Someone worthy of the pride of his long dead parents. But then he was wed to Marared, and the solid foundation he'd built his life on began to crumble. He could feel it slipping away, like a coastline undermined by the relentless force of the sea. It was extremely unsettling. The way he felt about Marared gave her far too much power over him.

But what could he do? He seemed to be helpless before his yearning for her. No matter how he tried not to, he longed for her regard. Conquering her body and winning her maidenhead wasn't enough. Especially since the act seemed to mean so little to her. She still saw him as beneath her, a pawn to manipulate. Her actions this evening made that clear.

The seneschal, Dunstan, appeared beside him. "Milord, we spoke of going over the accounts tomorrow."

Gerard motioned impatiently. "We will do that, of course. But for now there is another matter I wish to discuss. I need to send a message to Caer Brynfawr to a Lady Aoife. Who would you suggest for the task?"

"Lady Aoife? Not Lord Caradoc?"

"'Tis a message from my wife to her cousin.

The messenger must be someone who knows how to get to the fortress, but does not have close ties to the household. Someone trustworthy. And, of course, I will need Father Anselm to write the message."

"I believe Lady Marared knows how to read and write. She said something to that effect when I was showing her the tally sticks and tax accounts."

"Then I will need someone who can read Welsh."

"Milord?"

Gerard gave the seneschal an exasperated look. "So I can know exactly what she's written."

"Of course, milord."

His wife could read and write. Few women had the skill. Caradoc clearly considered his daughter's education to be as important as that of his sons. The Welsh outlook was very odd. They treated all their sons as their heirs, gave women alarming amounts of authority and freedom, and made little of the difference between lord and commoner. Their leaders appeared to gain their status not from their titles, but from the respect they earned from those who served them.

Of course, now that he thought of it, the situation was not that different from how things were at his overlord's castle. Fawkes de Cressy had started out as a squire and ended up a lord. His wife, Lady Nicola, not only ran the household, but exerted a great deal of authority in other matters. And she could read and write, while Fawkes had only begun to learn the skill.

But Lady Nicola was cool-headed and shrewd. Nothing like his flighty, mercurial wife. And she loved Fawkes and was intensely loyal to him. While his wife...Gerard's insides twisted, the rich stew roiling in his belly. He found his wife fascinating, endlessly compelling. But he did not trust her for a moment.

SHE'D DONE IT! He'd agreed! Marared's body throbbed with excitement as she hurried to the bedchamber. It would be so good to see Aoife again. To have someone with whom she could talk freely. Not that she intended to tell Aoife about letting Malmsbury consummate the marriage. Her cousin didn't need to know about that. No one did.

A flash of shame swept her. She couldn't believe she'd allowed Malmsbury to do those things to her. To kiss and caress her. To use his mouth to make her so aroused she was helpless to push him away when he...she gasped as she remembered the feel of his body inside hers. Sudden pain, followed by spectacular pleasure. She sought to recall the pain, but the memory of all the other magical sensations blotted it out. Even now her body pulsed with delicious yearning. The whole time she'd been in the hall, speaking to Malmsbury, her body had been screaming at her: *Nay, I don't want food. I want him!*

His hard flesh inside her. His arms wrapped around her body. His lips nuzzling and probing hers. Blessed Mary, it was appalling! How could her body betray her like that? What sorcery did he know that he was able to guess exactly the means to render her helpless?

All the more reason she must do this. Find a way to get him to give up on the marriage and send her back to her father. She had to make this scheme work. She had to!

Marared let herself into the bedchamber and hesitated. Her plan was underway. But what was she to do in the meantime? It would be several days before the meeting could be arranged, and having bedded her once, Malmsbury would expect to do so again. She could not let that happen.

She glanced around the cozy room, lit with the golden glow of late sunshine. Why had she come back here? She should have gone to the garden, where everything didn't remind her of the shocking things she'd done with Malmsbury.

She turned and left. On the way down the stairs, a solution came to her. She would tell

Malmsbury her courses had come. She could have Edith convey the information to him. Surely that was part of the duties of a lady's maid. She hurried to the kitchen, thinking the young serving woman might be there.

GERARD WALKED SLOWLY back from the barracks, still puzzling on his wife's request. He'd done as she asked. A message would be sent to Caer Brynfawr in the morning. But a half-dozen questions haunted his thoughts. Questions he could not ask Marared, lest he risked breaking the fragile peace between them. He'd gained some ground with her and he didn't want to lose that. Because he wanted her to let him make love to her again. He longed to explore her sensual beauty in a more leisurely fashion.

The thought of it made him almost dizzy with arousal. As if he was under some kind of spell. His wife bewitched him. Around her, all his sensible, practical thoughts deserted him. There were many things to arrange for the trip to Abergavenny, but he couldn't focus on any of them. His world had narrowed down to the bedchamber, his wife, what their bodies had already shared, and what they might do in bed tonight.

He'd never understood men who let their cock run their life and guide their decisions. And now here he was, in thrall to his wife and willing to endure all sorts of insults from her, as long as she allowed him near. As long as she let him kiss and caress and make love to her.

He entered the hall and started for the stairs. Young Edith hurried toward him, her youthful features etched with a frown. "Milord, if I could speak with you a moment."

He halted. "Of course."

She paused and took a deep breath, looked at him and then looked away. "Milord, I…I must tell you something."

He went rigid. *What now?* "Go on."

"I…I…" She swallowed. "'Tis very awkward."

Awkward. So, not something life and death. He relaxed fractionally. Biting back his impatience, he nodded encouragingly.

Her eyes were downcast. "Milady asked to tell you that her…her courses have come. So she…that is…" She hazarded a quick glance at him. "She would prefer you did not share the bedchamber with her for a few days."

Was this normal? Something any gentlewoman might ask of her husband? He had no idea. "I must fetch a few things." He gestured toward the stairs. "I promise I won't disturb her." The saints save him. Here he was, placating a servant because he feared to displease his wife.

He strode up the stairs. She'd gone too far this time. Sending a servant to convey her wishes. Sending a servant to tell him what he must do. He was lord here, and *he* would decide where he slept!

His temper was still high when he reached the solar. She stood by the window, as if soaking in the last of the fading light. "Madam." He spoke sternly.

She turned, her expression wary. "Did Edith…did she…?"

"She did." He watched her face, wondering if she would start hurling insults at him. It didn't matter. "We are man and wife, bound together by God and law. If you have something you wish to speak to me about, something that concerns matters between us, you will not send a servant with a message. You will come to me yourself."

She stared at him, green eyes wide. Mayhaps this is what he should have done from the beginning. Instead of trying to appease her, he should have insisted she do what he wished.

She broke off her gaze. "I was only thinking…I thought you would want to…"

"Want to what? I'm not going to be banished from my own bedchamber for several days every month." He studied her face, trying to understand her motivation. Was it possible she was truly embarrassed? Was that her real reason for avoiding him?

She nodded. "You're right, of course. I wasn't thinking clearly." She gave him a swift, sudden smile. "I've never been married before."

She looked so lovely. So desirable. Maybe it *would* be better for them to sleep separately. Did he truly want to be this close to her and know they could not make love? It might actually benefit him to heed her request. Some time apart might help restore his reason, and sort out the contradictory messages of her behavior.

But where the devil was he supposed to sleep? He didn't want to return to sleeping on a pallet on the floor. He'd made love with her on the bed, and having experienced that intimacy, he wasn't going to give it up. "Whatever it is that's troubling you, you'll have to get over it. You're a married woman now. There will be other awkward things we must deal with."

Her auburn brows drew together, and her dazzling green eyes turned cold. The transformation from demure maid to fiery vixen was so swift, he felt like he'd been kicked in the belly. This was the real Marared; the other one was all pretense. She feigned shyness and uncertainty when it suited her. When she thought it would soften him up and make him feel sorry for her.

For weeks he'd endured her insults and flashes of temper. He'd let her have way in almost everything she asked, deferring to her tender female sensibilities. Indeed, there were many times he'd actually felt sorry for her. *Poor Marared. Torn from her home and family. Wed to a man she doesn't know. Surrounded by strangers.* But all she'd done with his sympathy and kindness was use it against him. Manipulating him. Making him into a witless dolt who would do anything to please her.

He strode across the room. She shrank back against the window-lined embrasure, all her haughty resentment gone. He seized her slender shoulders and glared down at her. "I am your husband. You will not give me orders nor dispute my wishes. You will behave as a proper gentlewoman and give me the respect I am due."

She swallowed and nodded. A tremor passed through her, and her normally rosy skin lost color. This time her meekness wasn't feigned. She truly was afraid of him.

He released her and stepped back, shocked by what he'd done. Laying hands on his wife. Making her think he might strike her. What was wrong with him? What had happened to his self-control? He took a deep breath, wrestling with his seething emotions. His sudden fury was gone, replaced by unease. Why was everything different with this woman? What did she do to make him into a raging madman?

With effort, he regained his composure. His first instinct was to apologize, but then he thought better of it. Maybe this was what it took to get this woman to respect him. She hadn't let him bed her until he'd lost all restraint. Now that she'd seen he could get angry, she might stop trying to manipulate him.

But some part of him insisted he must temper his domineering stance. He didn't want his wife to be afraid of him. That was no basis for a marriage. He inclined his head to her. "My apologies for losing my temper. 'Twas inappropriate. You made a simple request of me and I refused it. There was no need for me to take out my frustration on you."

She gaped at him. As if he was as much of a mystery to her as she was to him. The thought calmed him further. But it didn't weaken his resolve. He did not intend to abandon his own bedchamber.

"We are man and wife now. 'Tis fitting and reasonable we share a bed. I can think of few circumstances when it would be otherwise. For you to have your courses is a natural thing, and you should not feel embarrassment or shame because of it. If you do, you will have to overcome your feelings. I will not agree to being banished from our bedchamber. Nor from our bed." He nodded to the massive piece of furniture.

Some of her defiance returned, and she looked as if she was on the verge of protesting. Then she seemed to think better of it. She nodded. "As you wish, milord."

CHAPTER ELEVEN

MARARED MOVED AWAY from the window, uncertain what to do next.

Malmsbury's hazel eyes still bored into her. At last he broke off his gaze. "There are a few more things I must see to for the trip to Abergavenny. I'll send up Edith to assist you."

As the left the room, she exhaled, feeling the tension drain away. The feeling did not last long. In moments, she started pacing.

Gerard of Malmsbury was like no man she'd encountered. She'd thought him weak and easily controlled. He was not. She'd thought him cold and aloof. He was not that, either. She was used to overwhelming people with her volatile moods. That didn't seem to work with Malmsbury.

He'd met her wild temper with dispassionate reserve. Responded to her sensual nature with a fiery ardor of his own. When she coolly rejected him, he stood up to her, intimidating her with his size and strength. And then, after he'd well and truly frightened her, he turned into back into the perfect gentleman.

Which was the real Malmsbury? How was she ever to know? How was she to outwit someone who always seemed to be one step ahead of her?

She felt hopelessly frustrated. It was bad enough she had no idea how to deal with Malmsbury. Worse, she did not know how to deal with her feelings for him. He infuriated her, frightened her, and enticed her. She was drawn to him, her body craving his.

She paced, struggling with her dilemma, until Edith arrived. "Milady, I brought some cloths." The maid indicated the basket she carried.

"I don't need them. I only said that to avoid Malmsbury." Marared glanced at the serving maid and saw she'd shocked the young woman speechless. She fixed Edith with a stern look. "Don't ever get married. Avoid it if you can. You might be able to do so, since you're not from a noble family. You may think I'm very fortunate to have been born a chieftain's daughter. I *was* fortunate. Until I was forced to wed Malmsbury. Now I have no power over anything. My life is not my own."

"That's not true." Edith spoke softly, and yet

her tone was confident. "You have great power. Anyone at Tangwyl will obey any order you give."

"Unless it contradicts my husband's wishes. Then they will not."

This seem to appall Edith even more. She frowned, her blue eyes disbelieving. "But that is as it should be. The scriptures say a woman must obey her husband. 'Tis the natural way."

Marared snorted. "Natural for whom? I'm quite certain the scriptures were written by a man. Or several men. There were no women involved."

Edith was silent for a few moments. Then she asked, "Was it not like that in your father's household? Did your mother not defer to your father?"

Marared tried to recall the interactions between her parents. "My mother died when I was fairly young, but I don't remember my father ordering my mother to do things. Nor do I recall that she always did as he wished." *And yet...she always supported him. She loved him and was unfailing loyal and devoted to him.*

She would not tell Edith that. To do so would point out the glaring differences between her parents' relationship, and hers and Malmsbury's.

Edith went to the chest and put the cloths away. Her tentative manner suggested she was trapped in the room with a wild beast, and she feared making any sudden moves lest she startle it into attacking.

If only Malmsbury saw like her that. *He* wasn't afraid of *her*. Indeed, it was the other way around. She feared him. Not because she dreaded he would strike her or abuse her. Nay, it was his kindness and utter reasonableness that terrified her. That and the desire he aroused. Even now, she longed for him to return. She wanted to be near him, to have his body close to hers.

THE RAIN POURED down and the sky was a dull, gloomy gray. Despite the fact that she was on the way to meet Aoife and her plans were the falling into place, Marared's mood was as bleak as the weather.

It had taken three days for the message to get to Aoife and for her to respond, and they had been miserable days for Marared. Although, the nights were what really took their toll. Nights when she lay beside Malmsbury, listening to his slow even breathing, his body shifting the rope supports of the bed when he moved or turned over. Every little thing seemed to remind her of the intimacy they'd already shared.

She couldn't forget what they'd done in the

bed a short while before. The memory haunted her, and her body felt horribly, wretchedly deprived because they weren't doing it again. Her skin ached for his. Her breasts throbbed, longing for the touch of his big, warm hands or the delights of his mouth suckling and nuzzling.

It was torture to lie beside him and know what she was missing. Her deprivation fueled her anger and determination, and made her resent him all the more. She couldn't wait to be quit of him. Of his stubborn, calm reasonableness. It wore her down like the steady, relentless waves of the sea. Breaking through her defenses and making her vulnerable.

The thought of it made her want to urge Gwenevere into a run and flee Malmsbury and their escort at this very moment. But even if she could get away for a time, he would track her down and take her back to Tangwyl, and then she would be trapped forever. Nay, she must keep to her plan.

She peered through the falling rain, seeking comfort in the thought they were getting closer to her beloved homeland. But it was hard to see anything through the blur of water. The rain beat steadily on the hood of her oiled leather cape, and the dampness and chill seeped through her layers of clothing to make her shiver. Malmsbury was probably right. They should have sent another message, delaying the meeting until the weather cleared. But she hadn't wanted to wait, and so she'd insisted they set out as planned.

She grimaced as she thought of poor Aoife, also forced to travel in the awful weather. After this, she would owe her cousin even more than she already did. Maybe she could ask her father to insist Rory marry Aoife. But that wouldn't be right. And it wouldn't solve Aoife's dilemma, that the man she desired had no interest in her.

She and Aoife were certainly a pair, Marared thought glumly. Aoife longed to be married, even though the man she'd chosen, Rory, didn't love her. Marared, on the other hand, knew she would be quite content if she never married anyone. She had no use for love, or any of that silly nonsense. She wanted to be free, the same way Rory did.

There were other similarities between her and the handsome Irishman who was the object of Aoife's desire. Rory longed to return to his home country. Only his duty as one of the warriors bound to serve at Caer Brynfawr, held him in Cymru. Marared felt sorry for Rory. The weather in her homeland was harsher than that in Ireland, especially in the mountains. The scenery was also different, too. The territory Rory hailed from in Munster was open pastureland, with broad, glistening lakes and small fishing villages along the coast.

But at least he was a man, with the freedom to come and go as he pleased. Her father could have insisted Rory be one of the men who traveled to Tangwyl with Marared. But he had not, knowing Rory would be even more homesick further inland. Of course, if Rory had come to Tangwyl, then Marared could have easily asked Aoife to join her there. Although then there would be no way to set her plan in motion.

Her plan. Would it work? Would her cousin Rhys agree? There were risks. Raids were always dangerous, especially when made on a prosperous, well-defended keep like Tangwyl. And the raids might not be enough to break the truce. Her father could argue he had no control over the rebel warriors and therefore, their actions did not invalidate the alliance.

But Malmsbury would have to spend time and resources dealing with the raiders. If the raids became frequent and disruptive, her husband might finally decide this alliance, and marriage, weren't worth it.

Although it wasn't entirely his decision. He'd wed her on the orders of his overlord, Fawkes de Cressy. And Malmsbury did not strike her as a man who would go against his overlord. Especially after de Cressy had raised him up from an ordinary knight and made him a lord.

Seeing the flaws in her plan aggravated her despondency. All she wanted was for her life to go back to the way it had been. To be able to ride freely in the hills at home and watch the new lambs frolic. To admire the goshawks floating majestically on the downdraft. The play of light over the landscape as the sun peaked out from the clouds. The golden blaze of gorse on the hillsides, and blue speedwell and pale daisies gleaming in the grass, with orange and white butterflies fluttering above them.

She sighed. Although she hated to admit it, part of what she yearned for most was her childhood. But even if she remained at Caer Brynfawr or wed one of her countrymen, her life would be much less carefree than it was back then. Indeed, living at Tangwyl, she probably had more ease and freedom than she would if she returned to her homeland.

But she hated it at Tangwyl. Despised being idle and useless. The tedium of sewing for hours in the garden or grooming Gwenevere until her coat gleamed. But what else could she do? There was no place for her at Tangwyl. The household functioned perfectly without her. The only reason for her to be there was to seal the alliance, and to provide Malmsbury with an heir.

That thought aroused another, unsettling one. She might be pregnant right now. Despite her excuses to Malmsbury, her courses hadn't come. If there was a child on the way, her father would never let her return home, even if the alliance was completely shattered.

She would not think about that. But she would focus on her plan. It had to work. She couldn't keep coming up with excuses as to why Malmsbury couldn't bed her. And if she gave in and let him do as he wished, she would eventually lose all will to fight him. She could not let that happen. She could not.

They followed the river north to Hereford, a bustling market town. As they entered the settlement, Marared glared at the square-towered church. "I can see the English have taken over this place and built their ugly buildings."

Malmsbury raised a brow, but didn't respond.

Marared knew her words were peevish and spiteful. The English had controlled this area for many years. The locals had clearly come to accept them. They probably even considered themselves English.

The weather had cleared and as they rode past the town, Marared could easily make out the gray stone of the priory, with the great arches of the church rising above the other buildings. Malmsbury rode ahead to speak to the porter at the gate. Marared scanned the trackway leading from the other side of the valley. Had Aoife and her escort already arrived?

Malmsbury returned, his expression unreadable. "Lady Aoife and her party are not here yet." His mouth quirked, as if he was amused. "I must say, the abbot is not exactly pleased by your visit.

You will only have a short while to speak to your cousin. Are you certain you wouldn't rather meet Aoife somewhere else in the valley, now that the weather has cleared? You'd be able to talk more at your leisure."

Marared shook her head. In the priory, they would be allowed to meet in a private room, and she would not have to think about Malmsbury waiting nearby.

"As you wish," he responded.

Marared urged her horse forward. Her plan was set in motion; she would see it through.

Inside the priory, a holy brother took Marared's horse and another led her to the guest house. Her guide was young, with full lips and dark, mournful eyes. Marared couldn't help wondering how he'd ended up at the priory. He didn't seem happy at all. Or maybe he was dismayed at having a woman invade his private realm.

As they made their way along the little-used pathway, Marared had the sense the young brother was trying to keep her out of sight of the other monks, as if she were something shameful or dangerous, something that should be kept hidden. She thought angrily of some of the scriptures Father Idwal quoted. They implied women were not only inferior to men, but a source of evil, since they led good men astray.

What nonsense. So far, in their relationship,

it had been Malmsbury who had led *her* astray. He'd made her forget her vow to do everything she could to escape this marriage. Now she was back on course again.

The brother took her to a small guest house, furnished only with benches and a rough plank table. But there was a blazing fire in the grate and the room was warm and comfortable. On the table was a platter of bread and cheese, and an earthenware ewer.

Marared ate and drank eagerly, not caring that the wine was sour and the bread tough and hard. Then she sat restlessly, fidgeting as she worried Aoife wouldn't come.

Finally, her cousin arrived and collapsed on the bench across from her. She looked out of breath and harried. "What is it, Marared? What's happened?"

Marared went around the table and hugged her cousin. "Nothing's wrong. I'm sorry if I worried you."

"If nothing's wrong, why am I here?"

"Take a breath and have something to eat and drink. I'll explain while you do so."

Aoife nodded and took a drink of the wine Marared offered her

As her cousin began to eat, Marared remained standing, her body alive with the nervous energy as she tried to decide how best to explain. "Nothing awful has happened, Aoife. Indeed,

Malmsbury has been a perfect gentleman and everyone at Tangwyl Castle treats me well. But I haven't forgotten that my husband is my enemy. I still intend to escape this marriage."

Aiofe paused in eating. "By the rood, you are stubborn. I thought by now you would have adjusted to your new life. You say nothing is wrong, that your husband treats you well. Then why are you so dissatisfied?"

"Malmsbury is the enemy. Don't you see? I can never be content married to him. To do so would be to give up all my convictions. To forget everything I've been taught."

"Taught by whom? Your father? 'Tis clear he's changed his mind. If he can come to view the English differently, then so can you."

"But what about my brothers, who died at the hands of the filthy *Saeson*?"

"They didn't die at the hands of the English. They died because they chose to fight them. There's a difference."

Marared clenched her jaw. Aoife would never understand. But her cousin did. Rhys would help her, if she could convince Aoife to get word to him. "I'm determined in this. You won't dissuade me."

"I suppose I won't." Aoife resumed eating. Marared waited until she was finished, then sat down across from her. She leaned over the table and spoke in a quiet voice. "I need you to get a message to Rhys ap Cynan."

"What does he have to do with this?"

Marared glanced around the room and spoke in even softer tones. "I want him to raid Tangwyl. I must convince Malmsbury my father has broken the truce so Malmsbury will send me back to Caer Brynfawr."

Aoife looked alarmed. "I don't think it will work. Your father only has control over his own warriors. He can't be held responsible for the actions of renegades like Rhys and his men."

"We have to make things difficult for Malmsbury. We have to make him see the truth. That his kind doesn't belong here and never will."

"The English have been in this country for hundreds of years."

"Exactly. Our people have been here for far, far longer than that. Since our ancestors erected the ancient standing stones."

Aoife's expression grew wry. "I might remind you that you're half-Irish, and your mother's people were once bitter enemies of the Cymry. Since her blood runs in your veins, you can hardly claim to be a pure Cymraes."

"But I feel like I am! I feel like the very essence of my homeland runs in my veins!"

"Perhaps Malmsbury will come to feel that way, too. Or at least your children will."

At the mention of children, the sickening thought returned. She might already be carrying

Malmsbury's child. She pushed the horrifying notion away and glared at Aoife. "You won't help me?"

"I didn't say that." Aoife's dark eyes grew tender. "You are my kinswoman and I love you. I want you to be happy."

"Then do this for me." From her cloak, draped over the chair, Marared took out the missive she'd written. "Get this to Rhys. I beg you."

Aoife took the missive reluctantly. "You know Rhys can't read. Nor can any man in his warband."

"Rhys is resourceful. He'll find someone to tell him what it says."

"You're certain you want to do this?"

"I'm certain." In truth, Marared wasn't certain at all.

A moment later, she asked, "How are things with you and Rory? Has he shown any sign of warming to you?"

"Nay. But it doesn't matter so much now."

"Why not?"

"One of Malmsbury's knights, he..." Aoife looked away.

"You mean you don't care about Rory anymore? You've already switched your allegiance to one of the enemy?"

Aoife's gaze turned clear and direct. "'Tis not like that. Guy's different than the rest of the

Saeson. He's always smiling and jesting. He makes me laugh."

"I vow, it sounds like the cunning wretch has already seduced you."

"Don't be silly. I would never dally with a man I'm not wed to."

Marared's whole body felt tight with shock and betrayal. She'd never imagined her cousin would get over her yearning for Rory and end up besotted with someone else. Especially one of the knights Malmsbury had left at Caer Brynfawr as part of the marriage agreement. And it had all happened so quickly, in the few weeks since the wedding. "No wonder you don't want to do this. No wonder you keep finding excuses for why you should not to carry this message to Rhys."

"I said I would do it, and I will."

Weak. Her cousin was weak. That was the difference between them. Aoife might give in to the enemy, but she would not.

Marared forced herself to calm. She dared not reveal her true feelings to her cousin. Aoife's cooperation was essential to her plan. "How is everything else at Caer Brynfawr?"

GERARD SCRUTINIZED MARARED and Aoife as they left the priory, observing that neither woman looked happy. Marared appeared deep in thought, her eyes downcast and her mouth set in a grim line. Aoife also appeared discontent. For the dozenth time, Gerard wondered if he'd made a terrible mistake in agreeing to this meeting. But it would have been churlish of him to deny his wife an opportunity to meet with her cousin.

He should have insisted they meet at Caer Brynfawr. That would have been the normal arrangement. But he'd worried if she went back to her former home, it would make it even more difficult for her to accept her new life at Tangwyl.

He struggled to shake his gloomy mood, reminding himself that having done this favor for Marared, she had no excuse not to be intimate with him. Her courses must be over, so there was no reason for her to refuse him. If she tried to, he would remind her he'd done everything she wished and now it was her turn to accommodate him.

Although he didn't want it to a matter of *accommodation*. The thought of her letting him bed her out of obligation or duty was distasteful. He wanted Marared to desire him as much as he desired her.

His passion seemed to grow stronger every time he looked at her. All he could seem to think about was getting his wife home and alone so he could kiss her and caress her and explore her beautiful body.

He hurried to help her onto her horse. "Did you have a pleasant visit?"

She smiled, although it appeared forced. "Aye. Very pleasant. Very satisfying."

Chapter Twelve

G ERARD TRIED TO make conversation with Marared as he rode beside her, but her responses were terse. Aye, everyone at Caer Brynfawr was well. The weather there had also been wet, but not exceptionally so.

"And your father's hounds? You mentioned one of his favorites had whelped."

"Oh, aye."

"How many males and how many females?"

She glanced at him, seemingly irritated. "What does it matter?"

"Don't you recall that we discussed the idea of one the puppies coming to Tangwyl?"

She gave a distracted wave. "Aoife agreed to bring up the matter with my father."

He felt certain she was lying; she and Aoife had discussed nothing of the sort. Why was she deceitful about the most trivial things? He considered confronting her, but decided there was no point. She'd only give him more lies, or grow angry and insulting. He didn't fancy being called names.

Giving up on the conversation, he spurred his horse forward. There were times when he wondered if anything was worth enduring this miserable sham of a marriage. But he'd agreed to take control of Tangwyl, and that meant arranging this truce with Caradoc, which required him to wed Marared. He could not back out now, no matter how difficult things became.

He glanced around, hoping the spring scenery would ease his mood. After the rain, the vegetation was so green it was almost blinding, and blossoms were everywhere: white daisies, golden buttercups, purple madder, and delicate blue mountain pansies. The sweet fragrance of hawthorn and yellow root hung in the humid air. In a few hours they would reach the Tangwyl demesne. *His* lands, at least in the sense he was overlord.

There was no reason to be morose about his circumstances. He was very fortunate. How many landless knights, let alone bastards, ever had such an opportunity? He might bemoan his fate in being married to a difficult, exasperating woman, but a lot of knights never got the chance to marry at all. And while Marared might vex and frustrate him, she'd also given him the most transcendent sexual experience of his life.

The memory of their coupling instantly took over his thoughts. The feel of her silken skin. The delicious, beguiling scent of her, as lovely as the fragrance of any flower. Her silken mouth. Her passion, so intense and wild, it was like being carried away in a thunderstorm. He would give a great deal to have a chance to love her like that again.

Nay, he would not give up yet. As soon as she allowed him near, he would show her even perfection could be improved upon. There was so much left for them to explore. All he needed was a chance, and he would make her pleased she had married him.

MARARED WAS VERY relieved when Malmsbury pulled ahead and she no longer had to make conversation with him. Being near him made her stomach churn. She couldn't help thinking about what Aoife had said about the knight named Guy: *He makes me laugh.* Malmsbury had done far more than that to her. He'd given her intense pleasure. Made her moan and sigh with delight. What if Aoife was right? What if she was simply being stubborn? What if it would be better for everyone if she accepted her marriage and moved forward?

Back when Malmsbury had been an unknown, foreign-looking knight, it had been so easy to reject him. Now it became harder and harder every day. It took all her will. All her energy.

And it wasn't merely the memory of their lovemaking that made things so difficult. In the past few weeks she'd learned what sort of person he was. Not arrogant and rude, but thoughtful and considerate. She'd never known him to be short or condescending with anyone: groom, page, or kitchen wench.

Maybe you've made a terrible mistake. Maybe you should turn around and go after Aoife. Tell her you've changed her mind. But then she'd have to explain to Malmsbury what she'd done. He'd never trust her after that.

But why did she want his trust?

Because he'd bedded her. Her feelings for him weren't real. It was simply her lust suborning her will. Which meant she must not let him bed her again. The excuse of having her courses would no longer work. She'd have to come up with some other reason to keep him at a distance.

The dilemma gnawed at her, making her weary. By the time they reached Tangwyl, she was so tired she could hardly wait to get off her horse. Malmsbury saw how fatigued she was. They were barely into the bailey when he dismounted, handed the reins to the ostler, and hurried over to help her down. He settled her on her feet. "What's wrong? Are you ill?"

His worried expression gave her an idea. She let herself wilt against him. "I think the food I ate at Abergavenny disagreed with me. I must lie down."

"Can you walk? Do you want me to carry you?"

By the saints! That was all she needed. To have him hold her in his arms! "Nay. I am not that unwell. I can walk." She straightened and gave him a quick smile.

He nodded, his hazel eyes dark with concern. "I'll fetch Edith to tend you."

She breathed a sigh of relief as he walked away. This was the means to get a reprieve from Malmsbury's attentions. He was used to noblewomen who were sickly and frail. If he thought she was ill, he would never consider exerting his marital rights.

The plan should have soothed her mood, but it didn't. Maybe she truly was ill. Or maybe she suffered from that dreaded disease the poets wrote about: she was heartsick.

GERARD PAUSED BEFORE to the bedchamber door

and gathered his resolve. It was time to confront his wife. When they first returned from Abergavenny, he'd believed her illness was real. That the food at the Priory had been tainted or she'd taken a chill in the rain. But he'd soon become suspicious. Especially since Marared seemed to feel well enough to go to the garden when the weather was fair. It was at nightfall she appeared to decline. She would claim she was not up to joining him in the hall for the evening meal and then be in bed and asleep—or pretending to be—by the time he retired for the night.

He had a very good idea why Marared was pretending sickness. On the first night home from Abergavenny, when he'd attempted to join her in bed, she'd asked him to sleep elsewhere, saying she didn't want him to catch whatever afflicted her. Later she spoke of sleeping restlessly and her worry she would disturb him if he tried to sleep beside her.

He'd quickly come to doubt her claims, yet remained reluctant to confront her. But he knew he couldn't keep on like this. It was time to act. He opened the door and strode in.

Marared was seated on the padded window seat wearing a crumpled shift. As soon she saw it was him, she stiffened. "Milord."

"Milady. How fare you today?"

A swift, calculating look crossed her face. "I thought I was better, but now I'm feeling faint again."

He folded his arms and fixed her with a steady gaze. "I don't believe you."

"What?"

"I don't think you're ill. I think it's an excuse to force me to keep my distance."

Her eyes went wide, although he felt certain her shock was feigned. "I truly have been ill. If I shun you, 'tis because I don't want you to catch whatever it is I suffer from."

He approached the window seat and stood over her. "I accept the risk. Go back to bed if you wish. But I intend to join you there."

"Now?" Her expression grew wild.

"Aye. Now."

"But...I..." Her eyes narrowed and a hard look came over her face. "Of course."

She rose slowly, her shoulders slumping, and made her way to the bed. He followed, wary. Did she guess his words were a bluff? If she refused him, he wasn't going to force her. Even if the law said he had the right, he wouldn't take her against her will. That was rape, a repulsive, cowardly act.

She slid beneath the blankets and lay flat on her back, eyes closed, as stiff and still as a corpse. A part of him could not help but be amused. So this was her plan, to pretend lovemaking was an onerous, unpleasant duty she must endure. His anxiety fell away, replaced by a keen sense of challenge. He felt certain he could get her to respond.

He removed his boots and undressed. When he was naked, he slid in bed next to her.

CURSE HIM! HE intended to go through with it! Well, she would not open her eyes. Or give him any sign she knew he was there. He could take her body, but he could not make her feel anything while he did so. She would be naught but a vessel for his lust. An empty shell. He could not say she'd denied him; he would get what he wanted, but it wouldn't have anything to do with her.

She felt his mouth on hers and kept her lips tightly closed, resisting. He caressed her neck and shoulders. His calloused fingers were gentle and coaxing. She fought to control her response, but his touch seemed to leave a trail of fire in its wake. The smoldering heat grew more intense. It surged hotter when he fondled her breast and played with her nipple.

She told herself she was being tortured and willed herself to feel pain, to imagine the mounting pleasure as excruciating and miserable. But her body had a mind of its own. She struggled to hold back a moan.

His touch was delicate. Subtle. Enflaming. Unbearable. He seemed determined to explore every inch of her. His fingers lingered on body parts that should not have been sensitive: her arms, along her ribs, the curve of her hip, her belly. All the while he kept getting closer to the area she longed for him to touch. She would burst apart if he did not touch her there.

But, nay, she could not want that! She could not!

She took a deep breath, determined to quell her response. As her mouth opened, he took full advantage, kissing her deeply and using his tongue to tease and tantalize hers.

She jerked her head away. "Nay! Stop!"

"Why?" His breath was warm against her cheek. He kissed her again. She murmured her protest against his lips, then gave in and kissed him back. Even as she did so, she felt tears seep from beneath her eyelids. *'Twas not fair he could do this to her! 'Twas not!*

He stopped kissing her. "You're crying."

"Aye."

"What's wrong?"

"I don't want to do this."

"I think you do."

"Nay, I do not!" She let out a sob. Her lower lip trembled.

With a sigh, he drew away. She immediately felt bereft. He climbed from the bed, his movements heavy and defeated. Her sense of loss and regret caused the words to slip out. "Nay, I didn't mean…"

He turned to gaze at her, head cocked. Then, still staring at her, he climbed back into bed. He stroked her cheek. She closed her eyes and gave a little hiccup of resignation. What did it matter if she let him bed her? He'd already taken her maidenhead. There was no point resisting him now.

You'll regret it. You'll lose more of your will to fight him. Everything will be more difficult.

He silenced the warning voice inside her with another long, searching kiss. In moments she'd forgotten everything but the feel of his lips on hers. His taste, so warm and delicious. His kisses were leisurely. Tender. Exquisitely arousing. When she began to squirm and moan, he paused. "Mayhaps you should take off your shift."

She nodded, lost in some mindless, languid haze. He helped her sit up, and she let him pull her shift from underneath her and over her head.

He eased her down on the bed and pushed the bedding aside. She shivered with expectation and her breathing quickened. Every inch of her seemed to pulse with excitement.

She struggled to remain still as his gaze moved over her, searing her skin with shimmering sensation. His caresses followed. His fingertips grazed her nipples, then he cupped her breasts, molding the flesh in his hands. His big, long-fingered, warm hands.

She pressed herself against the bed and tried

not to writhe. Her breathing came hard and fast. If only he would move his tormenting hands lower, to the pulsing center of her body, the lodestone of her thoughts. She could feel wetness seeping out of her and she longed for him to fill the burning void inside her, the part of her that demanded to be joined with him.

He played lazily with her breasts, as if he had all the time in the world. Streaks of fiery need swelled inside her and overwhelmed her patience. "Please," she whispered.

The slow, tender stroking halted. She met his enigmatic hazel gaze and knew he saw her desperation, her helpless desire. But she didn't care. If he stopped now, she would surely die of frustration and regret.

His mouth twitched into a smile and a dimple she'd never noticed before appeared on his cheek. She held her breath, silently begging him. Would he reject her now that he knew how much she wanted him?

His eyes grew hooded and distant and his nostrils flared. He sat back on the bed and moved the covers away. She could see his erection jutting out. Now he would take her. They would be joined. Her womb stirred inside her, taut with expectation.

He ran his fingers along her thighs and they fell open, splaying wide. She closed her eyes in mortification, even as she waited breathlessly for him to continue. She gasped as she felt his mouth on her most sensitive parts. When her hips jerked, he grasped her thighs and held her still. She gave in to the sublime sensations as he used his lips, his tongue, even his teeth, to work magic on her sensitive flesh.

Quivers of delight raced through her. She felt the building pressure, the impossible spiraling need. She keened her helpless surrender and soared into the rapturous heights, flying wildly in a star-studded, magical realm.

Gradually, she floated down to earth. She sought to catch her breath and slow her racing heart. Then she opened her eyes and met the gaze of her lover. He looked pleased and satisfied, as if he'd been the one to experience such dazzling sexual pleasure. She should be angry that he'd won, furious over the unfair methods he'd used. But having been so deliciously gratified, she had no will to fight him.

"Where did you learn to do that?" she whispered.

GERARD HESITATED. WOULD she twist his answer around and somehow find fault with his skill in pleasuring her? "A woman taught me."

Her eyes narrowed. He could see the gleam

of jealousy flickering in their darkening green. "A lover?"

"Not exactly. I paid her."

Her suspicion turned to confusion. "Why?"

"Why? Why, what?"

"Why would you pay her to learn how to…"

"Please a woman?"

"Aye."

He shrugged, trying to hide his amusement. "It seemed a worthwhile skill to acquire."

She contemplated this. Then she looked at directly at him, her expression intent. "What else did she teach you?"

He let out a helpless laugh. Then he smothered back another guffaw and grinned at her. Slowly, warily, her lovely coral lips curved into a smile. Her radiant loveliness seemed bright enough to light the darkest gloom and bring hope to anyone who beheld her.

Her eyelids swept downward, then she coyly met his gaze. "Well?"

He pounced, pushing her back against the bed as he straddled her. "Well, what?" he growled back.

He didn't wait for her answer. Instead he showed her the rest of what he'd learned from a patient, very skillful whore.

CHAPTER THIRTEEN

MARARED SAT UP in bed and stretched. Her body felt delightfully content and relaxed. But in the back of her mind, the familiar doubts and guilt loomed. She climbed out of bed, as if that would help her escape the tormenting thoughts. But they followed her, reminding her of the message she'd sent to Rhys, and how it was in direct opposition to her amazing experience last night. How could she betray a man who made her feel so wonderful? How could she betray herself?

Outside the cozy bed, the room was cool, and she hurried to don her shift, draped over one of the chairs. Malmsbury must have put it there. That was the sort of man he was, careful and considerate. She thought again of the things he'd done to her and felt a flush of embarrassment. He was a wonderful lover, playing her body as an adept musician might play the crwth or harp. How confident he'd been he could bend her to his will and make her helpless with desire. She wanted to despise him for that. But even though she stoked the ashes of resentment, they refused to catch ablaze.

She dressed and went to the window, staring out at the overcast sky. Malmsbury might give her great pleasure in bed, but the rest of her life was bleak and purposeless. At this moment, she did not entirely regret plotting with Rhys to sabotage the alliance and her marriage. She could not live like this, a pampered, aimless life. She missed her home. She missed Aoife, her father and her brother, and everyone at Caer Brynfawr. She missed the horses and her father's hounds. Even the sheep and the cattle. And she missed the wild hills and all the animals that lived there: foxes, hares, squirrels, pine martins and deer, the hawks and gyrfalcons and the other birds.

Undoubtedly, some of those creatures lived around Tangwl. But she didn't know where to find them, and she felt certain Malmsbury wouldn't let her go riding alone to seek them out. And what about her mother's family in Ireland? Now that she was wed, would she ever see them again?

The losses piled up, making her want to weep. But that was what children did, and she was a woman. Women took charge of their lives, as she had done in sending the message to Rhys. Even though her stomach clenched whenever she thought of what she had set in motion, every time she reasoned things out, she came to the same conclusion. Escaping this marriage was the only hope she had of ever being happy again.

Feeling slightly calmer, she put on her stockings and shoes and sat in the window seat to begin the struggle to tame her hair. She needed Edith's help. But the young maidservant hadn't come, and it seemed foolish to go searching for her simply to have the girl tend to her hair. But after a few minutes of fighting with tangles, she decided she had no choice. She usually slept with her hair braided, but Gerard had undone her plaits so he could run his fingers through the waist-length strands. Then the vigor of their lovemaking had turned her hair into a snarled mess.

She smoothed her hair as best she could and tied it at her nape with a ribbon before going to fetch Edith. After searching the hall and the kitchen, she finally found her in the weaving shed. The girl jumped up from her loom when she saw Marared. "Oh, milady, I'm sorry. I was supposed to come and see to you. Lord Gerard said to let you sleep and then I forgot."

"Where's Malmsbury?" Marared asked. A moment later, she regretted the question. She must get used to the idea that in a few weeks or months, he would no longer be a part of her life.

"He's in the stables. One of the mares is foaling and having a difficult time."

Marared felt an instant surge of anxiety. So many things could go wrong during birthing.

"I came here to get your help dealing with this rat's nest." She motioned to the tangled mass trailing down her back. "But it can wait. I think I'll go see how the mare is faring."

"Milady?" Edith looked startled.

"Oh, I know it's not something gentlewomen are supposed to do, but I always helped my father with the lambing, and this isn't much different. I'm very fond of animals; I hate to see them struggle and suffer."

"Very good, milady. Come and get me when you are ready to have me do your hair."

Marared left the weaving shed and headed toward the stables. As she crossed the mucky yard, she wished she had worn her pattens to protect her slippers from the mud. They were going to be a mess, maybe even ruined. But helping an animal was more important.

She found Malmsbury and the stablemaster outside a stall. Looking in, it was obvious the mare was struggling. Her head drooped and her brown eyes were listless.

Both men regarded Marared with surprise. "What is it, Marared? Is something wrong?"

Malmsbury asked.

"I just heard about the poor mare. How long as she been in travail?"

"All night," Ormond the stablemaster answered. "I think the foal is placed wrong."

"Have you tried to turn it?"

"I've done that with cows, but this mare is so small, I feared to make things worse."

"I could try," Marared said.

Malmsbury and Ormond looked at her as if she'd grown two heads.

"I used to do that with the ewes. Especially when they were carrying twins. Sometimes the two lambs get tangled up, and you have to reach in and rearrange their limbs to get them out safely. Or pull one of them out, to keep the other from dying."

Ormond glanced at her hands. "I suppose it's worth a try. The question is, are your arms long enough to reach the foal?"

Malmsbury said nothing, and Marared felt a flare of anger. He clearly didn't think she knew what she was talking about. But at least he hadn't refused to let her attempt this. "I need some hot water to wash with. It's important to keep things clean during the birth process."

"Who told you that?" Ormond asked.

"The midwife."

"But midwives deliver babies. Animals are hardier. The straw is fresh, but I wouldn't want to think of a woman giving birth here in the stables."

"It hurts nothing to follow Anwen's advice," Marared retorted. "She's delivered many healthy infants over the years."

"Very well, I'll have Edgar fetch hot water from the kitchen."

While they waited, Marared entered the stall to let the mare get used to her. The poor creature. Malmsbury said her name was Star. The animal was so weary and exhausted she paid little attention to Marared. Marared touched the mare's side. It was taut, the skin was stretched as far as it would go. But the rest of the mare's skin seemed loose. Marared turned to Malmsbury. "She needs water. It will give her strength."

Malmsbury took a bucket and headed to the rain barrel outside the stable entrance. When he returned, Marared sought to coax the mare to drink. She didn't seem interested, as if she'd given up and was waiting to die. Marared felt a stab of fear. If things were too far gone, both the mare and her foal *would* die. Then everyone would think she was a fool.

But that didn't matter. She didn't care if what she was doing was futile; she had to try to help this poor suffering creature.

Ormond returned with the hot water.

"Hold her head." Marared motioned. "Hopefully she's too weary to struggle or kick me."

"Marared." Malmsbury's tone was sharp. "I'm not sure you should do this. It seems risky. What if the mare kicks you or knocks you down?"

Marared shot him a look. "You're worried you'll have to tell my father that some harm has come to me. If that happens, remind him what a headstrong, stubborn wench I am. He'll understand. Especially if he knows an animal is involved."

Her gown had long sleeves, which would get in the way. Marared shot Malmsbury a defiant look, then unlaced the front of her gown, slid her arms out of the sleeves and tied them loosely around her breasts. This left her arms bare and her shoulders covered only by her thin linen shift. It was indecent to have Ormond see her like this, but she didn't care.

She rinsed her hands and arms in the near scalding water, wishing she had some soap. After shaking the excess water off her hands, she approached the mare's rear. She gently touched the animal's flank. When the mare didn't become agitated, she carefully slipped her hand into the mare's birth canal and searched for the foal. She immediately found the head, but the front legs were tucked behind it. She needed to straighten them so they would come out more easily.

She strained deeper, until she could grasp one of the legs and slowly ease it forward. The mare had a contraction, squeezing Marared's arm like a vise. She gritted her teeth, pleased despite the crushing pressure. The mare's body had not given up.

When the birth spasm passed, she again sought out the delicate ankles of the foal and maneuvered them bit by bit until they were straight. Then she held on to one of them tightly, waited for the next contraction. When it came, she pulled hard. The leg slipped from her grasp and she cursed heartily, using words no lady should know. Now Malmsbury would realize she truly was an uncouth Cymraes.

Again, she sought out the delicate limb. Grasping it tightly, she waited. It seemed like forever until another contraction came. When in finally did, she gritted her teeth and pulled, hanging onto the frail leg with all her strength.

Nothing happened. Her spirits sank. The mare did not have enough strength to push the foal out. But she waited for another contraction and tried again. This time the foal seemed to move. She waited, panting, for the next contraction, then braced herself and pulled. The horse whinnied, a cry of pain. Then the foal slid out, pitching Marared backwards.

Ormond immediately knelt by the foal and wiped the glistening membranes from its face and rubbed its body with straw, hoping to stimulate it to take a breath. Malmsbury knelt beside Marared and helped her sit. "Are you hurt?"

She was too exhausted and dazed to speak. Ormond's voice came from a distance, full of triumph. "It's a little filly and she's alive!"

Marared let out a sigh of relief.

"You're a true heroine," Malmsbury said. "You saved two lives today."

Aye, she had. She'd done something worthwhile. Something she could be proud of. It had been a long time since she felt like this. Strong and capable.

With Malmsbury's aid, she stood and approached the foal, laughing with delight as she watched it climb shakily to its feet. It went down again, but got up more quickly the second time and balanced on its spindly legs. She could not help turning and smiling at Malmsbury. He smiled back broadly, showing the dimple she'd noticed recently. His hazel eyes shone with warmth and tenderness, and she realized his look of fond happiness was not directed at the foal, but at her.

For a few seconds she felt a bond with him, a much different sort of connection than the one they had in bed. This time, it felt as if their spirits touched.

She looked away, unsettled. This could not be happening. She couldn't be feeling this way. Not with Malmsbury. He was the enemy. She could not forget that.

"What will you name her?" she asked Ormond, who was coaxing the foal closer to its exhausted mother.

"That is for Lord Gerard to decide."

"What do you think, Marared?" Malmsbury asked. "What shall we name her?"

She focused on the wobbly creature and the weary mare, sniffing her baby uncertainly. It was so important the mother accept the foal. Otherwise they would have to find another nursing mare and hope she would let a second foal feed. Or they could try to raise the foal themselves. But hand-fed animals seldom thrived.

When the mare began to lick the foal, Marared felt tears of relief forming in her eyes. She said a silent prayer of thanks.

Malmsbury came up beside her. "All is well now. Thanks to you."

She nodded, but didn't look at him. Now that the crisis was passed, she realized she was cold. The sticky birth fluids covering her were rapidly chilling her.

He touched her shoulder. "You're shivering. We should get you back to the castle."

"A hot bath would not come amiss." She tried to untie the sleeves of her gown so she could dress properly, but it was difficult now they were wet.

Malmsbury began to undo his belt. "Here. Let me give you my tunic to wear."

"Just get me a horse blanket." She gestured.

"It's far too late to worry about how I look anyway."

He fetched a horse blanket from the next stall and put it around her shoulders. "I vow, you still look beautiful."

"Then you are a madman." She reached up to touch her hair, which had come loose from the ribbon. Her tangled tresses spilled in wild waves over her shoulders. "I'm not sure even Edith can unsnarl this mess."

"Let's you get you to the bedchamber so she can make an attempt. After your hot bath."

Malmsbury took her arm but she slipped away and approached the little filly, which the mare was now devotedly licking. The foal was a gray, like its mother, a common color for local horses. She didn't touch the foal, not wanting to disturb the tender scene. Its coat was now the hue of a stormy sky, but would probably grow lighter as it matured. Marared was reminded of bluebells in the spring. "What don't we call her Bluebell?"

Ormond made a sound in his throat that suggested he didn't approve, but Malmsbury nodded. "A lovely name, for a lovely little filly."

A WARM GLOW spread over Gerard's body as his

wife gazed adoringly at the little creature whose life she had saved. This was a side of Marared he hadn't seen before, this maternal tenderness. The last hour had been full of surprises. He hadn't known his wife could be so strong and so determined. He'd thought of her as mercurial and passionate, charming qualities in bed, but not very helpful the rest of the time. It was a revelation to realize that beneath her wildly changeable temperament was a bedrock of strength and determination.

Few women would have been able to do what she had done, and no gentlewoman of his acquaintance would even have tried. His pampered wife was not selfish and spoiled after all. If a crisis demanded it, she could act with decisiveness and fortitude. She was also deeply compassionate. Seeing the mare was in trouble, she hadn't hesitated. Although her resentment of him as a *Sais* had caused him more than a bit of aggravation, he'd always admired her proud determination to defend her homeland and her people. Now he had other reasons to admire her.

At the same time, he felt the familiar anxiety. This was a woman who would do anything to achieve her goals. He'd already discovered it could be unpleasant to interfere with her wishes. Now he could see that it might be dangerous. Would he ever truly win her loyalty? Or would she always choose her people and her beloved

Cymru over him?

As they walked to the castle, Gerard realized she was still shivering. She needed that warm bath immediately. "Go up to the bedchamber. I'll have hot water brought up and fetch Edith."

She hurried toward the castle, holding the horse blanket tightly around her. Her rose gold hair floated like a cloud around her shoulders, reminding him the feel of it as he ran his fingers through the silky tresses when they made love. He half wished he could be the one to bathe her, rather than Edith. But he knew nothing about untangling hair. But perhaps afterwards, when she was warm and clean and comfortable…

Nay, he must not let his thoughts go there. He was already obsessed with his wife. She had too much power over him.

CHAPTER FOURTEEN

MARARED SAT WRAPPED in a blanket as Edith patiently combed out her wet hair. The maidservant had used goose grease to unsnarl the worst of the tangles before helping her wash her hair in the bathing tub. As the maidservant finished untangling the knots, Marared brooded. For once she'd had a useful role at Tangwyl, but it was over now. Her life would go back to its usual tedium. Of course, she still had the pleasure of making love with Malmsbury to look forward to.

The thought made her clench her teeth in self-disgust. It was disgraceful to enjoy her husband's lovemaking even as she plotted to end the marriage. But Malmsbury was the enemy, which excused her behavior. Except, if he was the enemy, she should not have allowed him to get so close. Oh, she was a hypocrite, a wretched, disgusting hypocrite.

She shifted restlessly on the stool, wondering if Edith would ever finish.

"Almost done, milady. Then I will braid it to keep it from being tangled again."

Why bother? Marared almost responded. Why bother with anything? Aiding the poor struggling mare had briefly roused her from her sense of hopelessness and frustration, but now there was nothing to look forward to. Nothing except this endless battle between the yearnings of her body and the cold, rational pathway her head had already chosen.

"Milord!" Edith exclaimed as Malmsbury strode into the room.

"I don't mean to intrude."

He was always so courtly and polite. Why didn't he ever get mad?

"Why are you here?" She faced him sullenly, not caring that Edith drew a sharp, dismayed breath.

His calm, reasonable demeanor did not crack. "I thought perhaps you would like to ride out with me and look at the mares in the far pasture. Several of them are near to giving birth. After our experience with Star, it seems wise to keep an eye on the others."

"Do you really have time for such things?"

"We need quality horses to see to the castle's

defense, and we can't afford to purchase them all. Seeing to the breeding stock is obviously part of my responsibilities."

But it wasn't part of his duties to take her along. He was doing that because he thought she would enjoy it. Curse it. As hard as she tried to see this man as a villain, he refused to cooperate.

"Aye. I would like to go. Although I will need to dry my hair a bit and get some warm clothing."

Malmsbury gave a slight bow. "I'll wait for you in the hall."

GERARD FOUND HIMSELF grinning as he left the bedchamber. At last he'd thought of a way to involve Marared in life at Tangwyl. She clearly cared about horses and other livestock. Involving her in their care might make feel like she was part of her new home and help thaw her coldness. And also ease her resentment of him. She'd responded to him eagerly on a physical level, but he had no illusions she'd come to care for him. There was a part of her that still viewed him as the enemy. As stubborn and proud as she was, that animosity would not be easy to overcome. But he'd made a start.

He met her in the bailey a short while later.

Her hair was in braids and she wore a warm cloak. It was obvious from her expression that she was excited by the prospect of going riding.

For all it was May, the day was misty and cool. The drifts of fog hanging over the hills made him worry they might have trouble finding the herd. But with luck the mist would lift. Despite all that already had transpired, it was not yet after *nones*.

Once they'd left the castle, Marared started to ask questions about the herd. He answered as best he could, half-wishing he'd had Ormond come with him. But the stableman was busy with Star and her baby, and another mare that had foaled recently. Besides, he wanted to be alone with Marared, somewhere besides their bedchamber.

He spoke conversationally. "I'm surprised you know so much about birthing horses."

"The Cymry have been breeding horses since long before the English arrived. 'Tis said some of the bloodlines go back to the days of King Arthur, when he bred native ponies to horses left behind when the Romans left Britain."

"King Arthur? You speak as if he was a real person. I thought all those tales of him were legends."

"Of course he was a real person! And he was a Cymro, as well. Although he might have been born at Tintagel on the Cornish coast, and his father half-Roman, his mother was a Cymraes. Her name was Igraine, after all." She made a sound of disgust. "Your people seek to steal our greatest king and pretend he was from Brittany or some such place, but the evidence is clear. Although he fought the Saxons in east Britain, Arthur grew up in Cymru, and we are the ones who have kept his history alive."

Gerard made a gesture of surrender. "I know little enough of the lege…man. All I've heard are tales told by bards."

"Most bards are Cymro. Or they were. Before the English decided to overrun Britain and steal everything."

Most of the bards Gerard had encountered were from Aquitaine or Normandy, which made him dubious of Marared's claim. But he wasn't going to argue the matter. Better to try to soothe things over by making much of Arthur, whose reputation was impressive, whether he was real or not. "You should be proud the tales of Arthur have spread so far and he is so well-known. Clearly, he was an extraordinary man."

Marared raised her jaw. "He was a visionary, a man who saw Britain as one kingdom, not an island divided among warring tribes. He fought valiantly against the Saxons, but there were too many of them, and too few of our people. 'Twas the same when we faced the English."

It seemed a curious idea to Gerard, that

Britain could ever be united as one land. Twould be like Normandy, Aquitaine, Brittany and the other duchies around Paris all being joined together in one country. "I truly know little of these things. My father was a hired knight from Anjou."

She turned to look at him. "Then why are you known as Gerard of Malmsbury?"

He felt the flush creep up his neck. No matter what he did to prove himself, every time he faced the facts of his birth, the sense of humiliation came roaring back. "I'm a bastard. I couldn't take my father's name."

She gave him a quick smile. "Among the Cymry, 'tis no shame to be born on the wrong side of the blanket. As long as your father recognizes you, you're treated the same as his other sons."

He would never understand this woman. A moment ago, she was resentful and angry. Now she sought to reassure him. "The Cymric way seems fairer. Although what I believe is that a man should be judged by his deeds and accomplishments, not by his father's position or title."

"That sounds sensible enough. Although we both know the world isn't like that. And if you think all men should be judged by their actions, what about women? If being born a bastard shaped your life, consider how being born a woman has shaped mine."

"But a woman isn't the same as a man. Thank heavens." He smiled at her, hoping to remind her of what they had shared in bed.

"Oh, aye. I know. A woman is weaker, frailer, less fit in every way. And her mind and character are deficient as well. The scriptures say so."

"That doesn't mean it's true."

"You would question the Holy Scriptures? Is that not blasphemy?"

"The scriptures say one thing, but my experience says another. That doesn't mean the scriptures are wrong. It simply means they don't apply in all situations. For example, my lord's wife, Lady Nicola, she is the equal to any man in terms of her mind and character. In addition to her skill in managing the whole castle household, she can tally sums and read and write."

After a time, Marared shot him a defiant look. "If you believe women can be the equal of men, does it not seem unfair we have so little power? I had no choice in wedding you. Yet you were eager enough to take me to wife, even though 'twas clearly not what I desired."

He was on treacherous ground now. Mayhaps he'd been unwise to bring up Lady Nicola and his thoughts on women. Then the perfect response came to him. "I had no choice in wedding you, too. Lord de Cressy bid me do whatever I must to arrange an alliance with your father. Your father was the one who insisted the marriage to you be part of the agreement."

"You didn't want to wed me?"

He'd walked into a trap. If he spoke honestly, he would insult her. If he lied, she might think all his previous words were false as well. Somehow, he must find a balance, a way to make the truth seem less harsh.

He gave her a rueful smile. "I must admit I'd always imagined myself marrying a more ordinary woman. One who was plainer, less keen-witted, and more biddable. But now that I've been spoiled by your beauty, your intelligence, and your fire, I realize it wasn't such a bad a bargain after all."

"Even though I'm a Cymraes?"

"*Especially* since you are a Cymraes. After you, all other women seem plodding and dull."

He saw that he'd pleased her and exhaled in relief. Now, if only he could find a way for her be happy with her lot as mistress of Tangwyl. He hoped her interest in the horses might lead to that.

They left the main trackway and started into the hills. The sun burned off the mist and when they reached the top of a rise, in the pasture below they could see more than a dozen mares, many with their foals beside them. The sight of the beautiful animals, their coats glossy gray, chestnut, and bay against the vivid green of the knee-high spring grass, made Gerard's breath catch. It seemed to him that at this moment, there could hardly be a more fortunate man in all of England. He glanced at Marared, his beautiful wife, and knew that it was so.

She smiled back at him, obviously affected by the thrilling scene as much as he was. They started down into the valley. Gerard's mood dampened when he saw the herdsman. He'd forgotten the man who looked after the horses was Welsh, or a *Cymro*, as Marared would refer to him. At least Gerard felt certain that the man must be Welsh, with his short, stocky build, dark hair and slightly swarthy skin. But he couldn't remember the man's name, which made it awkward. Would Marared think he hadn't bothered to learn it because the man was only a herdsman and a Welsh one at that?

They dismounted and secured their horses at the gate in the hedgerow, then climbed the stile into the pasture. The herdsman approached. "My lord," He nodded to Gerard, then his gaze turned to Marared. "Lady. What do you here?"

"We've come to see the horses," Gerard answered.

"Of course." The man turned and motioned. "There are three mares left to foal. The other two...one didn't conceive and the other had a stillborn colt a fortnight ago."

Gerard gazed out at the mares, focusing on

the ones without offspring. "Ormond didn't tell me we'd lost one."

"It happens. There was naught anyone could do. She dropped the foal during the night."

"Ormond said we bring the younger ones into the stables when they start labor."

The man shrugged. "You can't always tell. This one wasn't showing much. And her colt was very undersized. 'Tis likely it wouldn't have survived even if it had been born alive."

Gerard felt a sharp sense of loss. Foolish. What was one foal, out of more than a dozen? And yet it was a young life lost, and he could not help mourning it. He glanced at Marared, expecting her to also react with sadness. To his surprise, she seemed to be studying the herdsman. All at once Gerard felt disinclined to leave her alone with the man, even though that had been his plan.

He glanced sharply at the Welshman. His weathered face gave nothing away. "Which one lost the colt?"

The man jerked his head in the direction of the herd. "The bay. Might have been too soon to breed her."

"Who decides which mares will be bred?"

"The lord of the castle, I presume."

The coldness of the herdsman's dark blue eyes pierced Gerard, arousing a sense of warning. He shook it off. "When the time comes this fall to breed the mares, I will ask your advice. And Marared's." He nodded to his wife. "That's why she's here. She has some knowledge of birthing animals and tending livestock."

The next moment he realized he should have referred to her as Lady Malmsbury, or at least Lady Marared. But he did not think the oversight would trouble her.

The herdsman's expression remained unreadable. "Is that so?"

"I thought you could show Marared the herd. Have her familiarize herself with the animals, especially the mares that have yet to foal. She already saved one little filly, and likely its mother as well."

Gerard looked at Marared, who didn't seem as pleased by his praise as he'd expected. He had the sense he was missing something.

He pushed aside the twinge of warning. "I have things to do at the castle." He met the herdsman's gaze, wishing again that he could remember the man's name. "I'll depend on you to look after Marared and see that she gets back to the keep safely."

"Of course, milord."

Gerard gave Marared a quick smile and headed for the gate. He climbed the stile, untied the reins, and mounted before looking back. Marared and the herdsman stood facing each other, their stances stiff. He wondered if the herdsman resented having to deal with a woman. Marared had probably picked up on the man's cool manner and was angered. But she could handle the situation, Gerard felt certain. His wife was not one to be put off by anyone.

"DAFFYD, WHAT ARE you doing here?"

"I might ask you the same."

"I would think that was obvious. My father wed me off to Lord Malmsbury. I had no choice in the matter."

"Ah, but 'tis a fine life, isn't it?" Daffyd jerked his head in the direction of the castle. "A warm, spacious keep. Servants to do your bidding. A fool of a husband who you clearly have wrapped around your little finger."

"It isn't like that!"

"What is it like, Marared?"

She wanted to say that even now she was plotting to be rid of Malmsbury. But then she remembered her husband's warm smile as he left her, and knew a sudden sinking feeling.

She focused on Daffyd. His blue eyes burned with hostility and anger. "How did you come to be employed here?"

"Malmsbury needed a herdsman, and I have the skill."

Among other skills. Daffyd had accompanied her brothers on raids many times. He was a shrewd and ruthless warrior. "You know what I mean. You wouldn't willingly work for a *Sais*, not unless you had some plan to undermine him."

Daffyd's mouth twitched. "Not *undermine*. That would be too good for the puling worthless coward."

"He's not a coward!"

Daffyd smiled unpleasantly. "Is that so? I see the fine life of being the leman of a *Saeson* swine has won you over."

Marared jerked back. "I'm his wife, not his mistress! And I'll thank you to remember my father is your chieftain. Not to mention, my *husband* is not uncouth, evil or ruthless, or anything you might associate with the English race. He not only treats me well, he treats everyone well, from the lowliest kitchen boy to the knights in his garrison. He rose from humble beginnings himself, and he hasn't forgotten what it's to be an underling."

"Strange. You defend him now, but only a few days ago you were so anxious to be rid of him that you asked your cousin to lead a raid on Tangwyl."

Marared let out her breath in a hiss. "How do you know about that?"

"Rhys and I are in regular contact."

Her heart fluttered like a frantic bird in her

chest. "How long have you been employed here?"

"Since last winter. Not long after Lord FitzAdam died."

"Who hired you?"

"The first man de Cressy sent here, as soon as the king made him overlord of the castle."

"What was his name?"

"Reynard. The name means fox, and he looks like one, with a bush of red hair. But he's clearly not as wily as his namesake. Otherwise he wouldn't have–" Daffyd's eyes narrowed. "What does any of this matter to you?"

She sought to regain control. "I came here to look over the mares. We'd best get on with it."

Daffyd gave her a lazy, assessing look. "What do you want to know?"

She followed him around the pasture as Daffyd pointed out different animals, gave her their names, or at least the names he used for them, and their histories. He discussed whether they had had a difficult or easy time giving birth, whether they took to their offspring quickly and if their foal was thriving. The few who hadn't yet dropped their foals, he assessed in terms of how soon they might go into labor.

Daffyd *was* very knowledgeable about horses. Marared could well imagine why de Cressy's man decided to hire him.

As they talked, she agonized. It was disturbing to realize Rhys had spies here. But since he was her ally, why did it bother her? Perhaps because it pointed out so starkly that her loyalties were no longer clear and certain. She didn't want anyone at Tangwyl to suffer or be hurt in any way due to a raid, or any other conflict with her countrymen. But this was war. People were bound to be hurt.

She'd been so intent on taking back control over her life that she had not considered the effect of her actions on other people. Now she could see how naïve and selfish her plan was. But how did she change things? The plot she'd set in motion could not easily be ended.

When they finished discussing the herd, Marared went to her horse. Daffyd followed. "There's still a chance to redeem yourself. Prove you're a true *Cymraes* and help us throw off the yoke of the *Saeson* usurpers."

"How would I do that?"

He fixed her with a keen look, then shook his head. "Nay. I'll not share our plans with you. 'Tis clear you're too far gone."

Marared wanted to protest, but knew it would be a waste of breath. Daffyd could read her too well. She might fool Malmsbury, but she could not fool this man.

She rode back to the keep, her mind whirling. Somehow she had to find a way to get word to Rhys that she'd changed her mind. But if what

Daffyd said was true, it was too late. What else could she do, except go to Malmsbury and confess everything? But if she did that, he would know how untrustworthy and deceitful she was. He would never trust her again, and might well have her watched and controlled every moment.

Her turmoil made her feel sick, and she wondered how she was going to sit beside Malmsbury at the evening meal and pretend all was well.

CHAPTER FIFTEEN

A S SOON AS she joined her husband at the high table, he gave her surprising news. "A messenger came while you were gone." He motioned with his head to a slim, dark-haired youth who was shoveling mutton stew into his mouth as if he was starving.

Marared stared at him. "Cynan?" Turning back to Malmsbury, she asked, "What message did my father send?"

"He's wants us to meet with Prince Gwenwynwyn of Ceredigion at his stronghold along the coast."

"What?" She'd heard of Gwenwynwyn, but could not fathom what he wanted with them. "What's the purpose of this meeting?"

"King John has wed his illegitimate daughter Joanne to Prince Llywelyn of north Wales.

Gwenwynwyn is furious. Your father wants to us to meet with him and convince Gwenwynwyn that his own alliance with de Cressy is not part of some English plot to take control of this part of Cymru as well."

Marared tried to make sense of this new development. "I suppose I can reassure him regarding my father's intentions, but it will be up to you to discuss de Cressy's plans. Llywelyn..." She shook her head. "The prince of Gwynedd obviously has some sort of scheme in mind, but I doubt anyone here in the south knows what it is."

"I can see why your father wants you to go. You understand these matters much better than I do."

"But what can I do? I'm a woman. I have more rights under Cymric law than English, but I have no say in matters of politics. After all, my father did barter me off like a piece of livestock."

"Nay. He passed you on to me as if he was offering me a precious jewel, the most valuable thing he possessed."

Marared felt herself flush. Must Malmsbury always be so unfailingly chivalrous? It made her feel even worse about her arrangement with Rhys. No matter how it made her look, she had to get word to her cousin that she had changed her mind. Convince him Malmsbury was a good lord and no threat to Cymru. Nay, the real threat was the constant power struggle between the princes who controlled different parts of the country. If they had agreed to work together long ago, instead of fighting each other like dogs over a bitch in heat, the English would never have gained control over her beloved homeland.

What did it mean that Prince Llywelyn had agreed to marry an English princess? Was he really accepting John's authority over his lands in the north? She wondered what her father thought. Suddenly she realized the perfect plan was staring her in the face. "I will go. But we must talk to my father first. Caer Brynfawr is on the way."

"I agree. Mayhaps while we are there, your father can choose some of his men to join us on the journey.

She breathed out in relief. Now she could eat without feeling every bite stick in her throat. While she was at her father's stronghold, she would find a way to get a message to Rhys. "When will we leave?"

"Whenever you can be ready. Is tomorrow morning too soon?"

"Nay. The sooner the better."

GERARD USED A hunk of bread to mop up the last bits of the savory stew. This was what marriage was supposed to be like: two people talking reasonably and working together. For a time, he'd thought they would never get to this place. It was a huge relief to think they finally had. Although he still had doubts. Was Marared being too agreeable? And what had transpired between her and the herdsman?

"What do you think of the herdsman?"

"You mean Daffyd? I think he is capable."

"What about the mares left to foal? Should we bring them in to the stables?"

"I think so. Daffyd said all of them should foal within the next fortnight."

"Then bringing them to the stables is probably wise. Although if something goes wrong, we'll have to hope Ormond can manage without you." He looked at her meaningfully, wanting to show his admiration for what she'd done.

She didn't seem to want to meet his gaze. Something was troubling her. She remained quiet through dinner, and as soon as she finished eating, she announced she was very weary and retiring for the night. By the time he arranged for horses and an escort for the morrow and went up to the bedchamber, Marared was in bed, apparently asleep.

He was keenly disappointed. On the journey they were about to undertake, there might not be any opportunity to engage in intimacy. He wondered if, in the morning, he could coax her into lovemaking.

But she woke before him and was quickly out of bed and dressing. It almost seemed as if she was avoiding being alone with him.

It took them all day to reach Carodoc's fortress. They were damp and weary when they arrived, and after a meal of mutton stew before the fire, Gerard and Marared met with Caradoc in the chieftain's private chamber to discuss how to deal with Gwenwynwyn. Caradoc suggested they should flatter the prince and pretend to share his scorn of Llweylyn and the king.

Gerard shifted uneasily. "But isn't that...I don't know...a bit treasonous?"

"'Tis a private conversation, not an oath of fealty. Even if you are uncomfortable speaking ill of John, you can still express your disdain for Llywelyn for wedding the daughter of his greatest enemy."

Gerard stared at Caradoc. "And how can I do that? Did I not also wed the daughter of a man, who if not an enemy, then who has not always been on the side of my people?"

Caradoc waved dismissively. "A very different situation. Although we might not have the same goals, you and I were never enemies. Nor have our houses been at odds for centuries. The animosity between Gwenwynwyn and Llywelyn runs deep."

Gerard glanced at Marared, wondering what

she thought. She appeared distracted, as if she wasn't even listening to her father. A moment later, she rose. "I'm going to find Aoife. I've scarce seen her since we've been here."

Gerard watched her leave, feeling more unsettled than ever. Here he was, about to venture into a country that considered men like him their bitter enemies. Although he no longer saw all Welshmen as treacherous and unprincipled, he was unable to truly trust them either. The only ally he had was Caradoc.

He looked the chieftain square in the eye. "If something happens to me on this journey, or while we're in Ceredigion, will you seek justice for me?"

Caradoc's dark brows drew together and his blue eyes were fierce. "Of course I would. You're my daughter's husband, and the father of my future grandchildren." He cocked his head. "You're working on that, aren't you, Malmsbury? All is right between you and my daughter? She is doing her duty as your wife?"

"Of course." Gerard hoped his embarrassment wasn't too obvious.

Caradoc nodded. "I'm glad to hear it. I wasn't certain how long it would take her to accept her new circumstances. But as for this other matter. Gwenwynwyn needs allies. He wants reassurance you and I are on his side, rather than Llywelyn's."

IT WAS CHILLY and windy in the courtyard. Marared paced, as much to keep warm as due to her nervousness. What if Rhys didn't come? She'd asked Diarmad to fetch him as soon as she arrived, and his steading wasn't that far away. She wished she could have sent him another message, but it was clear she must explain her change in plans to him in person.

By now, Rhys might know about their impending journey to Ystwyth. She expected he had spies here at her father's fortress, men who were loyal to her father in everything except this matter of the alliance with Malmsbury. One of them might have told Rhys. If she didn't get him to change his plans, Rhys might seize the opportunity to raid Tangwyl while Malmsbury wasn't there to defend it.

Dread made the stew she'd eaten congeal in her stomach. She took another deep breath, seeking to calm herself. A sound behind her made her whirl around.

Rhys laughed sourly. "You've been spending too much time with the *Saeson*. You've grown soft."

Marared bristled. "I was preoccupied with my thoughts."

"Oh, aye, and what thoughts might those be?

Are you contemplating your pampered life at Tangwyl and worrying you might lose it?"

"Hardly. I was worrying whether you'd come."

"What is so important you must speak to me face-to-face? Last time you sent a message through Aoife, as if I was your lackey who should do your will, no questions asked."

"I thought I was giving you what you wanted. You've always been keen to raid and cause trouble with the Marcher lords."

"And now? I'd heard you revel in the luxuries your wealthy husband can provide you and fully enjoy your life as a fine English lady. I remember a conversation we once had before you were wed. At the time you vowed to do all you could to rid our lands of the wretched, greedy foreigners."

Marared sought to compose herself. She must not lash out angrily and look weak and foolish, Rhys clearly thought she was. "'Tis true, I have reconsidered my stance, at least toward Engli... *Saeson* like my husband, who care for their lands and the people who live on them. Those who are honorable and decent."

"Ah. I am supposed to believe this husband of yours is some paragon, a noble and compassionate saint. Well, if he is that, why doesn't he give back the lands his people have stolen and sail back across the channel? You could go with him and continue your comfortable life there."

"Malmsbury was born in England. Besides, he's not free to make such choices. He owes fealty to Fawkes de Cressy. Without his lord's support and favor, he is a landless knight with no prospects."

"And if he were to go back to being a landless knight with no prospects, I doubt you would stay with him. Nay, you'd go running back to your father and beg him to find you another rich *Sais* for a husband. Maybe you could do even better this time and marry a *real* lord. You're comely enough, and if you could tame your fiery temper and learn to be biddable and meek, I'm certain some *Saeson gwat* would be interested."

This was going nowhere. She would never convince Rhys that Malmsbury was a decent lord and a good man. Even if she did, that would not change her cousin's outlook. She was going to have to come up with something better. "'Tis true I've changed my mind about raiding Tangwyl. But not for the reasons you think. The people there are loyal to Malmsbury. They have accepted their circumstances. Nay, I believe they've decided their circumstances are actually better. They've been treated well and have comfortable lives at Tangwyl. If you decide to raid the demesne, do not expect the locals to aid you."

"I doubt all of the people at Tangwyl are as

content as you say. Indeed, I know more than a few who are not. They would not speak openly to you, knowing how you feel about Malmsbury." Rhys smiled suddenly. "You'd be surprised how many spies I have in the castle. You might think about that before you get too cozy with Malmsbury. If he goes down, you might well end up going down also."

"No one would dare harm me! They know if they did, my father would wreak revenge!"

"And where will he find the men to avenge you? Caradoc has angered many of his allies. Do you really think any of his clients are going to risk their necks fighting their own countrymen for your sake?"

Marared snorted. "That's ridiculous. Cymry have always fought against Cymry. Why do you suppose the first the English were able to gain so much power and control so much of our territory? 'Twas because the princes of Cymru have always been at each other's throats."

Rhys's expression was deadly. "I never thought to see the day you would defend the enemy."

"I'm not defending them. Merely pointing out how often *we've* been our own worst enemy. If the Cymry are to have any hope of keeping the lands they still hold, our leaders must learn to work together."

"Is this the nonsense Malmsbury has been

feeding you?"

"Nay, it's what I've observed on my own. 'Tis the constant fighting among our own people that has allowed the English to prevail and prosper."

"Nay, they prevail and prosper because they have more men and better weapons. And because they are greedy and ruthless, unprincipled, lying cheats."

Marared sighed. This was a waste of time. She might as well give up and go back inside. If Rhys decided to raid Tangwyl, there was nothing she could do about it. Except tell Malmsbury so he could warn the people there. But she didn't want to do that yet, not when she had this journey to make with him.

⇒⟫⟪⇐

AFTER LEAVING CARADOC, Gerard had returned to the hall and looked around for Marared. When he didn't see her, he went to the guest bedchamber and lay down.

But he couldn't sleep, so he went back to the hall. There was movement near the door. A slim, hooded form entered, glanced around, then headed toward the wing where the unmarried women slept. Gerard went rigid. He felt certain the woman was Marared. He wanted to catch up with her and demand to know what she'd been doing. But if she'd been up to something deceitful, she was unlikely to admit it.

A sick feeling built in his stomach. What if she'd been meeting a lover? What if there was a man she'd yearned for at Caer Brynfawr? Now that she was no longer a virgin, Marared could lie with any man she wished and not worry if she got with child. Any babe she gave birth to would legally be considered his offspring. She would face no shame or censure. She could keep her lover and her husband, and no one would be the wiser.

Bile filled his throat. Would she do such a thing? Was she truly that faithless?

Nay. He would not believe that. He would not. If their marriage was to have any chance at all, he must give her the benefit of the doubt. He must trust her until she proved herself untrust-worthy.

He returned to the bedchamber and sought to fall asleep. But the image of the surreptitious form of his wife, sneaking in from the outside, would not let him rest.

He eventually fell into an uneasy slumber, waking as soon as a servant came to stoke the brazier. Getting up, he made his way outside, intending to relieve himself in the midden near the stables. As he peered into the early morning mist, a mounted figure rode across the yard. The rider said something to the guard at the gate. The gate creaked open and the horseman rode out.

Gerard strode to the gate. To his relief, he knew the guard. After greeting Corbi, he asked the man about the rider who had just left the fortress.

"That was Rhys ap Cynan." Corbi jerked his head the direction the man had ridden. "He's a nephew of Lord Caradoc."

Marared's cousin. Was that what Marared had been doing last night? Meeting with him? But why?

"Does Rhys ap Cynan come often to Caer Brynfawr?"

"Not often. Caradoc and he don't usually see eye-to-eye." Corbi assessed him carefully before adding, "Rhys would never have agreed to allow an Englishman to marry his daughter."

Gerard's belly still felt tight with unease, but he told himself there was no proof Marared had met with Rhys.

When he went inside, Marared greeted him with a warm smile, as if she was genuinely pleased to see him.

"Did you have a good visit with Aoife?" he asked.

"Aye. 'Twas delightful to catch up with her. When we met at Abergavenny, it was so rushed."

Exactly as I told you it would be. "Has there been any talk of her wedding this fellow she yearns after?"

Marared looked thoughtful. "I think she has changed her mind about how she feels about him."

"Then there's no reason for her not to come to Tangwyl for an extended visit."

"Mayhaps."

Gerard motioned to the bread and cheese on the table. "We should break our fast. We must leave soon."

Marared nodded and reached for the knife. Gerard watched her cut the bread. She seemed weary, as if she had not slept well. Perhaps she had stayed up too late visiting with her friend.

They left Caer Brynfawr, accompanied by three of Gerard's knights, Guy, Rob and Anselm, and three of Caradoc's men, Owain, Madog and Ifan. Gerard wondered if it was a large enough escort. But he told himself this was a diplomatic mission. Marared's presence should safeguard their journey through Powys. When they reached Ceredigion, they had the missive from Gwen-wynwyn.

Caradoc had advised them the best route to Gwenwynwyn's fortresss, Castell Ystwyth, was to head west along the River Wye.

They crossed brilliant hills ablaze with golden gorse bushes. The trackway dipped down into the river valley and they rode through a woods where the last of the bluebells carpeted the ground in a haze of violet. Chiffchaff, thrush, and cuckoos called to their mates in the trees above them. When they climbed the hills again, heavy-fleeced, pale gold sheep were everywhere, as well as a herd of small black cattle. The harshness of winter was gone, and the landscape seemed bursting with life. Observing the beauty all around them, Gerard understood why the Welsh fought so hard to keep control over their wild lands.

They saw only the occasional farmstead, and Gerard thought how different this place was from the area around Malmsbury, where settlements and villages were everywhere. Here, you might ride for miles and not see any people, nor any sign of them. When he first came to Wales, he'd thought the landscape lonely and bleak. But now he was starting to see the pleasures of living in a place like this. When it was clear, the sky was a dazzling blue and he felt as free as one of the goshawks that rode the air currents above.

MARARED'S STOMACH CHURNED as she rode. She'd lain awake half the night trying to figure out what to do. She wanted to warn Gerard about Rhys's possible plans, but if she did that, she'd have to admit her part in them. And if she betrayed Rhys, didn't that prove him right, that she was turning her back on her own people and giving up any hope that Cymru might some day be free of outsiders?

But she genuinely cared for Malmsbury. And not only because of the spectacular lovemaking they'd shared. Her husband was kind to her, unfailingly considerate. Over time, she'd come to admire him. His calm, quiet authority. His respect and concern for the inhabitants of Tangwyl. He seemed to be a good man, much better than many of the men opposing him.

She didn't think Rhys was a good person at all. He was cynical and ruthless, and had little concern for the people who might be hurt in his quest for power. She wished she'd realized that before she'd sent him the message encouraging him to raid Tangwyl. How could she have been so wrong about her cousin? If only she'd seen his true nature sooner. Before she'd been so foolish as to ask for his aid. Now if anything happened, it would be her fault. But the only way to thwart his plan was to warn Malmsbury.

Even if she could convince herself to do that, it might not work. She had no idea when or in what form the raid might come. Even if she told him now, Malmsbury would not be able to do anything. They were headed away from Tangwyl and couldn't spare any of their escort to ride back with a message.

All at once, she realized how risky this journey was. They were a small traveling party, traveling to Cerdigion and meeting a ruthless prince who clearly had no love for the English. If she wasn't Caradoc's daughter, they would be in grave danger. Her father clearly thought his authority as the overlord of Powys was enough to protect them. What if it wasn't?

As they neared the coast, the tangy, wild scent of the sea filled her nostrils. Marared immediately thought of one of her early crossings to Ireland, how the violent wind had buffeted the ship as the gray-green waves heaved and tossed around them. She told herself she had survived that experience, and she would endure this one.

Gwenwynwyn's stronghold was a castle set high on a ridge above the Ystwyth River. But unlike most Cymry fortifications, the walls of this stronghold were of stone. Marared was impressed that Gwenwynwyn held such an impressive citadel. Then she realized Castell Ystwyth had probably been built by the English and Gwenwynwyn had only taken it over recently.

She said something in this regard to Ifan, one of her father's men who had accompanied them. He nodded in the direction of the fortress. "Aye. It was originally built by an Englishman named Gilbert de Clare near a hundred years ago. Since then it has been added on to and rebuilt several times, changing hands through several Welsh princes."

"And Gwenwynwyn is the latest?"

Ifan nodded, his expression wary. "I would not set much store by what Gwenwynwyn tells you. He's not an ally I would seek out myself."

"Then why do you think my father has sent me here?"

"It doesn't hurt to have friends in several corners. As little as I trust Gwenwynwyn, I trust King John even less."

"And what of Llywelyn?"

"I've not met the man, but he seems shrewd and clever. And he must have impressed John, that he would agree to give his daughter to the man. Although she is illegitimate and not a true princess, as the English account it."

"And so my father's plan is that we appease Gwenwynwyn, in case we need his support at some point?"

"Your father is like a maiden with two lovers these days. He must work hard to keep them both happy, and at the same time, prevent them from learning about each other and realizing he keeps faith with neither of them."

Marared did not like the implications of that. She wished her father had discussed these things in more detail before he sent her on this mission. But of course, he had not, because she was merely his daughter, not his son. It was galling how men treated women, as if they had no brains in their heads and could not think things through for themselves.

Although Malmsbury had never dismissed her opinions because she was a woman. Why was he different? Was it because he'd had to struggle so hard to find his own place in the world, and that struggle had taught him to judge everyone on their own merit? She glanced in Malmsbury's direction. A sudden yearning to be near him sprang up. She squashed it down.

They slowly made their way around the trackway leading up to the castle gate. As they rode single-file on the narrow pathway, the view of mist-shrouded river valley below was both thrilling and terrifying. Marared was used to steep, treacherous pathways, but she didn't usually climb them while mounted and with a sheer drop on one side. She spoke soothingly to Gwenevere and avoided looking down.

They finally reached the fortress entrance and rode in through the narrow gate. She was helped from her horse. A young servant girl with reddish brown hair and a wan, narrow face gestured for Marared to follow her. Marared glanced at Malmsbury, thinking he would come as well. But her husband appeared to be deep in conversation with one of the knights guarding the gate.

The servant girl, who said her name was Melangel, led Marared to a small, but lavishly furnished chamber. Here, too, she could see the influence of the English. The high, round window, the carved bed, and elaborate tapestries on the wall weren't luxuries usually found in Cymric holdings. It was obviously the best bedchamber in the castle. Prince Gwenwynwyn was treating them as honored guests. That was something.

The servant helped her out of her traveling cloak, and Marared washed her face and hands in the basin of water on the carved wooden sideboard.

"What of my clothing?" Marared asked as she dried her hands on the cloth the servant girl provided. "I would like to change before going to the evening meal." Gwenwywyn would presumably hold a banquet in honor of their visit. He might even have a bard perform. She would enjoy that, as she had not experienced such entertainment in a long while.

"Your clothing will be brought to you," Melangel answered. "Is there anything else you require at the moment?"

It might be awhile until the banquet and she was very hungry. "If it's possible, I would like something to eat. Nothing elaborate. Cold food will do."

Melangel bowed, her face expressionless, and left the room.

Marared stared after her, wanting to call her back. Why had there been no mention of when the meal would be served, or when Malmsbury would be joining her?

Perhaps Malmsbury intended to sleep elsewhere. But the bed was clearly meant to accommodate two people. It seemed a waste if he did not sleep here. And disappointing. She had looked forward to being alone with him and being intimate.

She sat down at the stool near the sideboard and undid her plaits. Until her baggage arrived, she had no brush. But she could at least rebraid her hair and try to tidy it with her fingers.

It was a challenge to smooth her thick wavy tresses, which always became curlier and more unruly in misty weather. She was on the verge of giving up and seeking out someone to help her when there was a knock at the door. Exhaling in relief, she called out, "Come in."

She had expected Melangel, returning with the food. It was a shock when a well-dressed, dark-haired man entered the room. Marared got up from the stool so fast she knocked it over. "Milord? Prince Gwenwynwyn?"

The man gave a slight bow. "Greetings, Marared ferch Caradoc. Welcome to Castell Ystwyth."

Gwenwynwyn's deep blue eyes moved over her, taking in her unbound hair and moving down her body, clad in a simple traveling gown. The intensity and obvious interest of his regard unnerved her further. He was not behaving as a nobleman greeting a married woman. She wanted to grab her cloak and cover herself.

"I'm afraid you have the advantage of me, Lord Gwenwynwyn. No one has brought my baggage, so I've not had a chance to change my clothing nor tidy myself."

Gwenwynwyn smiled, his expression wolfish. "I'm not concerned. What we need to discuss doesn't require formality. In fact, perhaps it's better this way."

He seemed pleased he'd caught her off her guard. Did he truly think she would be more amenable to whatever he said if he approached her like this?

She stood up straighter. "I would prefer to discuss things in a more formal atmosphere. I don't keep secrets from my husband. As lord of Tangwyl, he needs to be aware of whatever we agree to." *If we agree to anything.*

Gwenwynwyn laughed. His eyes glinted as he drew near. "No secrets? You and I both know that's not true. You have many secrets from your husband."

Marared went rigid. Someone must have told him of her arrangement with Rhys. "'Tis not as you think. At one time I was at odds with my husband and unhappy in the relationship. That's no longer true. I might once have foolishly spoken to someone of some scheme to weaken

Malmsbury's hold on Tangwyl in order to cause him to disavow the marriage. I no longer think such a plan is in my best interests. Nor is it in the interests of the people who reside at Tangwyl. Malmsbury is a fair and honest lord, and I am content to have him as my husband."

"A pity." Gwenwywyn spoke in a mournful tone, although his expression showed glee. "This would all be so much easier if you'd kept to your original plan to rid yourself and Tangwyl Castle of the foul English scum."

Marared gasped and took a step back. She'd feared coming here, worrying she would end up over her head in the treacherous waters of Cymric politics. Clearly, it was too late to worry about that. Right now she was drowning. She shot a look at the door. "What have you done with him?"

"With whom?" Gwenwynwyn's voice was maddeningly calm.

"My husband?"

"'Twould be very awkward for you to wed me if you were still wed to him."

He's killed him. Anguish hit Marared like a blow to the belly. A moment later, reason returned. They'd barely arrived. Besides Gwenwynwyn was already worried about Llywelyn, who'd made an alliance with the king. He must know that murdering an English lord, no matter how minor, would bring down the wrath of King John. Gwenwynwyn must have some other scheme to be rid of Malmsbury besides killing him.

Marared was astonished by the incredible relief she felt. But she could not think about that. She must focus on thwarting Gwenwynwyn. No matter what happened, she didn't want to marry this man, sneaky, slimy snake that he was.

But she dare not let Gwenwynwyn know how she felt. Not until she'd figured out a way to defeat him. She cocked her head and gave him a thoughtful look. "What's the advantage to me in going along with your plan? What do I stand to gain? Tangwyl castle is a fine, comfortable keep. I'm pampered and cosseted and allowed to do whatever I wish. I don't even have to order the household or serve as chatelaine."

She'd chafed at her life at Tangwyl, feeling useless and bored. But Gwenwynwyn wouldn't know that.

Gwenwynwyn made a dismissing gesture. "I wouldn't expect you to reside here at Castell Ystwyth. I have other holdings where you could live."

"Not castles though." She layered on the condescension.

"Nay, not castles." His expression was sour. "But I can offer you something Malmsbury cannot."

She regarded him dubiously. "And what is

that?"

"With you as my wife, all of the midlands would be under Cymric control. You would be a princess. A princess of *our* people."

"But what of Llywelyn? He won't stand by and let you seize control of that much territory. And now he's allied with King John."

Gwenwynwyn's expression darkened. "I have a plan. I mean to see that traitorous bastard pay for allying himself with the enemy."

Luring her here and making her his wife was obviously only a part of Gwenwynwyn's scheme. He must be allied with someone in Gwynedd who resented Llywelyn and sought to undermine him. She must find out who that was and warn Llywelyn.

But why would she do that? Who was the enemy here? A part of her believed any man who allied himself with the hated English was a traitor, even it was her own countryman. But that would make her father a traitor as well. Blessed Jesu! She couldn't unravel her own thoughts, let alone deal with this man. She looked down at her hands, trying to buy time.

Gwenwynwyn approached. She kept her gaze focused downward, fearing he would guess her thoughts. Every fiber of body was tense and alert.

He reached out and cupped her chin in his hand. She jerked back. "Milord! This is unseemly.

I'm married to another man. 'Tis not right!" She widened her eyes at him and shuddered, praying he would think it was from shock and fear rather than revulsion. He watched her steadily. "Please, milord. Don't shame me like this. 'Twill put a stain upon all that passes between us after this." She exhaled slowly, thinking about the small knife she always wore strapped to her leg. How could she distract him so she could retrieve it? She feared he meant to rape her.

He watched her for long, still moments, while her heart beat wildly and she took frantic breaths. All at once, she observed Gwenwyn-wyn's desperation. The sagging pouches beneath his vivid blue eyes spoke of a man pushed to the limit. This was his last chance. If he failed in this bid for power, his importance as a prince and his say in Cymric politics would dwindle to nothing. She must stand up to him, but also give him a way out.

She exhaled slowly. "If you can get the Church to disavow the marriage, I will agree to wed you. But that..." she raised her chin defiantly, "is the only way I will agree."

His eyes narrowed. Then he nodded. "We don't currently have a priest here at Castell Ystwyth. But I will send for one."

"A lay priest will not do. The marriage must be voided by an abbot or bishop. Only someone who is recognized by the Church as having real authority can make such a decision. I think it unlikely you can get someone like that to travel here. We will have to go to them. The only places nearby where we would find an abbot or bishop are St. Dogmael or Strata Florida."

She saw his brows go up as she mentioned St. Dogmael. The priory was to the south, and far too close too to the lands of the Deheubarth chieftains for him to want to travel there. That was fine with her. She much preferred they go to Strata Florida, which was to the east and nearer to her father's territory and some hope of help.

He frowned as he considered the matter. Although his hair was reddish, his stocky build and blue eyes were typical of a Cymro. This man was exactly who she once would have wanted to wed. But now she much preferred Gerard, with his skin tanned the warm hue of oak leaves, his thick, wavy brown hair and his enigmatic hazel eyes. The thought shocked her, but only a little. Her once-strong preference for her countrymen had vanished.

Gwenwynwyn seemed to decide. He faced her as if confronting an enemy. "Very well. I'll make arrangements to go to Strata Florida."

He started to turn away. Marared took a step toward him. "Although I would understand if you don't take Malmsbury's knights, my father's men must go with us. My father would not want me to travel without his warriors protecting me."

Gwenwynwyn took time to consider this. Perhaps he was trying to decide how his own warriors would fare if confronted by her father's men.

"Their loyalty is to my father," Marared said. "Their only duty is to protect *me*." Her words implied that her father's men bore no fealty to Malmsbury. She doubted that was true. She believed even the Cymric men in her escort would take Malmsbury's side against this man. Once that would have incensed her. Now she was glad.

Gwenwynwyn nodded. "Perhaps one or two of them can come. The rest of your escort will stay here."

Stay here, but where? Anxiety for Malmsbury made her ask, "What are you going to do with my…my current husband?"

Gwenwynwyn glared at her, his patience clearly at an end. Then he turned and walked out of the room. She could hear the latch click closed behind him. Long seconds passed. She went to the door. It was locked from the outside. She was trapped here, with no way to get help. If Gwenwynwyn chose to, he could leave her here to starve. Or go mad.

She rushed to the window. Panic made her throat grow tight and her heart race. She climbed onto the cushioned seat and pressed her face against the small round window. The river was directly below. Even if she could find a way to break the thick glass in the window and crawl out, she would fall to certain death.

The dread building inside her made her almost consider that choice. Might not death be preferable to being trapped like this? At the mercy of a man who saw her only as a means to an end? Her freedom was gone, and with it, any hope of a happy, contented life. Might it not be better to end things now, flying from the window like a goshawk and enjoying a few moments of joyful release before the brutal end?

She took a deep breath, and then another, fighting the fear clawing at her insides. Somehow she must slow her racing thoughts and reason this out. She wasn't a goshawk or gyrfalcon. If she jumped from the window, she wouldn't fly free, soaring over the river valley, but fall to a gruesome death. And she already had a plan. Unless Gwenwynwyn changed his mind, by tomorrow she would be out of this place and in a much better position to escape. But how was she to endure in the meantime?

The terror over being trapped in the small bedchamber continued to gnaw at her. It ate away her resolve, threatening to throw her back into a panic. She tried breathing slowly and evenly. She reminded herself she wasn't in some small, underground cell—as Gerard probably was. Gwenwynwyn had likely put him in the dungeon, or whatever foul accommodations a fortress like this possessed. She imagined Gerard trapped in a cold, dark, filthy chamber with nothing more than some filthy straw to warm him. An arrow of pain lodged in her breast.

She realized suddenly she had thought of him by his Christian name. He was no longer *Malmsbury*, the name of the town where he grew up. He was *Gerard*. Her husband. Her lover. Tears sprang to her eyes at the thought of him, alone and suffering. Although Gwenwynwyn had probably also imprisoned the English knights in their escort. Gerard would likely have them for company. But one of those knights was Guy, the man who had won Aoife's affections. If anything happened to him, her dear cousin's heart would be broken, the same as Marared's if she lost Gerard.

She struggled to force away her suffocating dread and consider what Gerard would do in her situation. His controlled, careful nature, which she'd once scorned, now seemed like a very fine way of dealing with life, at least when facing a crisis like this.

Gerard would eat the food Gwenwynwyn had brought to keep up his strength, so he would be ready when he had a chance to escape. Then he would carefully think things through, weighing all the options.

Her instinct was to flee. But she must accept

that even if she could get out of the fortress, it would not be easy to get away. Gwenwynwyn would probably take a large escort. Not only to guard his prisoners, but also because he risked encountering Gryffyth ap Rhys, the other man who was fighting for control of this region.

Her country was like a nest of vipers and she and Malmsbury were caught in the middle. For the dozenth time, she thought what fools most Cymric chieftain and princes were, always fighting their own countrymen for more power for themselves, even as their homeland was being whittled away by the English.

Stupid men. If women ran things, they would behave more shrewdly. Or would they? Only a short time ago, she had blindly hated the English, making no distinctions between those who were noble and good and those who were corrupt and power-mad. It had taken intimate contact with one of them to make her see the difference. And she had no doubt Gerard was an exception among English nobleman. He was certainly the exception among men. No other man in her life had ever treated her as he did. He behaved as if what she felt and thought mattered. As if her ideas were meaningful and useful. No other man had ever her treated as his equal. Not even her father, and certainly not her brothers. Nor her cousin, Rhys.

She grimaced as she thought of the foolish

plan she'd concocted. What had possessed her to think her cousin could be trusted? He was exactly like most of the other Cymric warlords and chieftains, concerned with amassing as much power as possible. That was probably at least as important to him as defeating the English.

She felt a stab of disgust she had been so blind to her cousin's character. But there was nothing she could do about that. She could only move forward and take the next logical step. Which means she must eat so she would be strong for the next challenges she faced.

She'd barely started on the cheese and chewy maislin bread when there was a sound at the door. Seconds later young Melangel entered. "I brought you some wine." She nodded to the silver ewer she carried. "Lord Gwenwynwyn wanted me to make certain you had everything you needed."

Gwenwynwyn must think she'd gotten used to such luxuries and wanted her to know he could offer her those things. Despite his earlier attempts to intimidate her, he was now treating her with respect and courtesy. Perhaps if she went along with the pretense, he would let down his guard. She must convince him that her objection to marrying him had to do with her moral qualms, rather than her distaste for him or her feelings for Gerard.

She took a sip of the wine, hoping it would

fortify her. Desperate schemes were already racing through her head. She imagined subduing the serving girl and imprisoning her, binding her mouth with a cloth so she could not shout out for help. But even if she could escape the bedchamber, she still had to make her way through the tortuous maze of the castle, find her horse and get out the gate. She might succeed at some of those things, but not all of them. And even if she did manage to get out of the fortress, pursuit would be rapid. Gwenwynwyn knew this area and she did not.

She took another swallow of wine. It would be foolish to try such a thing, no matter how desperate she was. Her current plan—to leave Castell Ystwyth with Gwenwynwyn and his escort, and then attempt escape—made much more sense.

But what about Gerard? If she left him behind, what would happen to him? Gwenwynwyn might decide to have him killed. But if he was going to do that, why go to all this trouble to have the marriage voided? The knife blade of fear for her husband twisted deeper, making the little food she'd eaten feel like a lump in her belly.

"Melangel." She tried to make her voice pleasant. "I'm certain you've been told not to speak openly with me. But, I beg you, can you not at least tell me how my escort fares? Some of them are my countrymen, men I've known for years. And Lord Malmsbury, he may be English, but I have lived with him as my husband for over a month. I would know he and his men are alive at least, and not being mistreated."

Melangel shook her head, looking very young and sad. "I know nothing, milady. I have no knowledge of the circumstances of your escort."

"But you must know what Gwenwynwyn does with…with hostages." She'd almost said prisoners, but she feared the term would make Melangel even more wary.

"I'm afraid not. Gwenwynwyn hasn't been at Castell Ystwyth for long."

"Who was your overlord before then?"

"'Twas Maelgwn ap Rhys, lord of Deheubarth. But he was very seldom here. Maelgwn made an arrangement with the king that gave him this keep."

"The king? You mean John?"

Melangel nodded solemnly. "But since then, Gwenwynwyn has broken with Maelgwn. And Maelgwn is in the south, fighting his brothers."

She'd come here thinking the goal was to pacify Gwenwynwyn, who was unsettled by Llywelyn's marriage to John's daughter. But Gwenwynwyn apparently held Castell Ystwyth due to Maelgwn, who was allied with John. The convoluted politics of Cymric princes were enough to make her head spin. But one thing was clear. Gwenwynwyn had convinced her father to send her here not because he wanted Caradoc's support, but because he had planned this scheme of marrying her to consolidate his hold on Ceredigion.

The thought made her furious with Gwenwynwyn all over again. But she could not reveal her animosity to the serving girl. Instead, she sniffed, as if holding back tears. "Is it possible you can find out how my escort fares? It would relieve my mind greatly to know they are well."

"I'm not certain how to do that, milady."

"Where do you usually work, when there are not guests to serve?"

"In the kitchen, milady."

"Then you should be able to find out if any food has been provided to my escort."

Melangel looked doubtful. Marared continued to press her: "Think how you would feel if someone you cared for was far from their home and in unknown circumstances. Would you not worry about how they were being treated? It would relieve my mind greatly to know they are at least being fed."

Melangel nodded timidly. "Perhaps I could ask one of the other serving girls. But I would not want to ask Einion, the cook. He gets angry over every little thing."

Marared smiled at her sympathetically. "There's no reason to bother the cook. I'm certain one of the other girls will know if anyone has taken food to men who recently arrived."

At least she hoped some of the servants were aware of such things. Or, were they all like this timid young woman? Too downtrodden and meek to take note of anything? If circumstances were different and her father had wed her off to Prince Gwenwynwyn rather than Gerard, she definitely would have made some changes around Castell Ystwyth. Such as making certain the serving maids were better treated and certainly better fed.

Of course, Gwenwywywn was probably the sort of man who wouldn't allow his wife to have any power, even in household matters. Marared shuddered. She was very fortunate to have wed a man like Gerard, who showed the utmost consideration for her decisions and cared for her happiness. But now that life she had failed to appreciate was threatened. If she could not escape Gwenwynwyn and his awful scheme and free Gerard, everything she cared about was at risk.

Melangel was still standing there, waiting patiently. Marared made her tone gentle. "That will be everything. Unless you would like some food." She gestured to the bread and cheese left on the platter.

Melangel gave her a horrified look. "I could not. I would get in trouble for certain."

"You can say I ate it all. Sit now, and have

something to eat. That is an order." She motioned to the stool.

Melangel crouched on the stool, reminding Marared of a cornered coney. She began to nibble on a chunk of bread. Marared went to the window. If she left the girl alone, perhaps she would relax.

Marared gazed unseeingly out the small window. If only she knew more about Gwenwynwyn and what sort of man he was. Her instincts told her he had not planned things out, but impulsively seized this opportunity to make her his unwilling bride. Perhaps when he saw the size of their escort and realized how far they were from any help, he'd come up with this scheme. Or, maybe her cousin Rhys somehow had a hand in it. Gwenwynwyn seemed like a wary, careful man, and this plan spoke of someone shrewd and ruthless. Someone like her cousin. Maybe he'd left Caer Brynfawr immediately after they spoke and ridden here ahead of their arrival. Was he here even now? Advising Gwenwynwyn on every step of the plan?

The thought unnerved her. Rhys would immediately see through her insistence that the marriage be annulled by an important church official. He would know she was buying time to escape. He would also make certain Gerard and his English escort never left Castell Ystwyth alive.

Another shiver of fear swept her, and she

glanced over at Melangel, still eating. If she made a dash for the door, the small, underfed serving girl would be no match for her. But then she'd have to make her way around this sprawling, unknown fortress, find Gerard and his men, free them and hope they could get safely out the castle. Even if she freed Gerard, she knew he would never agree to leave her. He would not save his own life and leave her at the mercy of Gwenwynwyn. She knew that much about him.

Besides, if she attempted to escape, she'd get poor Melangel into terrible trouble. Gwenwyn-wyn would have the girl beaten, perhaps killed. She'd started to earn the girl's trust; she could not betray her now. Nay. She'd have to stick to her original plan. And hope against hope that nothing happened to Gerard until she could get free and find help.

Melangel finally finished, and after thanking Marared profusely, scurried from the room. Marared gritted her teeth as the latch fell into place, locking her in. It would be a long, agonizing night. It would take all her patience and self-control to endure it.

CHAPTER SIXTEEN

GERARD SHIFTED, TRYING to ease his body's discomfort. The cellar was dank and chilly, and the shackles on his ankles and wrists chafed. With six other men in the small space there wasn't much room to move. At least Marared wasn't enduring such miserable conditions. He'd seen a young serving girl leading her away to the living quarters of the castle. Gwenwynwyn would not treat a woman like this, especially not the daughter of an ally.

He was also relieved he hadn't been separated from his companions. If he'd been brought down here by himself, he would have been certain Gwenwynwyn meant to kill him. Or imprison him indefinitely. But his captor wasn't such a fool to think seven men could disappear and no one would ask questions or pursue the matter. Especially since it was well known Gerard and his men were on their way to this place.

Of course, Gwenwynwyn could always kill him and let the rest of them go. But Gwenwynwyn must know de Cressy would seek justice if his vassal was killed. De Cressy might even go to the king. That would give John an excuse to send knights into Wales, which surely Gwenwynwyn didn't want to happen. Or, perhaps John would have Llywelyn ap Iorwerth handle it. Then Llywelyn would have an excuse to come south and seek to enlarge his territories. Hardly the outcome Gwenwynwyn was seeking either.

Nay, he didn't think Gwenwynwyn would kill him. But what was the man's plan?

Slumped on the floor beside him, Owain grunted. "It may seem we are in a bad way, milord, but don't fret. Caradoc won't abandon us. If we don't return, he'll send men to find out why."

Unless he's in on the scheme. But it made no sense for Caradoc to insist Gerard marry his daughter and then knowingly send his new son-in-law into this viper pit. If anyone was working with Gwenwynwyn, it had to be Marared.

He wished he could ask Owain whether he thought she might be involved. But he didn't want Owain to realize he was so unsure of his wife he feared she had betrayed him. Nor did he want Owain to be offended and angered by the suggestion his chieftain's daughter was untrustworthy. He must keep his dark musings to himself. Which was not such a strain. He wasn't a man for prattling on about whatever was on his mind.

Perhaps that was partly why Marared hadn't wanted to wed him. She was used to men like her father, bluff, sociable men who spoke openly. She might find him cold and distant. But he'd tried so hard to show her he cared for her. Could she not see it? Even if he'd never spoken of his affection for her, surely she must know how he felt.

But perhaps not. He'd never told he loved her. The only men who spoke of such things aloud were poets, jongleurs and courtiers. Not knights.

The sound of footsteps. The souterrain door creaked and there was a flicker of light. Gerard caught a glimpse of a tray and a pitcher being pushed through the opening.

"At least they don't mean for us to starve," young Anselm said cheerfully. "That's a good sign, isn't it?"

IN THE MORNING when Melangel returned to the bedchamber, her face had more color and she moved more quickly, as if having a decent meal had heartened her. She put a bowl of pottage and some dried apples on the small table. Drawing close to Marared, she spoke in a barely audible voice. "Your escort is being held in the souterrain. Food and water was taken down to them."

Marared let out her breath in relief. "Is that where prisoners are usually held?" She also spoke quietly. It seemed unlikely anyone was spying on them, but it didn't hurt to be cautious.

"I think so, milady. Apparently, that part of the castle hasn't been used in some years."

The souterrain was probably damp and foul and horrible. But there was nothing she could do to help them.

She forced herself to eat some of the bland pottage, then motioned for Melangel to finish the rest. While Melangel ate, Marared washed her face and tidied her clothing. Then she sat on a stool while the serving girl brushed her hair and braided it. Melangel seemed quite adept, as if she dressed ladies' hair everyday. When Marared commented on it, Melangel pointed out that smoothing hair was not much different than carding wool, which she'd done for years.

Before Melangel had finished braiding, there was a sound at the door. Gwenwynwyn entered. Marared rose to face him.

He gestured curtly. "Are you ready?"

"Almost." Marared resumed her seat so the serving girl could finish braiding her hair. She could feel Gwenwynwyn examining her and was surprised by the revulsion she felt. He wasn't an unattractive man, but the thought of being intimate with him made her skin crawl. Was it because she didn't know or trust him? But she'd never felt that way with Gerard, even when she considered him her enemy.

As soon as Melangel finished her hair, Marared retrieved her cloak from the clothing pole, pulled it on and fastened it. She feared Gwenwynwyn might try to help her and if he got near, she worried he would sense her distaste for him.

He started for the door. Marared shot Melangel a warm, encouraging smile and mouthed the words "thank you". She had to let Melangel know she was grateful for all the girl had done for her.

She followed Gwenwynwyn as he led her rapidly through the twisting corridors of the keep. It was a good thing she hadn't tried to escape the night before or she would have gotten hopelessly lost. Several mounted knights waited in the bailey, although none of them were men she knew. Marared fought the discouragement she felt. She would have no allies on this journey, and would have to manage everything herself. At least Gwenevere was saddled and ready to go. Thank heavens. She worried Gwenwynwyn wouldn't let her ride her own mount and she needed her swift, obedient mare, or her plan was useless. Gwenwynwyn must think she had accepted her circumstances. Either that or he didn't believe she had the courage to try to escape.

Her plan might work, but it would not be easy. She'd have to wait for the perfect circumstances. Play the dutiful, refined lady and bide her time.

A squire helped her onto the mare. Gwenwynwyn mounted his own horse and gestured for her to follow. They rode through the gate and slowly made their way down the pathway winding around the hill. Marared's dread of the sheer drop off to the side was tempered by her relief at being out of the castle. She savored the fresh air, tinged with the faint scent of the sea and the fragrance of flowers and grass. After the musty staleness of the fortress, it smelled wonderful.

The winding trail finally reached the other side of the hill. Marared caught a glimpse of the landscape to the east, a rich tapestry of gleaming green pastureland interspersed with the golden green of newly-leafed oaks and the creamy white of hawthorn blossoms. She wanted to ride off immediately, but she knew she couldn't. Gwenevere might be fast, but these men were familiar with this territory and she was far from any refuge. She must be patient and wait for the right opportunity.

She kept Gwenevere to a sedate pace, forcing Gwenwynwyn and her escort to ride slowly as well. The prince glanced back at her a couple of times, his expression stiff with impatience. But she kept to her pretense of being a refined lady who rode with timidity and caution. Let him think she was a delicate flower who had to be treated with care. She rather enjoyed the deception.

They followed the river, picking their way along the marshy land where yellow flag irises gleamed among the reeds. Then they turned and climbed into the hills. They saw a herd of cattle grazing, the recently-born calves the same black-brown hue as their mothers, bucking and chasing each other in the tall, green grass.

They passed a farmstead of ancient stone. It was wildly overgrown with brambles and moss, and looked as if it had been there for centuries.

How many chieftains had claimed authority over this area in all those years? Probably dozens, each claiming to be *prince* of some territory or other. But the folk of the hills knew better than to involve themselves in the disputes of chieftains and princes. For them, life went on the same no matter who was supposedly their lord.

Marared and her escort moved into a broad valley. When she saw the dense woodland ahead, Marared's heartbeat accelerated. This was her chance. As they neared the edge of the woodland, she urged Gwenevere forward so she was riding next to Gwenwynwyn. "Milord, I must stop. I am in need of…I must relieve myself."

Gwenwynwyn halted, and his eyes narrowed. She gazed at him with what she hoped was helpless innocence and motioned to the forest. "I need a bit of privacy."

She didn't wait for his response, but rode for the trees. Although she'd feared he would send one of his men after her, no one followed. She rode slowly at first, searching for a pathway. At last she found a game trail and urged the mare faster. Any moment Gwenwynwyn might sense something amiss and send someone after her. By then she must be out of the woods so she could give Gwenevere her head and ride swiftly.

The forest thinned, but the ground was marshy. She still couldn't go as fast as she'd like, lest the horse stumble in the soft wet ground and throw her or be injured. She gritted her teeth as she continued on at a measured pace.

Finally, they reached open ground. She glanced around warily and then urged the horse up a steep hillside. When she reached the top, she pushed Gwenevere into a full gallop. The wind was in her face, tearing at her hair and making her eyes water. But exhilaration and excitement flooded her with energy. Up one hill and down the other she rode, putting as much distance between herself and Gwenwynwyn and his men as she could.

Gwenwynwyn would expect her to head east, back toward her father's keep. Instead, she chose a route south. Even if he was able to track her, he was less likely to pursue her too far. He wouldn't want to risk encountering men loyal to the southern princes.

Of course, she faced risks with this route as well. By heading south, she might have more difficulty finding her way back to Caer Brynfawr. And if she fell into the hands of one of the southern princes, they might seek to ransom her. But she would deal with that when the time came. At least for now she was away from Gwenwynwyn. Having lost his prize, there would be no reason for the prince to keep Gerard and his men captive.

At least she hoped he would take the sensible course of action and not kill the captives in a fit of anger. Gwenwynwyn didn't seem like a rash, vindictive man. But he was a Cymro, and possibly Irish as well. She well knew that both races were known for their volatile temperaments.

The hills around her were bare and open. If Gwenwynwyn or his men were anywhere near, they could easily spot her. She must keep to the valleys. She guided Gwenevere down the steep hillside. It was midday, and the air was thick and humid. She could feel her face getting burned by the sun, but it was too hot to pull up the hood of her cloak. Sweat soaked her underarms and chest. The horse was also lathered and spent. They both need to rest.

A small stream flowed through the valley. She rode the horse into it and let Gwenevere drink. When the animal had quenched her thirst, Marared dismounted and led the animal to a copse of elm. She returned to the stream and splashed water on her face. She was desperate for a drink, but the bank was muddy and churned up, and the water didn't look clean. She would have to look for a place where the creek flowed more swiftly. For now, she must content herself with the meager moisture of the half-dried apples Melangel had given her, which she'd stored in the pocket of her cloak.

She sat on the bank and ate the apples, aware of Gwenevere eyeing her and nickering softly. The poor horse didn't understand why she didn't share the apples. "I'm sorry, Gwenevere. This is all I have, and it might have to last me awhile. I can't eat grass like you."

The next moment there was a loud *moo*. Marared scrambled to her feet as a dozen cattle came down the hillside and splashed through the creek. A herdsman trailed after them. His skin was weathered to the hue of walnut juice, his hair and eyes black as raven's feathers.

Heart racing, Marared faced the herdsman. Despite her disheveled appearance, she hoped he could tell by her clothing and her horse that she was someone of consequence.

She straightened, trying to appear regal. "Good day. I was riding and lost my way. Can you tell me where I am? And where the nearest fortress or settlement is located?"

The man examined her and then her horse. His eyes widened, the whites of them stark against his dark complexion. She reached out her hand, hoping to soothe him. "I mean you no harm, sir. If you will help me, I will see that you are rewarded well."

The man took a step back, his eyes still wide with alarm. He shook his head, then turned and raced past her. He ran pell-mell toward the herd of cattle, waving his arms and shouting, seeking to drive them out of the stream and down the valley. They snorted and bellowed in fear as they bucked and ran.

Marared stared after the man in puzzlement. Why was he so alarmed? She glanced down at herself. Her summer cloak of blue and red checked wool was muddy, and her braids had come undone during her frantic ride. Her hair billowed around her shoulders in mass of russet waves. Still, her unkempt appearance hardly explained the man's extreme dread.

She looked over at Gwenevere, the elegant pale gray mare, with her bridle and saddle of dark red leather, a wedding gift from one of her father's allies. Gwenevere was a mount fit for a queen—a *fairy* queen. Marared gave a rueful laugh. When the herdsman came upon her—a young, well-dressed woman out in the middle of nowhere, riding a beautiful horse—he must have thought she was one of the Fair Folk, come to seduce him and steal him away to the dark enchanted realm of the fey, from which he might never escape. Or if he did, he would find a hundred or more years had passed and everyone he knew was long dead.

Old tales like that still had power, especially in isolated places like this. Marared let out a sigh. Although it was flattering to be mistaken for a fairy queen, how was she to get help if everyone she encountered fled in fear?

GERARD CLENCHED HIS jaw, his thoughts roiling with turmoil. Earlier in the day, a guard had come and called out for Madog. Gerard had tensed with dread, thinking Gwenwynwyn meant to execute them one-by-one, starting with his escort. But the brief exchange between Madog and the guard soon made it clear the Welshman was in on the scheme to imprison them.

The other men were as appalled as he was. But that did little to ease the sting of knowing there'd been a spy in their midst. The betrayal had caused Gerard to doubt everything. Once again, he began to wonder if Caradoc was also involved. After all, the chieftain was the one who arranged this meeting with Gwenwynwyn. Perhaps Caradoc's cheerful, hearty outlook was merely a mask to cover his deceit.

And what of Marared? Had she also known? Nay, he would not think like that. If he lost faith in her, he would have nothing to cling to. He needed the memory of her to survive. When things were the worst, he allowed himself to remember the silky feel of her skin. Her warm, feminine scent, a mingling of the herbs she bathed with and her own unique sweetness. Her beautiful eyes, which could glow with magical light, or flash brilliant green with fury.

Ifan coughed, and Gerard felt a stab of compassion for his companions. Guy had told him there was a woman at Caer Brynfawr he was growing fond of. But what of the other men? Did any of them have a sweetheart? Or some other pleasant memory to sustain them? He could not fathom how they must feel, if they had nothing to brighten the darkness of their prison.

Perhaps anger would give them a purpose. They might rage against Madog, cursing their former companion's falseness and deceit, and plotting how they might get revenge, once they were free of this place. Indeed anger had been what had motivated Gerard for most of his life. He'd been determined to prove he wasn't worthless. Determined to show the world that even though he was a bastard, he was as courageous and skilled as any well-born knight.

Although that was not much comfort in his current circumstances. If Gwenwynwyn had no luck getting de Cressy to pay the ransom, their captor might well quit feeding them and let them starve.

But de Cressy would pay, wouldn't he? He and Fawkes had been through so much together. The first few years, de Cressy's hold on Valmar and Mordeaux was precarious. They'd endured great uncertainty while King Richard was held captive by the emperor, and then even more when Richard died and John became king. It could have all gone horribly awry. Fawkes was Richard's man. John could have seized Lady de Cressy's dower lands, snatching away all that Fawkes had fought so hard to win. Instead, he had rewarded Fawkes with more property and power, including the honor of Tangwyl Castle. Which Fawkes had then offered to Gerard. Having chosen him for such a fine position, it seemed unlikely that someone as loyal and principled as Fawkes would abandon him now.

Gerard thought back to his first few weeks after learning he was to command Tangwyl. The sense of exhilaration and vindication he'd felt.

The idea that he—bastard son of a minor knight—had risen so high. His elation had dimmed slightly when he learned he must wed Marared and realized she despised him. But he'd quickly discovered that beneath her prickly, challenging exterior, Marared was an intensely passionate woman. He'd done all he could to woo her, and it seemed as if she was warming to him. Now he'd lost her.

He should have listened to his instincts. As soon as he saw Castell Ystwyth, he'd known the wisest course was to turn around. He'd been convinced it was a trap, and yet he'd ridden in willingly. Now, here he was, deep in Welsh territory and buried beneath a fortress that seemed as formidable and impregnable as the high ridge it was built upon.

He must have let out an involuntary sigh because, because Owain spoke beside him. "There's no reason to lose hope, milord. As Anselm said, at least they're feeding us. We could fare far worse."

"Why keep us alive?" Ifan asked. "What is he planning?"

"Maybe he intends to use as hostages," Guy said. "Hold us for ransom. De Cressy would pay, I feel certain."

"Of course, he would." Gerard sought to sound confident.

"What good will gold do Gwenwynwyn?"

Ifan's tone was bitter. "Gold isn't going to help him hold this fortress or expand his territory."

"'Tis not about ransom," Owain said. "Marared is what he wants. We're merely in the way."

Gerard tensed. More than once, his thoughts had gone down this same pathway, but he dreaded hearing these things spoken aloud.

"Marared? What does he want with her?" Ifan asked. "He can't wed her; she's married to Lord Gerard. And he doesn't seem like the type for rape."

Owain response was terse. "If he marries her, he has a hold over Caradoc and can claim his territories to the east."

No one spoke for a time. Finally, young Anselm broke the oppressive silence. "But if that's what he's planning, why is Lord Gerard still here with us?"

"There's more than one way to get rid of an unwanted husband," Owain said. "A marriage can also be annulled or invalided. Kings do it all the time. John had the Pope annul his marriage to Isabel of Gloucester so he could marry lovely young Isabella."

Anselm sighed. "'Twill be weeks, if not months, before Gwenwynwyn gets a response from the Pope."

"Don't be foolish," Owain spoke impatiently. "He's not going to petition the Pope. He'll find some church official around here to end the marriage."

"But on what grounds?" Guy asked. "He can hardly say they are related."

"If Gwenwynwyn can get Marared to say her vows were coerced, that would be grounds," Owain answered.

"But why would she do that?" Anselm was still clearly puzzled.

Gerard knew exactly why, but he certainly wasn't going to speak of it. No reason to let these men know how resentful and angry Marared had been with the marriage arrangement. Although he'd truly thought she'd gotten past that and begun to care for him.

Rob spoke for the first time. "He might threaten to have us all killed if she doesn't agree."

Now there was a thought. What if Marared was forced to choose between his life and remaining married to him? If she cared for him at all, she would have to go along. Not to mention, he couldn't imagine anyone would want the deaths of five other men on their conscience.

It seemed there was no way out, Gerard realized. He would not get to keep his life *and* his wife. He would be happy to have his life, but it would not be the same without Marared. At one time, he would have been relieved to be free of this marriage. Now he felt the very opposite. He loved Marared and would fight to get her back. That is, if he ever got out of here.

CHAPTER SEVENTEEN

I T HAD BEGUN to rain. At first it was a fine mist, but it rapidly turned into a real downpour. Marared had stopped and retrieved her oiled leather cape from her saddlebags as soon as it started. But now she could ride no further. She could barely see.

She guided the mare to the first stand of vegetation she saw, a copse of gorse bushes. Dismounting, she pulled the cape farther over her head and crouched down beneath the branches, trying to avoid the thorns. Bright yellow blossoms glistened among the green leaves. She shivered as a gust of wind drove rain under the cape. At least she had plenty of water. All she had to do was stand up and hold her face to the sky, and she would be able to drink her fill. But without food or shelter, how long would she last?

She had tried to do the reasonable thing and not act impulsively. But what had seemed perfectly logical at the time now seemed witless. She'd escaped Gwenwynwyn, only to face an unknown fate, alone in unfamiliar territory. If she did encounter someone, how was she to convince them to help her? Like the herdsman, they might flee at the sight of her. Although no one could imagine she looked like a fairy queen now. More like a drowned rat.

She shivered again, trying to warm herself. Nay, she would not give up. 'Twas only a rainstorm. Although she needed to find real shelter.

When the rain started to ease, she mounted Gwenevere and rode on. Several ravens flew by, making her wonder if perhaps a sheep had died and the birds were drawn to its carcass. If there were sheep, there must be a lambing shed or farmstead nearby. She guided the horse in the direction the birds had flown. A short while later, she spotted an opening among the rocks on the side of the hill.

She rode near, dismounted and left the reins trailing. As she approached the opening, she tensed. The Fair Folk were said to live under the hills. Maybe this was the entrance to one of their abodes.

Nonsense. She could not let childhood fears control her. The light was fading. She needed to find shelter quickly and this cave looked promising.

The entrance was small, about half her height. Bending down, she peered inside, but it was too dark to see much of anything. Half holding her breath, she inched in. The cave might be the lair of a wild animal; she needed to be cautious.

All she found was dried leaves and pinecones, probably cached there by a squirrel or marten. The cave smelled musty and acrid, but it would do for a shelter. Crawling out, she tied Gwenevere's reins to the saddle so the mare could graze freely, then returned to the cave and spread out her raincape. Wrapping her cloak around her, she lay down.

It began to rain hard again. The steady sound of the downpour outside the cave reminded her how alone she was and how far from home. The burning hunger in her stomach added to her bleak mood.

At Tangwyl, her life had been so easy and comfortable. She'd always been warm and well-fed, and spoiled by having servants to wait upon her. Once she'd scorned that life, but now it sounded very pleasant. She'd been so caught in her anger and resentment that she hadn't appreciated how fortunate she was.

The same was true of Gerard. She'd been so intent on seeing him as the enemy that she'd ignored his true nature. She shunned his consideration and kindness, thought him foolish for being so patient, and seen his tolerance as a sigh of weakness.

Ah, his patience. It was a miraculous thing. The way he endured her rudeness and insults. Her anger and hostility. If she were a man, she'd never have put up with being wed to such a shrew. Gerard had not only tolerated her, but also sought to please her. He'd indulged all her requests, including her ill-fated scheme to meet with Aoife so she would carry the traitorous message to Rhys.

Bitter tears pricked her eyelids. What a fool she'd been. If not for her meddling, it was likely she would not be here, lost, alone, and facing an uncertain future. And Gerard would not be where he was, imprisoned in a dark, cold cell at Castell Ystwyth.

At least she hoped he was still imprisoned. What if Gwenwynwyn had killed him? The thought aroused a crushing grief. He deserved so much better, including a wife who honored and cherished him. She would be that wife, if she were given the opportunity. Resolve filled her, sweeping away her cold, gloomy thoughts and helping warm her.

She slept fitfully, waking a half-dozen times. When at last she roused, morning light was filtering into the cave and the faint trills of birdsong could be heard in the distance. Her limbs were cold and stiff. Hearing the low of a cow, she was suddenly impatient to face the world. She scrambled out of the cave and discovered a heavy mist had settled over the area. The cow let out another bellow, but because of the fog, she couldn't tell the direction the sound came from.

She called for Gwenevere, and the horse nickered back. Still disoriented, she gathered up her things in the cave and again called out for her horse. The mare whinnied in response. She moved toward the sound, stumbling on a rock and then running into a bush. Finally, she made out the shape of the horse in fog.

She hurried to Gwenevere and rested her head against the mare's side, taking comfort from the animal's warmth and bulk. Her clothes clung to her skin, clammy with dampness and making her shiver. She normally loved the wild hills of her homeland, but today they seemed harsh and forbidding.

After what seemed like a long while, the mist finally faded and she mounted Gwenevere. She soon encountered a flock of sheep and relief flooded her. No farmer would let his flock stray too far untended. There must be herdsman nearby. She spotted the shepherd. His tattered sheepskin tunic and rough brown wool trousers hung on his thin frame, and he wore no shoes.

Like the other man she'd encountered, his hair was dark and his skin dusky and weathered.

He watched her approach, his gaze steady. As she neared, she realized he was older than she thought. Whiskers darkened his narrow jaw. Wanting to take no chance that he would think she was one of the fey, she called out a greeting and introduced herself. She explained her circumstances and asked directions to the nearest farmstead. The man turned and pointed.

Marared thanked him and rode on. Perhaps someday she could return and bring him some shoes. Her father and Gerard always made certain the people who worked for them had proper attire for being out in the weather.

A short while later she crested a hill and spied the farmstead. An enclosure of hawthorn bushes and ancient stonework surrounded a barn and other outbuildings with animal pens around them. In the center was a large dwelling, also of stone.

As she approached, two very short-legged tan-colored dogs greeted her. She'd seen this kind of dog before. They were called corgwn and used for herding cattle, although her father's herdsmen did not use them. A man soon appeared, dressed much like the shepherd. He did have shoes, although they were nothing more than pieces of leather wrapped around his feet and tied at his ankles.

The man appeared more curious than wary. She explained who she was, and he helped her down from her horse. He took the animal, and in a roughly-accented voice said he would was see the mare was looked after. Marared approached the dwelling. She hesitated a moment, then stepped inside the open doorway. Near the hearth, several women were busy at looms. In the dim interior, it took her a moment to make out the rough but simple furnishings. There were several benches and a large table pushed out of the way, a tall coffer and a chest in the corner.

One of the women—with strands of reddish hair sticking out from under her cap—left her loom and approached Marared. She gave a slight bow and introduced herself as Bronwen.

Marared explained who she was and where she was headed. She also gave a vague story of being separated from her traveling party and how she was trying to find her way back to her father's fortress. She mentioned nothing of Gwenwynwyn nor her traveling companions being imprisoned in Castell Ystwyth.

Bronwen said her husband, Talhern, was hunting and should be home soon. She asked one of the women to fetch water for Marared to wash her hands. Another brought Marared buttermilk and oakcakes, along with a bowl of mutton stew from the cauldron hanging over the fire.

Marared sat on a rough-hewn bench at the

table and began spooning the hearty stew into her mouth. As she started on the oatcakes, she observed the household. All four women wore plain woolen gowns, but Bronwen's was brown and cream checked and of a finer weave, marking her as the mistress. Her reddish hair and light skin also set her apart.

Marared was surprised there were no children in the dwelling. Perhaps Bronwen's children were grown, the girls married off already and the boys with their father. But the women were all clearly of childbearing age. Had all the younger children died?

Marared felt a pang of melancholy. Children were so vulnerable. Even if they reached adolescence, tragedy could still befall them. They might succumb to injuries from tending livestock or using an axe or other implements. Young men of noble blood also faced the dangers of being a warrior or knight. She'd never before considered such things. It had saddened her to lose her brothers, and she had grieved deeply when her mother died. But neither experience compared to the pain a woman would feel at losing a child.

Her hand strayed to her belly. For all she knew, a babe might already be growing inside her. She half hoped it was so. Then if anything happened to Gerard, she would have something to cling to and distract her from her guilt and grief.

Tears blurred her vision as she thought of Gerard and his companions, trapped inside dark, forbidding Castell Ystwyth. If Gerard was killed, his death would be on her conscience. What a wretched, stubborn fool she had been. But she would not mourn over what she could not change. She must find a way to rescue Gerard and his men.

Restless, she stood and motioned to the door. Bronwen looked up from her weaving but said nothing. Outside, the weather had cleared, although it was still cool and breezy. Marared found the midden by smell and made use of it. Wandering around the farmyard, she saw newly sprouted bean and turnip plants in the vegetable garden. Small brown and white chickens pecked in the dirt. A bramble-fenced pen held white, spotted pigs wallowing in the greasy mud. A black cow stood in another pen, likely kept there for milking.

Growing up, Marared had never had to worry about caring for livestock. Now she realized how much work went into providing for a household. A dozen or more people lived in this place, and all of them had to be fed and clothed. There were over three times as many at her father's fortress, and four times or more at Tangwyl. If she ever got back to Tangwyl, she would make more of an effort to help.

No wonder Hilda always seemed a bit harried. It didn't seem right that everyone at Tangwyl worked so hard while she had a life of leisure. It was also a life of boredom. If she were more involved in the running of the castle, her life would be more fulfilling. And if she got her husband back and he regularly shared her bed, she would be not only content, but happy.

Bronwen had said her husband would be home soon. But having eaten, Marared felt ready to be on her way again. Perhaps Bronwen could tell her about nearby landmarks that would guide her in the right direction.

She started for the house and turned at the sound of voices. Three men entered the farmyard. Behind them trailed a mule laden with the carcass of a deer. The oldest of the three men was clearly Talhern. With his heavy mustache and piercing blue eyes, he reminded her of a younger version of her father. One of the two youth accompanying looked like him, while the other resembled Bronwen.

Marared went to meet them, inclining her head politely. "I am Marared ferch Caradoc ap Maben. I'm trying to find my way home to Caer Brynfawr. Can you tell me which way to travel?"

Talhern also inclined his head in greeting. "I am Talhern ap Emrys. And these are my sons, Geraint and Elidon."

He gave the two youths a look and they both bowed awkwardly. Talhern dismissed them and met her gaze. His eyes were as clear and sharp as blue glass. "You're traveling alone?"

"I became separated from my companions."

"How long ago?"

"Two days."

"And you've wandered the hills for all that time?"

"I have a horse." She gestured in the direction of the barn.

"Where were you when you last saw your companions?"

"Near a forest." She pointed to indicate the direction she'd come from.

Talhern grunted. Marared grew uneasy. What if he took her back to Gwenwynwyn? Or, to some another man he considered his overlord?

"Mmm." Talhern cocked his head. "You have the look of him."

"Who?"

"Rhys ap Cynan."

She didn't know whether to be relieved or wary. "Rhys is my cousin. But his mother is a Cymrae and mine was Irish." *And I never thought we looked anything alike.*

"'Tis in the slant of your eyes when you glare at me."

Had she been glaring? She must learn to guard her expression better. And be very careful what she said.

"Rhys was here recently."

Marared tensed.

"He wanted my sons to join his warband. As if I would be willing to let the last of my blood be squandered on such nonsense."

The contempt in Talhern's voice surprised her. "Nonsense?"

Talhern made a face. "He wants to take back the lands that were lost to the English near a century ago. I told him I have my own land. And I don't think this is the sort of place the *Saeson* would fight to possess, do you?"

Marared looked around the farmstead. Although it was fairly prosperous, there was no river to bring in trade goods and it was too rainy and cool to grow wheat or many other crops. Talhern was right. Even greedy King John would not covet this place.

"You sent Rhys away?"

"Aye. I sent him away. Good riddance to him and the young fools who follow him."

Marared nodded. "He and my father also disagree."

Talhern cocked his head, still studying her. "None of this explains what you're doing here."

"I told you, I lost track of my escort. I went into the forest to relieve myself and got turned around. When I came out of the woods, I couldn't find them."

"I don't believe your father's men would lose track of you."

Her instinct to flee grew stronger. "They didn't know the area where we were traveling."

"*Where* were you traveling? And why? Your father must have had a reason to send you off on this journey."

It seemed she must tell him the truth, or at least part of it. "We were carrying a message to Prince Gwenwynwyn. He seeks an alliance with my father."

"Why send you?" Talhern's blue eyes grew calculating. "Or were you sent to wed Gwenwynwyn and that's why you ran away?"

Dread clawed her chest, making it hard to breathe. "I can't wed Gwenwynwyn. I'm already married."

Talhern's brows jerked upwards.

Marared licked her dry lips. Talhern might not want to fight the English, but he still considered them the enemy. But she could think of no other reasonable response but the truth. "His name is Gerard of Malmsbury. He holds Tangwyl Castle from the Marcher lord Fawkes de Cressy."

"Ah. And why does Gerard of Malmsbury allow his wife to roam the countryside with an escort too stupid to keep track of her?"

"'Tis complicated."

"We have time. 'Twould be witless for you to set out this late in the day."

Judging by the light, it was only a little past

sext. This time of year she could easily travel a good distance before it got dark. Was Talhern deliberately trying to keep her here?

The farmer was sturdily built and the way he was standing reminded her of large boulder. Solid and immovable. Unless she told him more of the truth, he would never believe her. Or let her leave.

"My husband accompanied me on the journey to Castell Ystwyth. But soon after we arrived, he and his men were imprisoned."

"And you?"

"I wasn't guarded. I was able to flee the castle and ride here."

Talhern looked skeptical, as well he might. If he knew anything about Castell Ystwyth, he would know no one simply rode out the gate of the massive fortress.

"Why do you suppose Gwenwynwyn imprisoned you? What did he hope to gain?"

She shrugged. "Perhaps he thought Lord de Cressy would pay a ransom for Malmsbury."

"And what of you? Would de Cressy pay a ransom for you?"

"Likely not. But my father would." Perhaps Talhern would help her if he thought her father would reward him for helping her.

The silence stretched out. A dog barked in the distance. Among the outbuildings, one man called to another. Talhern's blue eyes probed her, as if he could discover the truth of her words if he stared hard enough. Finally, he motioned toward the house. "Come inside. I would not have Lord Caradoc think I refused his daughter hospitality."

Marared hesitated. "Your wife has already fed me. I should be on my way."

"Go inside. I have to think on how best to handle this."

It was clearly an order. Although she might be of higher rank, she was a woman, so he felt he could command her. She felt the familiar rebelliousness and fought against it. She needed Talhern as an ally.

She followed Talhern to the house. He spoke briefly to Bronwen. She rose from her loom and gestured to the back of the dwelling. "Lady, you look weary. Perhaps you would like to lie down for a time."

Did they mean to lock her away as Gwenwynwyn had?

Bronwen's voice was gentle. "Your gown is a stained and torn. While you rest, I could wash and mend it."

She didn't want to spend the night here. Without her clothing, it would be even more difficult to leave. Yet, she didn't want to appear rude.

She forced a smile. "I'm certain my clothing will get even more soiled on my journey home. Although I would not mind lying down for a time." Perhaps once the rest of the household retired for the night, she could sneak out.

Bronwen took her to a spacious room at the back of the dwelling, which was clearly Talhern and Bronwen's private chamber. A fair-sized bed took up much of the room, but there was also a stool, several chests, and a coffer. On the bed was a thick woolen blanket dyed a lovely rose hue. Marared motioned to the blanket. "'Tis beautiful. Did you use madder for the dye?"

"Aye. My mother taught me the use of dyes and patterns for weaving."

"Did you grow up near here?"

"Nay. My family are from up north, near Conwy."

That explained why Bronwen didn't look like the rest of the people here. "How did you meet Talhern?"

"He came to Gwynedd looking for a bride. His family has ties there. This area is sparsely settled and he couldn't find a woman he wanted to take to wife around here."

"Yet there is good pastureland. I'm surprised there aren't more farms in the area."

"A fever passed through some years ago. Several farms were abandoned because there were no longer enough family members left to maintain them."

Bronwen waited expectantly. Marared realized she couldn't lie down on the beautiful blanket wearing her soiled gown. Despite her unease, she pulled her gown over her head. Bronwen took the garment and draped it over the back of the wicker chair next to the coffer. Marared removed her shoes and lay down in her shift.

Bronwen started toward the door. "If there's anything else you need, let me know."

"Thank you."

Marared stared up at the whitewashed ceiling. The bedding smelled of hyssop, lavender and some other sweet scent. Light from the one unshuttered window filled the room. She thought the brightness and her general unease would keep her awake, but after a time, her limbs grew heavy and her eyes drifted shut. She sought to open them but seemed unable to summon the effort. The room and all her doubts faded away.

SHE WOKE WITH a start. It was dark. How could she have slept so long? She climbed awkwardly from the sagging rope bed and fumbled around on the floor for her boots. When she couldn't find them, she made her way to the chair. To her relief, her gown was still there. Bronwen hadn't taken it away to wash, although she, or someone else, had been in the room and closed the shutters.

Marared put on her gown and padded to the door. She pushed the cowhide covering aside and peered into the main room of the farmhouse. In the faint light from the glowing hearth, she could make out vague shapes. She started forward and ran into a bench. The person sleeping on it jerked upright. "Watch yourself!" The next moment the serving woman gasped. "Beg pardon, lady, I didn't know it was you."

"I'm sorry. I didn't mean to wake you," Marared whispered.

The woman also lowered her voice. "Can I fetch you anything?"

"Nay. But do you know where my boots are? I need to go out."

"There's a chamber pot in the master's room. Likely under the bed."

"I'd rather go outside. I need my boots."

"They're by the fire. Mistress Bronwyn asked me to clean them."

"I also need my cloak. Is it hung near the fire as well?"

"Aye." The woman started to rise. "I can get your things."

"I'd don't want to disturb you any further. Although, thank you."

Marared carefully made her way to the hearth. No one else seemed to have woken. Her boots weren't quite dry, but good enough. Her cloak, hanging on a wooden stand near the fire, was toasty warm. She put on her boots and cloak and crept to the door. It creaked loudly as she opened it, making her cringe.

Outside, the air was thick with mist. She could barely see more than a few feet ahead. For a moment, she considered abandoning her plan. Then she decided she must try to leave while she could. She held her hands out in front of her and inched forward, guessing at the direction of the barn. After what seemed like ages, she encountered the scratchy branches of the hedge surrounding the farmstead. She must have gone the wrong way. Sighing, she turned around.

CHAPTER EIGHTEEN

GERARD HAD ALWAYS considered himself patient and calm. But the longer they were held captive, the more he felt his hope fade. He reminded himself he should be grateful they were still alive. If you could call this living—trapped in a nearly airless cell with no light or access to the outside world. He should also be glad he wasn't alone and take comfort in that.

As if prompted, Anselm spoke wistfully. "How many days do you think we've been here?"

It was Guy who answered. "If you base it on when they bring us food, I'd reckon three days."

"Nay, four," Owain said. "The first day, they brought us nothing."

The sound of a key turning in the lock interrupted their conversation.

"What is it?" Ifan whispered. "'Tis too early

for them to bring us food."

Gerard's heart skipped a beat. Was this when they came for him? How would they do it? Hanging? Running him through with a sword? If he had a chance, he would plead for the lives of his men. His muscles, already cramped from sitting for so long, tightened like the metal bands lashing a barrel.

"Lord Gerard." The voice was familiar. *Madog?* What the devil was he doing there? Had Gwenwynwyn decided he was finished with his young spy and sent him down to rot with the rest of them?

"I'm here," Gerard answered.

A deep breath and then a rush of words: "We don't have much time. And I didn't dare bring a torch, so you'll have to manage in the dark. Here. I'll bring you the key to unlock your shackles. Don't drop it."

Gerard reached out and after some fumbling, found Madog's hand and took the key. But it was still no easy thing to find the lock in his shackles and insert the key.

"What are you doing here?" Ifan voice was sneering. "Your conscience get the better of you?"

"Best not to talk too much," responded Madog. "I don't know for certain who we can trust."

"Not you, that's clear." Ifan let out another hiss of contempt.

"That's enough." Gerard spoke firmly.

After freeing his ankles, he moved on to his wrists. It felt wonderful to escape the punishing metal bands. With the full use of his hands, it was much easier to unlock the other men's shackles.

As he freed them, he could hear Madog's impatient breathing. Their rescuer was obviously very apprehensive. What was his plan for getting out them of the fortress? What of their horses? Without them, they had no chance of eluding pursuers. And they would be pursued, Gerard felt certain. If Gwenwynwyn had changed his mind and decided to let them go, he would not send Madog. Nor would the Welshman appear so agitated.

The last shackle fell away. They were free. Guy stretched and let out a groan. "I vow, I ache from head to toe."

"You'll forget how you feel as soon you breathe fresh air," Gerard said.

"Follow me," Madog whispered harshly.

Gerard grasped Owain's arm and reached out for Guy. The other men also linked hands until they formed a human chain. They moved slowly to the door and freedom.

Once outside their prison, they climbed single-file up the narrow stairs. The entrance to the dungeon was located in a corner of the castle yard behind the blacksmith's shop. The smith's forge was stoked, so instead of fresh air, they were surrounded with the acrid smoke of burning charcoal.

Rob coughed loudly. Madog gave him a stern look. Then he led them behind the smithy and past the other sheds and shops abutting the castle curtain wall. Gerard glanced back at his companions, wondering if they felt as anxious as he did. Why hadn't Madog waited until night to free them? Although then they would need a torch, and that might draw the attention of the guards in the watchtower. But it was hard to imagine anything would alarm the guards more than looking down and seeing their prisoners creeping through the castle yard.

At last they neared the stables and Gerard exhaled in relief. If they could get their horses, they might have a chance. But Madog didn't enter the long low building. Gerard started to protest, to say that they must try to get a couple of mounts. But to his amazement, when they reached the other side of the stables, he saw their horses were saddled and ready for them.

"How in the devil?" Guy murmured.

Madog shook his head to indicate they still must remain silent. Then he nodded his thanks to the stern-faced ostler and the two grooms holding the horses.

Within seconds they had mounted and followed Madog to the gate. This was clearly the most important hurdle. If the guards wouldn't let them leave, they had no chance. They could hardly fight their way out without weapons. With a pang of loss, Gerard thought of his beautiful sword, Conqueror.

The gate was wide open and there didn't appear to be anyone manning it. They rode out as easily as they'd ridden in. Then it was single-file down the treacherous pathway that wound around the castle motte. With the sheer drop to the side, they all concentrated on their horses' footing. It wasn't until they reached the bottom and had ridden to the shelter of the trees by the river that Madog halted.

Gerard rode up next to him and fixed the Welshman with a fierce look. "Explain."

Madog grimaced. "It wasn't supposed to be like this."

"How was it supposed to be?"

Madog looked away. "We weren't even supposed to come here. Rhys had it all planned."

"Rhys? Marared's cousin?"

"Aye." Madog glanced at Gerard, a glimmer of defiance in his blue eyes. Gerard glared back at him.

If Rhys had planned this, then it was likely Marared was involved. And she had probably met with Rhys when they stopped at Caer Brynfawr.

"Lord Gerard told you to explain." Ranulf prompted.

Madog cast him a sullen look. "Rhys and his men were supposed to waylay us on the way here. The plan was to abduct Marared and take her to Gwenwynwyn. When that didn't happen and we showed up here, Gwenwynwyn had no choice but take you prisoner, at least until his plan fell into place."

"Plan?" Gerard struggled for control.

"To wed Marared, of course. He was going to have a priest declare your marriage invalid."

Gerard sucked in his breath. He didn't want to ask the obvious question and find out if Marared was part of this. He couldn't bear to learn she cared nothing for him and was willing to disavow their marriage.

Ifan spoke for him, sounding incredulous. "And Marared agreed to this?"

"Not exactly." Madog's tone was sour. Gerard felt an absurd sense of relief.

"What does that mean?" Owain asked.

"It means she insisted a more senior church official must invalidate the marriage. Gwenwyn-wyn was taking her to the abbot of Strata Florida Priory."

Gerard's emotions flipped again, hovering near despair. Had Marared made this demand because she wanted to make certain her marriage Gwenwynwyn was valid?

"But then it all went awry." Madog snorted in disgust. "I can't believe she did it, a mere woman. They were trained, skilled men and Rhys had warned them to watch her. But she outwitted them all."

Gerard was too startled to respond. It was Owain who asked, "You mean Marared escaped?"

Madog threw his hands up. "Aye. Disappeared. Gone. As if she vanished into thin air. Gwenwynwyn and his men looked and looked for her. They're probably still searching. Although they did send a man back to the castle, on the odd chance she'd returned. That's how I know these things."

Gerard felt a swell of pride for Marared. His clever, fiercely independent wife. He could well believe she had done this. Aye, he could.

Owain spoke. "But why did you free us? Why were we allowed to ride out of the castle?"

Madog's defiance was back. "I had to talk them into it. A lot of the men argued you'd return with an army and attack. But I told them we had no choice but to let you go. Otherwise they would have to kill you, and I wouldn't have allowed *that*. I made it clear that killing you would anger Lord de Cressy and he would get the king involved, which is the last thing anyone wants. I didn't intend to let you rot there either. So I finally convinced the castellan you should be allowed to escape."

Gerard found his voice. "But without our weapons. Why didn't you see that they were given back to us?"

"I didn't want you to turn them on *me*."

Ifan snorted. "We might well have done so, you prick! What possessed you to go along with this fool plan anyway? I thought you had more sense!"

Madog glared at Ifan. "Rhys was certain it would work. He convinced all of us that once Marared was wed to Gwenwynwyn, Caradoc and his allies and freeholders would have no choice but to go along with his plan."

"Which was?"

Madog shot a cold look at Gerard. "To get the cursed English off our lands."

"Dullard." Ifan's tone was cutting. "'Tis far too late for that. You should be happy we have a decent lord." He gestured toward Gerard. "Rhys and the rest of you need to forget such nonsense. Find something better to do with yourselves than re-fighting battles already lost."

Madog glowered at Ifan, his jaw clenched. A few moments later he jerked his horse around and went crashing through the marsh.

"Should we…?" Guy motioned.

Gerard shook his head. "I know his kind. Nothing will change his mind. At least this way we know who our enemy is."

"Aye, we do." Rob's normally placid features were contorted with disgust. The knight had befriended young Madog. His sense of betrayal must run deep.

"But what about our weapons?" Ifan asked.

"Not much we can do," Gerard said. "Better we leave behind our weapons than lose our lives."

"'Tis a long way to Caer Brynfawr," Guy said. "Without weapons we'll be next to helpless."

"Then we'd best get riding, hadn't we?" Gerard turned his horse and urged the animal east.

MARARED FELT AS if she'd been trying to find her way through the mist for hours. The chill and the tension squeezed her body and made her neck and shoulders ache. She could only take tiny steps for fear of tripping over something. Surely by now she should have encountered something: a building, a pen, a gate.

A dog barked suddenly, sounding very near. Marared's heart lightened. "Here, boy! Come here!"

What if the dog attacked her? Despite her doubts, she called out again, making her voice soft and coaxing. She heard the dog approaching and bent low to offer her hand for it to smell. Then she petted its rough coat, feeling weak with relief. A moment later she grabbed the dog's collar. "Home. Go home."

With Marared hunched over, clutching its collar, the dog started off. They'd only gone a few paces when the mist abruptly ended and the farmhouse came into view. Marared released the dog's collar and patted it. "Thank you."

The dog whined and licked her hand before ambling off toward the barn. Marared stood frozen for a moment. It seemed as if some force wanted her to remain here. For good or ill, she must accept that.

She went to the house, opened the door and slipped inside. Everything was as when she'd left, although the fire in the grate had burned down and the room was cool. She hung up her mist-soaked cloak, removed her boots and tiptoed through the sprawl of bodies sleeping on benches. This time, no one woke.

In the bedchamber, a few rays of moonlight seeped past the shutters. She made her way to the bed, stripped off her clammy gown and shivering, climbed in wearing only her shift. Burrowing beneath the blanket, she stared unseeingly into the darkness. Her frantic struggle through the mist seemed like a dream. Yet she knew it had happened. Was the mist trying to protect her from her foolish urge to flee? Or was it a means of trapping her here?

She worried over the matter until she finally fell asleep. When she woke, sunlight gleamed around the edges of the shutters. She rose quickly and donned her gown, wrinkling her nose. The garment smelled of mud and sweat. Why had she rejected Bronwen's offer to wash it? Many of her actions the day before appeared foolish.

The main room of the farmhouse was nearly deserted. Bronwen and another woman were cleaning up after the morning meal. Everyone else must already be outside doing other chores. Bronwen greeted her with a smile. "Good day, lady. How did you sleep?"

"I slept well." If her hostess didn't know of her midnight escapade, there seemed no need to mention it.

Bronwen gestured to the table. "Have some freshly made oatcakes and cheese. Your boots and cloak are nearly dry. By the time you've broken your fast, my sons will be ready to escort you on your way."

"Thank you for your generous hospitality. It's kind of you and Talhern to look after me."

Bronwen nodded in response.

Marared ate quickly. Bronwen and another woman finished putting the food away. Then they dragged the two looms near the fire and unshuttered the windows at the front of the house so they would have light to work by. Two women, including the one she'd spoken to the night before, returned to the house. The women set to work, two of them spinning a pile of fluffy wool, the other two at the looms.

This must be what they did all day, everyday. Except when they were washing and cleaning the wool after shearing, dyeing the yarn, and other aspects of making cloth. Or doing other chores. Once again, Marared realized how fortunate she was to have been born a chieftain's daughter. And now she was an English nobleman's wife. That is, if Gerard didn't decide to set her aside after everything that had happened. *If he was even still alive.* A pang of dread shot through her at the thought.

She rose, again thanked Bronwen and went outside. Talhern's sons were waiting for her. They rode shaggy brown and white ponies that were barely tall enough to keep their legs from trailing on the ground. But the animals looked like sturdy, well-fed beasts, and even if there was no way the animals' short legs could match Gwenevere's gait, it would be much faster to travel with the two youths mounted than if they walked.

Talhern was holding Gwenevere's reins. The mare let out a nicker as Marared approached.

"A beautiful animal." Talhern handed Marared the reins.

"Aye, she is." Gwenevere was another reminder of her privileged status.

Marared focused on the two youths who would accompany her. Geraint was stocky and dark like Talhern. Elidon took after his mother, with reddish brown hair and fine features. They sat their horses stiffly, scarcely looking at her. She hoped that as they traveled, they would become more at ease and converse with her.

Their father motioned. "Look after Lady Marared. And give my regards to her father, Lord Caradoc, when you see him."

"Thank you for your hospitality. And for having your sons guide me on my way."

They set off. Marared struggled to keep Gwenevere to a slow enough pace for the ponies to keep up. The high-spirited mare was eager to be on her way.

Marared turned and smiled at Elidon. As the younger of the two, he might be easier to win over. "'Tis kind of you to guide me all this way. Or do you welcome this trip as respite from your usual tasks? What would you be doing this day if you were not traveling with me?"

The youth shot her a wary look. "We would probably be moving the flock to the north pasture. Or gelding the calves."

"Would you rather be doing this?"

She waited, but neither youth responded. At this rate, the journey was going to be long and tedious.

"Tell me, have you ever been to Caer Brynfawr before?" She gazed pointedly at Elidon. When he didn't answer, she turned to Geraint. "What of you? Have you ever been there?"

Geriant shook his head.

"Then how do you know the way?" The question sounded rude, but at this point she didn't care if she offended them.

Again, neither youth answered. Marared felt a stab of aggravation. She could travel much faster if she was alone. The day was sunny and clear and she had a fair idea of which direction to go. She really didn't need their help.

Her temper boiled over. "I don't see the point of having you escort me. You obviously have no desire to make this journey, and since you don't seem to know where we're going, I see no reason to inconvenience you to appease your father. You can tell him I rode off and you couldn't catch up. That would certainly be true. Your mounts are no match for mine."

She glanced at Elidon. Despite her cold tone, she wanted to give them one last chance to redeem themselves. No matter what the youths told Talhern, it was likely he would be angry with them.

Elidon did look distressed. He gave his brother a look, then glanced at her. "Please don't send us back. Although we haven't been to your father's fortress, we've traveled to the area."

"Aye," Geraint put in. "And you will be safer with us than you would be on your own."

She resigned herself to their company. At least riding this slowly she could appreciate the beauty of the countryside. The foxgloves were beginning to bloom, their tall rosy purple spikes rising above the thick green grass. The sky was a clear, rich blue. The sun on her face was warm and soothing.

Lulled into complacency, it took a moment for her to realize the landscape had begun to look familiar. Indeed, if they followed the crest of those hills to the south, they would be in sight of Caer Brynfawr in no time.

Even as she had the thought, Geraint called out, "It's this way." He pointed east, to a route she knew led down into a steep valley.

"Nay." She gestured. "I know where I am. This way is faster."

Geraint brought his mount up beside her. "You're wrong. We have to go this way." His blue eyes flashed with anger and threat. A moment later he urged his pony directly into her pathway. She turned her horse, only to discover Elidon on her other side.

She looked from one youth to the other. Did they really think they could control her so easily? If she gave Gwenevere the order to run, the mare would obey in a heartbeat.

As if guessing her thoughts, Geraint reached for the bow slung over his shoulder. "I'm a good shot. I'd hate to think of your fine horse being wounded."

Marared let out a gasp of horror. She could

not risk the safety of her beloved mare. She should never have trusted Talhern. He didn't send his sons along to guide her safely home, but to lead her into a trap. "Where are you taking me? What do you want?'

Geraint's eyes still glinted with warning. "You'll see." He motioned for her to ride east. The two youths stayed close, essentially herding her in the direction of the valley. Marared silently cursed herself. Would she never learn? Would she continue to make stupid mistakes and trust the wrong people? If her escort was taking her to Gwenwynwyn, she was doomed. She'd never escape him a second time. Regret cut her like a knife. What if she never saw Gerard again? The thought made her want to weep.

Above her, a hawk called to its mate. The fragrance of meadowsweet and chervil floated up from the tall grass. The moist air glided across her skin and gently lifted the curls and tendrils around her face. But she felt numb…except for her heart, which was like a cold stone inside her.

They crested the hill and descended into the valley. She could see a make-shift settlement sprawled along a small stream. There were lean-tos and tents made of branches and cowhides, and a pen for horses. More than a dozen men were gathered around open hearth. As they drew near, she saw one of the men was Rhys.

CHAPTER NINETEEN

MARARED GLARED AT her cousin, fighting the growing dread bubbling up inside her. Rhys would probably take her back to Gwenwynwyn. He would make certain she didn't escape.

Rhys nodded to her. "Greetings, cousin." To her escort he said, "Well done, boys. I'm glad to see you refused to listen to your father with his pathetic talk of keeping the peace and honoring his vow to Caradoc."

Marared glanced at Geraint. The youth looked very uncomfortable. She wondered if he was reconsidering his decision to defy his father.

She turned back to Rhys, her chin raised in defiance. "What will you do now? Take me back Castell Ystwyth? 'Tis a long way, and I will try your patience every moment."

Rhys snorted. "I'm sure you would, stubborn, difficult wench that you are." A muscle twitched in his jaw.

"Why so gloomy, Rhys? You got what you wanted."

"I would have, if it wasn't for worthless cowards like Gwenwynwyn and Madog."

Madog? What did he have to do with this? "What do you mean?"

"By now Gwenwynwyn is probably holed up in Ystwyth with his men, terrified that Fawkes de Cressy or your father will come and kill him. Or at least seize Ystwyth and send him into exile."

"Aye. They might do that. Gwenwynwyn was a lackwit to think he could get away with kidnapping me and forcing me to wed him."

"Nay, his *mistake* was in not killing Malmsbury and having done with it."

Rhys's words implied Gerard was alive! But she dare not react. "If he did that, de Cressy would almost certainly have sought revenge. He might even have involved the king."

Rhys's mouth curled. "Aye, the king. Let him send his army. Then perhaps my countrymen will understand they must fight. If we give in now, the cursed *Saeson* will only want more. They won't be happy until they've driven us into the sea and taken everything."

A part of her feared he was right. But she also knew there was no way her people could win back the lands already lost to the English. Her outlook was greatly changed from only a few months ago, when she'd been determined to fight the enemy to the death.

Rhys was still regarding her with cold contempt. She knew her cousin well enough to be certain he wasn't going to let her go. "If you're not sending me back to Gwenwynwyn, what do you plan to do with me?"

"You? Treacherous, traitorous bitch that you are? You've caused me a lot of trouble, and cost me an important ally. I'd like to see you pay with your life for your selfish defiance."

Her heart beat faster. Would he truly kill her, his own kin?

A faint, icy smile replaced Rhys's contemptuous glare. "But that would be short-sighted. You've cost me much. I intend to get some of it back. I'm going to hold you for ransom. If your doting husband wants you returned to him, he's going to have to pay me twenty marks of gold."

Marared inhaled sharply. "He doesn't have that sort of wealth!"

"Nay, but his overlord does."

"And how will he contact de Cressy when he is imprisoned inside Castell Ystwyth?"

Rhys's mouth twisted. "It pains me to say that Malmsbury and his men escaped, aided by the scheming, deceitful piece of *cach* known as Madog."

Gerard was free! He was safe! Her heart soared with relief.

Rhys had drawn his knife and was testing the sharpness of its blade against his calloused thumb. "Of course, another of my requirements will be that Malmsbury brings the gold himself." His chilling smile made his unspoken words quite clear. His real goal was to lure Gerard into a trap and kill him.

Marared breathed in sharply as dread seeped through her veins.

But maybe she could escape. She glanced around the camp. Most of the men here owed loyalty to her father. If Caradoc came for her, those who still honored him might refuse to follow Rhys's orders and set her free. They might do that anyway, if she could make them understand how foolish and dangerous Rhys's plan was. She grew calmer. There was no reason to despair. Not yet.

As THE OUTER walls of Caer Brynfawr came into view, Gerard tensed. What sort of greeting awaited them? Marared was likely here already, since she'd had a head start and knew the way. What had she told Caradoc? Where did her loyalties lie?

They were barely in the gate when Caradoc came out to meet them. He glanced around before approaching Gerard. "Where's Marared?"

Gerard sat up even straighter. Marared hadn't made it back. That was alarming. It could mean she'd joined up with Rhys. Or worse, something had happened to her. Gerard slid off his horse and handed the reins off to the waiting groom. "Can you see to it that my men and the horses are given food and water?"

Caradoc barked out the order. When he returned his gaze to Gerard, his expression was fierce. "Out with it, man. Has something happened to my daughter?"

"Let us go into the hall. I'll tell what I know."

Once inside, Caradoc seemed to remember his duties in greeting a guest. He had water brought so Gerard could wash, then urged him to sit at the large table. A servant brought a bowl of steaming stew, along with flagon and two cups.

"Drink some mead." Caradoc motioned to the flagon. "But then, by all that is holy, tell me what's happened to my daughter!"

Gerard would have preferred water to mead. But perhaps the potent beverage would help steady his nerves. He took a swallow and began to explain.

When he finished, the chieftain was silent. Gerard watched him uneasily. He had no idea how Caradoc would react. He might blame

Gerard for what had happened at Castell Ystwyth.

Caradoc let out a sigh. "I should never have risked sending my daughter to meet with Gwenwynwyn. Although I did think you'd be able to protect her. Of course, protecting her is always a chancy thing. You can't protect someone you can't control, and that's my Marared."

Gerard nodded. "I certainly wish I had done things differently. I was uneasy about entering the fortress. It seemed like a trap, and it was."

"And *I* should never have trusted Gwenwynwyn. I should have thought harder about what he had to gain. He's too far away for me to truly aid him in battle, which means an alliance with me is of little use to him. But this plan of his…what the devil was he thinking? Even if he convinced Marared to refute the marriage and wed him, what was he going to do with *you*? He surely couldn't let you go and expect you to do nothing after he'd stolen your wife. And if he meant to kill you, why didn't he do so immediately?"

"I know. It makes little sense. Perhaps he hadn't thought things through. Or maybe, rather than killing me outright, he intended to imprison me indefinitely." Gerard repressed a shudder. He'd almost rather die than languish in that dark, dank prison for months or years.

Caradoc flexed his shoulders. "At least Madog got a conscience before it was too late and freed you."

"I don't think he was motivated by his conscience, but by his fear of what was going to happen to him. I think once he heard Marared had escaped, he realized Rhys's whole scheme was falling apart."

Caradoc eyes widened. "Rhys? You're speaking of my nephew?"

"Aye. Madog said Rhys ap Cynan was behind everything. He was the one who convinced Gwenwynwyn to lure Marared to Ystwyth with the idea of forcing her to wed him."

The chieftain's expression grew hard. "That sneaky little weasel. I've had my conflicts with Rhys, but I never thought he'd do this to me…or to Marared."

"Ah, but Marared and Rhys have been working together for some time." Caradoc's son Maelgwn spoke from the shadows. Gerard hadn't even been aware of him sitting in a corner of the hall.

Caradoc turned to his son, glowering. "What do you know of it?"

Maelgwn took another swallow from the cup he cradled in his hands and jerked his head toward Gerard. "When you stopped here on your way to Ystwyth, she met with Rhys. And I know she's been in contact with him other times since you wed her. Ask Aoife. She'll tell you."

Gerard thought back to when Marared insisted on meeting with Aoife. At the time, he'd thought there was something odd about Marared wanting to travel all that way to meet with her cousin for such a brief time. Most likely she had used Aoife to pass on a message to Rhys. She'd probably asked his aid in getting rid of her unwanted husband.

Gerard felt sick. Marared had plotted to end the marriage. He'd known how she felt when they married but he'd thought she'd begun to warm to him. It was brutal to realize she'd been so unaffected. That she cared so little for him. But even so, he couldn't believe she'd been involved in Gwenwynwyn's scheme. Why go all the way to Ystwyth and then run away?

He said as much to Caradoc. The chieftain shook his head and didn't respond.

It was Maelgwn who answered. "That's where Rhys made his mistake. He thought he could use Marared to get what he wanted. But we all know better. Marared will bend her will to no man."

Caradoc gave his son a stony look. "By the saints, if you knew all this, why didn't you say something? Why did you let this wretched mess unfold and not speak out?"

"I didn't know anything about this scheme with Gwenwynwyn. As for Marared plotting with

Rhys, I didn't think that was any of my business. 'Tis Marared's life, not mine."

Caradoc pounded the table. "What did you think, that Rhys is doing this simply to get back at the English? Nay, his goal is to take my place as chieftain. If that happens, then where will you be? Do you suppose Rhys will see fit to let you drink wine and mead all day? He'll fortify this holding and use it as a base for his raids. And insist any able-bodied man join his warband. You'll have to get used to sleeping rough and risking your life. That is, if Rhys allows you to live. He's a canny wolf. The type to eliminate all potential rivals. He'll want my line to die out completely. Which means getting rid of *you*."

Maelgwn finally seemed to rouse from his lazy stupor. He stared at his father in shock. Seeing his son's expression, Caradoc's anger drained away. "I don't suppose Marared considered these things either. Catriona was right. I've been too soft on my children. I wanted you to have an easier life than me, to not always be fighting and strategizing. But I failed to prepare you for the grim realities and responsibilities that come with our status." He closed his eyes, looking weary. "And now my daughter may have allied herself with her treacherous, power-mad cousin and inadvertently brought us all down."

Tendrils of dread curled around Gerard's

heart. Had Marared's impulsive, stubborn nature brought ruin to her family? Caradoc was a loyal ally and a good man. If what he predicted came to pass, Marared, who had fought so hard for her freedom and independence, would not only lose all control over her own circumstances, but have to bear the guilt for the deaths of her father and brother. 'Twas a terrible fate. He would not wish it on any woman, let alone the fierce, maddening maiden who had stolen his heart.

But they didn't know for certain Marared was allied with Rhys. She'd fled Ystwyth and avoided marrying Gwenwynwyn, which suggested she was now defying Rhys. But where was she? The band of anxiety around Gerard's chest tightened.

An older man named Meurig appeared in the doorway, his weathered face set in grim lines. "A messenger came to the gate. Rhys ap Cynan has Marared. He says he's willing to ransom her."

Gerard looked at Caradoc, who appeared as stunned as he was.

"Bring the messenger here!" Caradoc ordered.

"He's left already. Didn't want to face you, I reckon."

"Who was it?"

"Young Hywel. Davy's youngest."

Caradoc exhaled in disgust. "Traitorous little fool!"

"What's the ransom?" Gerard was as shocked

as Caradoc, but also relieved. At least Marared was safe.

"He wants twenty marks of gold," Meurig said. "And he insists Lord Gerard bring the ransom…alone."

Caradoc swore an oath. "Scheming bastard has lost his wits! I don't have that sort of wealth. The wretched fool has vastly overreached himself this time. If I called up all the men who owe me fealty, my army would be thrice his, at least."

"But what about Marared?" Gerard asked. "If we don't pay Rhys, will he hurt her?"

Caradoc raised his brows. "They're kin. And she's a woman."

"You're certain she'll be safe?"

Gerard thought he saw a flicker of doubt in Caradoc's eyes. His own fear grew. When it came to seizing power, men could be utterly ruthless. It was rumored King John had killed his own nephew. And Richard's harsh betrayal of his father, King Henry, had almost certainly contributed to Henry's death. Even so, it seemed unbelievable that Rhys was power-mad enough to kill a woman, and his cousin.

Caradoc recovered his composure. "What good would it do Rhys to kill her? If he did that, even his own men would turn against him. We have some honor here in Cymru. We're not the savage beasts the English make us out to be."

Normally, Caradoc's words would have

made Gerard feel better. But they were talking about Marared. He wasn't willing to risk her life, despite her father's assurances. If there was even the slimmest possibility Rhys might hurt her, he had to do everything he could to rescue her. "Is Father Idwal or some other scribe around? I need to send a message to Fawkes and let him know what has happened."

Caradoc gestured. "I'll send for Father Idwal. If you want to apprize your liege lord of the situation, that's all well and good. But even if de Cressy agrees to the pay the ransom, I think it would be a grave mistake to do so. Rhys doesn't care a bit about the gold. His goal is to see you dead."

With him dead, Marared would be free to marry again. And this time, Rhys likely wouldn't bother finding someone to marry her off to, but instead wed her himself. Since they were cousins, the marriage would probably not be sanctioned by the Church. But that might not carry much weight here in Cymru.

Gerard thought about how much Marared would hate being a pawn in Rhys's schemes. Even if she had once plotted with her cousin, she would despise being coerced into marriage with him.

Caradoc motioned to Meurig. "Fetch Father Idwal. Then find some fit, young man to ride to Valmar Castle. Make certain the youth is trustworthy. Hard to know who is loyal these days, especially the younger men. I'm not entirely surprised Rhys has turned against me. But it's disappointing to think that others of my men have aided him."

Caradoc's face sagged. Gerard felt a sudden sympathy for the genial chieftain. Caradoc was a good man...perhaps too good. It often seemed the most callous and cruel were the ones who prevailed.

Men like Rhys. Fear coursed through Gerard. It would take several days to get a response from Fawkes. He couldn't wait that long. Marared was clearly being held someplace close to Caer Brynfawr. "Where do you think they are?" he asked Caradoc in a low voice.

The chieftain rose, making a tiny motion with his head in the direction of his son as he did so. "I've no idea. There are so many valleys around here, they could be anywhere. There's not much we can do until Father Idwal gets here. Might as well go out and look at the new foals. We had a fine crop this year."

Gerard also got to his feet. "I heard one of your hounds had puppies a few weeks ago. I was wondering if you would be willing to part with one."

"An excellent idea. They're in the main barn. The bitch whelped here in the hall, but we had to move them when they got big enough to get underfoot."

They went out to the yard. Caradoc spoke gloomily. "Sad to say, I'm not sure I trust my own son. For all I know, Maelgwn is spying for Rhys."

"My thoughts exactly. But now that we're alone, do you have an answer for me? Do you know where Rhys might be holding Marared?"

"I've some idea. Do you think we should try to surprise them?"

"Do you think it's possible? What's the risk of Marared being hurt if we do?"

"I told you, I don't think Rhys will harm her. You're the one he's after. If we attempt a rescue, I don't think you should be a part of it."

Gerard seized the chieftain's arm. "Marared is my wife. I must do whatever I can to free her."

Carodoc nodded, then wrinkled his brow in thought. "If we attack at night, and you dressed as a Cymro, you would not be so much at risk."

"But that means no helmet or mail." How could he go into battle without proper armor? He'd feel exposed and vulnerable. "Besides, if we're dressed no different than them, and it's dark, how will we tell our men from theirs?"

"We can smear our faces with charcoal. An old trick of raiding."

Gerard still felt uncomfortable with the plan. "But I'm taller than most Cymro, and I don't have a mustache. Nor long hair."

"With your face obscured by charcoal, your lack of facial hair will not be so noticeable. And, perhaps you don't realize how much your hair has grown since you first came here. 'Tis not quite as long as a Cymro, but passable."

"And my height?"

"One or two of my men are close to you in stature. And we'll have the element of surprise. That's the important thing."

"You don't think Rhys will anticipate an attack?"

"Nay. He'll expect you to behave like a *Sais*."

"Which means….?"

"Charge in on horseback in full armor. Or maybe he thinks you're fool enough to bring him the ransom. Everyone knows you're besotted with Marared."

"Is it so obvious?"

Caradoc grinned. "The way you look at her makes it very clear. You're normally stiff and cold, like the rest of your race. But when you gaze at my daughter, your face goes soft." Carodoc clapped him on the back. "I'm pleased to see it. I'd worried her fiery, independent nature would annoy you."

"And her…" Gerard hesitated, feeling like an utter dolt. "What do you think Marared feels for me?"

"When you stopped here on the way to Ystwyth, it seemed to me she was warming to you."

Warming to him. That was a far cry from what he wanted her to feel for him. And from the intense longing he felt for her. The deep need to protect her and do whatever he could to make her happy.

Caradoc slapped him on the back again. "Don't worry. Despite her temper and sometimes childish outlook, Marared isn't stupid. She'll come to admire your loyalty and steadfastness in time."

Admiration was hardly what he wanted either! Gerard struggled to shake off the aching disappointment. He would not give up. Once he got her back, he would find a way to make her love him. "Who will we take with us? What men do you trust?"

Caradoc turned grim. "After all that's happened, I can truly count only a handful of my warriors. I'll have Owain round them up. Meanwhile…" He motioned to an empty stall at the end of the stables. "Have a look at the puppies and decide which one you'd like to take back to Tangwyl."

Carodoc left. Gerard entered the stall and gazed down at the bitch surrounded by her squirming, whining puppies. The little creatures were very endearing, but he could not focus on them. Until he got Marared back safely, nothing else mattered.

CHAPTER TWENTY

GERARD FELT LIKE he might as well be naked. Bad enough that he wore no helm and his only protection was a boiled leather vest, which was too small and made him feel as if he couldn't breathe properly. But traveling on foot truly unnerved him. Not that they'd had a choice in leaving their horses behind. The countryside here was so rugged, even the most sure-footed mountain pony would be at risk of losing its footing and throwing its rider.

The hillside was dotted with crags and out-crops. Gorse and thorn bushes concealed piles of rough gray stones. The cloud cover was heavy, and allowed only the smallest hint of light to seep through from the half moon. Gerard felt like he was stumbling around in total darkness. Meanwhile, his companions seemed to move with nimble swiftness, as if they were part cat, part mountain goat.

His greater height and size were also a disadvantage. Caradoc had taken one look at him in his borrowed garments and shaken his head. "Even with the charcoal masking your features, you can't pass. Your build is too distinctive. You'll have to wait behind until we've freed Marared. Then you can help us if there's further need."

The man ahead of him halted suddenly and Gerard nearly ran into him. "Over this rise," the man murmured.

A few moments later, they all gathered around Caradoc. The chieftain spoke in a near whisper. "Ifan reports all is quiet." He motioned with his head to the young warrior. "But we still don't know for certain where they're keeping Marared. We need to get down there without being seen, find Marared, disable whoever is guarding her and get her out of there as fast as possible. Remember, this is not about inflicting damage or getting back at these men for being traitorous curs. Our only objective is freeing Marared. Do you understand?'

All the men murmured their assent. Gerard's clenched his jaw. *She's my wife. I should be the one to rescue her!*

But he had to think of the outcome, rather than the urgings of his heart. He must give Caradoc's plan every chance to succeed. Even so, as the troop of warriors set off, leaving him behind, his body was rigid with frustration.

He waited, listening to the usual night sounds: the hoot of an owl. The bleat of a sheep in the distance. The slow, musical trickle of water over rocks. Time crept by. Sweat accumulated under the suffocating leather jerkin and made him itch. He thought about what he would do and say when he got Marared back. How he would hold her in his arms and tell he loved her, even if there were dozens of people watching.

But what if she wouldn't let him near her? What if she didn't want to be rescued? What if she was a willing participant in Rhys's plan?

Nay, he would not believe that. Caradoc knew her as well as anyone and he was certain she wanted no part of her cousin's scheme. He would cling to that. He would—

Shouts echoed upwards. He couldn't make out words and strained to figure out what was happening. Was that faint scuffling noise the sound of fighting?

Unable to bear it any longer, he began a slow, careful descent. Halfway down, a woman's scream made his heart stop in his chest. He forced himself to take a deep breath and then another. When he had composed himself, he continued down the hillside, still moving with painful slowness. It was the most frustrating journey he'd ever made. But if he fell and was injured, he'd be no use to Marared.

At last, he reached level ground. It was even darker here in the valley. He could barely make out the shape of a tent ahead of him. Drawing his sword, he carefully circled around the tent. He could hear men speaking, but couldn't make out what they were saying.

He tripped on a rock and almost went down. *Patience.* Yet every fiber of his body screamed for him to hurry. At last he could see a campfire that made a circle of light in the darkness. Beyond the fire, Rhys held Marared fast against his body. Gerard took a step closer and saw the glint of Rhys's knife at her throat. He could not stop himself from moving nearer.

The Welshman saw him and called out, "Drop the sword or I'll kill her."

Gerard lowered his sword. "What about the gold? Don't you want the ransom?"

Rhys laughed. "Gold? What would I do with gold? 'Tis Marared I want. And you dead."

"Don't be a fool." Caradoc appeared from the shadows and moved toward Rhys. "Wedding Marared won't bring you what you wish. You can't stand against me."

"If that's true, then I might as well slit Marared's throat right now."

Nay! The panicked cry nearly escaped Gerard's lips, but he managed to hold back. He must not reveal how desperate he was.

Rhys's attention shifted back to Gerard. His eyes radiated hatred.

Gerard moved nearer. "'Tis me you want. What if I take Marared's place? Give myself up and you let her go?" He dropped his sword to the ground and took another step, his hands held out.

"Nay!" Marared's eyes met Gerard's, her expression desperate. In clear Norman French, she said, "Come no closer. Rhys might spare my life, but you have no chance at all!"

Relief flooded him. At least Marared didn't want him to be killed. Somehow, he had to keep them both alive so they could build from that. The knife concealed in his braies felt reassuringly heavy. He took a step toward Rhys. "Let her go and I'll take her place."

Rhys let out a cold, sneering laugh. "I don't believe a word you say, *Saeson* scum."

"What will convince you?"

"Come and stand in front of me and bare your throat for my knife. Then I will let Marared go."

MARARED COULD FEEL the blade of Rhys's knife pressing into her neck. Warm blood trickled from where he'd already cut her. If she tried to twist away, he would push the knife deeper. If she stamped on his foot or knocked her head against his chin—defensive techniques she'd learned from her brothers—she feared it wouldn't be enough to loosen his grip. But she wasn't completely helpless. She had her knife.

Rhys had never thought to have her searched when he first took her captive, so he didn't know about the small knife strapped to her calf. Even after his men had tied her hands behind her back, she'd been able to retrieve it. She'd been trying to use the weapon to cut the ropes binding her wrists when Rhys came for her. Now, she must use it to get him to release her.

But it was a puny knife, incapable of doing much damage. Her only chance was to hurt him where it counted. His leather jerkin didn't cover his groin, so his woolen trousers were his only protection. But she would have to stab hard and true. Difficult to do when he was behind her and she could only guess at the position of his body. Not to mention if she didn't hurt him badly enough, he might kill her. To succeed, she must wait until he was distracted.

Gerard moved nearer, his movements easy and unhurried, as if he was not facing an armed man who meant to kill him. In contrast, Rhys reeked of the sharp scent of fear. Marared needed him to relax and grow more confident, so he would be more likely to make a mistake. She let out a moan. "Rhys, please, you're hurting me."

He gripped her tighter. "You deserve it, bitch. You've cost me so much."

Gerard moved closer, looking very tall and formidable. Rhys would have to reach up to slash his throat.

But she couldn't let it come to that. Adjusting her grip on the knife, she drove it into back Rhys's body. He screamed and dropped the knife but didn't release her. She twisted and jerked, seeking to loosen his grip. Abruptly, he flung her away.

Then everything went black.

As soon as he saw Marared fall, Gerard rushed to her. He touched her face and called her name, but she lay unmoving. The wound on her neck wasn't deep. Why didn't she wake? He felt the back of her head and found a slight swelling, but nothing else. Panicked, he glanced around and saw two of Caradoc's men restraining Rhys on the ground. The rest of Rhys's companions seemed to have vanished.

He turned back to Marared. Caradoc came and knelt beside him. "She must have hit her head when she fell. *Marared bach.*" His voice was raw with anguish.

"We must get her back to the fortress. Find a

healer."

"Too dangerous to travel in the dark. We'll move her into a tent for now."

"I'll carry her."

Gerard picked Marared up and followed Caradoc to a tent. The chieftain moved aside so Gerard could duck into the leather shelter. He lay Marared on a pile of sheepskins. In the lamplight, her exquisite features seemed carved of pale stone. Anguish squeezed Gerard's chest and made it hard to breathe. He'd never felt so terrified. So helpless.

He smoothed Marared's hair away from her face and his fingers left a streak of blood. The dark smear intensified his horror. Did Marared have another wound? Frantically, he searched for another injury and discovered the back of her gown had blood on it. "Dear God, what is this? What has he done to her?"

Caradoc touched his shoulder. "Don't worry. The blood is Rhys's. Marared stabbed him. I'm sure she was aiming for his *ceilliau*, but she hit the big vein in the groin instead. That's why he went down so easily. He'll be dead soon, if he isn't already. There's no way to stop that kind of bleeding. Even if we desired to do so."

Gerard felt a surge of bitterness. Rhys was going to die and escape judgment. If Marared didn't recover, he'd have no target for his anger. "You've sent someone for a healer?"

"Aye. But there's likely little they can do. She'll either wake or she won't."

Someone brought a clean rag and a bowl of warm water. Gerard dabbed carefully at the dried blood on Marared's neck. The wound had already stopped bleeding, but the sight of it made Gerard sick with fury. He turned his attention to the lump on the back of her head. That wound hadn't even bled. Such a little thing and yet it might kill her.

Gerard closed his eyes and began to pray.

"The healer is here," Caradoc called from the entrance of the tent. "There isn't room in there for both of you. Come and sit by the fire."

Reluctantly, Gerard got up. To his surprise, the healer was Hew, the stablemaster. He gave the man a questioning look.

Hew gripped his shoulder. "I promise I'll do all I can. But head injuries are difficult to treat."

Gerard nodded stiffly. If the chieftain thought Hew was the best hope for Marared, he must trust that he was.

Before joining Caradoc, Gerard went to look at Rhys's body. He lay on his back, a dark stain spreading across his trousers. Marared had managed to wound him mortally, even as Rhys held a knife to her throat. His wife was an incredibly brave and resourceful woman. Tears pricked his eyes.

"Gerard. Come sit with us," Caradoc called.

Gerard joined the chieftain and his men by the fire. He refused the food they offered but took a few swallows of mead. The potent liquid burned his throat, but he was glad for it.

"I'm trying to decide what to do with the men who joined Rhys's warband," Caradoc said.

Gerard struggled to order his thoughts. In the world he was from, traitors were dealt with ruthlessly. "They broke their oath to you. I don't see that you have any choice but to hang them."

Caradoc nodded. "I see your reasoning. But here is mine. If I hang them, their kin will bear a grudge against me. And without these men—sons, husbands, brothers—it will be difficult for their families to survive. Women and children will suffer. And they had no part in this."

Gerard understood that killing able-bodied men would not help Caradoc's people prosper. Still, because of what these men had done, Marared might die. He wasn't certain he could forgive that.

"We have don't to decide immediately," Caradoc said. "The main thing is that Rhys is dead. Killed by a woman. A fitting end for a coward."

From the shadows, Ifan spoke. "I wonder how she got the knife."

"She had it strapped to her leg," Caradoc said. "I always insisted she do that when she went out walking or riding alone. I didn't want her to be entirely defenseless."

"Did you also teach her how to use it?" Gerard asked.

Maelgwn, seated next to his father, responded. "That was me. Along with Padrig and Dewi." Maelgwn's voice was choked. He looked genuinely shaken.

Gerard sat there a while longer, feeling numb. His thoughts seemed to run in circles. If only he'd been closer when Marared fell, he could have caught her. If only he'd listened to his instincts and they hadn't gone to Ystwyth in the first place. If only…

"Gerard, Hew says you can rejoin your wife."

He returned to the tent and met Hew outside. "The wound is on the back of the head, and up high, which is good," Hew said. "But I can't say when she will wake, or if she will be affected in some way."

Gerard nodded his thanks and ducked into the tent. Marared lay as pale and still as ever. Except for her hair, which gleamed brilliant red in the lamplight. It was a mass of tangles, but that didn't alter its beauty. Bright as fire, yet cool and soft to the touch. He knelt beside her and smoothed her hair away from her face, using his fingers to try to work out the tangles. If only he had a comb. Unsnarling her hair would give him something to do.

He took Marared's hand. Her nails were torn

and ragged. She'd been through so much already. "Marared, Come back to me. Please."

There was no movement. No response. The lump in his throat thickened and tears threatened. Nay, he would not weep. Not while there was hope.

Still holding her hand, he lay down beside her. He'd already sent a dozen prayers to heaven. Who else could he call on for aid? The spirits of this land? The Fair Folk, as Marared called them?

But everything he knew about the fey suggested they were cold and capricious, and cared little for humans. Unless they fell in love with one of them and stole them away. He imagined a troupe of the Fair Folk appearing in the doorway of the tent. Their hair and clothing, bright and dazzling. Their movements making a sound like the tinkle of bells. He could hear them whispering. Pointing at Marared. Admiring her beauty. They wanted her for their own. To carry her away to their kingdom beneath the hills.

He jerked upright. "Nay! You can't have her!"

There was no one there but him and Marared. He could see the first hints of light seeping through the opening of the lean-to and hear the call of a lapwing. But a sense of dread clung to him. It must have been a dream. But what if it was not? What if the Fair Folk had come and stolen her spirit already?

He touched Marared's face. Her skin felt cool and dry. Was she slipping away from him? He put his head to her chest. Her breathing was even and regular, as if she was asleep. And yet, she didn't rouse. She was caught in the place between life and death.

He reminded himself he didn't believe in enchantments or fairies. Marared had an injury inside her head. It would either heal or she would die from it. All these fanciful and terrifying thoughts were caused by his fatigue.

He lay back down again, but was afraid to close his eyes. He didn't want to dream about the Fair Folk. And it seemed important to remain vigilant. If he watched over Marared, not even magical beings could come and take her away.

Despite his resolve, he must have dosed.

Something alerted him and he bolted upright. Marared stirred beside him. "My head hurts."

No words had ever sounded so wonderful.

HER HEAD ACHED and she was dizzy and nauseated. Yet it was all right. Gerard was there. She squeezed his hand.

"What can I get you? Water?"

"Nothing." She didn't want him to leave her.

Gerard let out a deep sigh. He sat up, then

lifted her and held her against his chest. The movement made the dizziness worse. Her stomach lurched. She held very still, willing the sickness away. "I need to lie back," she mumbled.

"Of course. I'm sorry." He helped her recline and smoothed her hair away from her face. "I had a dream the Fair Folk came for you."

She gave a weak laugh. "They would have no use for me. Especially now. I must look and smell disgusting."

"Never. You are always beautiful."

His voice was so tender, so full of longing and love. She felt the same way about him. She'd been terrified when she thought Rhys would kill him. She stiffened and clutched Gerard's hand. "What happened? How did I get away from Rhys?"

"You don't remember?"

She didn't. It was all a blur, like a smashed pot where there was no way to tell how the pieces fit together.

"He's dead. You killed him."

Marared thought of her knife. It hardly seemed possible such a puny weapon could kill a man. "You're certain?"

"Aye. When you stabbed him in the groin, you hit the main vein in his leg. He bled to death very quickly."

She'd never intended to kill Rhys. But she wasn't displeased. By killing him, she'd kept him from hurting Gerard.

She stared up at her husband, thinking how dear he was. She would have given her life for him. He'd turned out to be everything she wanted in a man: loyal and courageous. Compassionate and fair. And handsome. She feasted her eyes on his sculpted features. His muscular neck and broad shoulders. His hair had grown out and dark whiskers emphasized the strong shape of his jaw. But even though he was dressed in the garb of a Cymro, he still didn't look like one. It didn't matter; he was the handsomest man in the world to her.

She smiled at him. "You are the one the Fair Folk would want." His eyebrows shot up. "Aye, it's true. I can easily see some fairy queen deciding to beguile you and carry you away her palace under the hills."

"If you think that, your injury has surely affected your wits." He grinned at her and she grinned back. Then he leaned down and kissed her.

CHAPTER TWENTY-ONE

ALTHOUGH GERARD OFFERED more than once to carry her, Marared's father's men used a litter to take her back to where the rescue party had left their horses. There Caradoc finally agreed to let her ride the rest of the way with her husband.

But it was not an easy journey back to Caer Brynfawr for Marared. Even cradled in Gerard's arms, every movement of the horse made her head throb and her stomach pitch and heave. She had to close her eyes and try to think of other things to keep from retching or losing consciousness.

She was trussed on a horse, being taken to the kingdom of the fey. They were stealing her away because it was the only way they could entice Gerard to their realm. He was the one they wanted.

She raised her head and saw him riding ahead of her, dressed in the bright, sumptuous garments favored by the Fair Folk. Satin and velvet in hues of green, his brow encircled with a gold crown glistening with emeralds and diamonds. She imagined how his hazel eyes would reflect the dazzling green of his attire. He rode like a sleepwalker, his body gently swaying with the movements of his horse. His chestnut gelding, Hearthfire, was also decked in splendor, the horse's green bridle and saddle were hung with tiny, golden bells. Their delicate tinkle sounded eerily like mocking feminine laughter.

The terrible foreboding increased. Gerard was deeply ensorceled, trapped in the spell of the fairy queen riding ahead of him. The queen turned back to look at her prize, and a scream of horror rose in Marared's throat. She expected a glamorous visage of beauty to match the woman's long golden curls. Instead the queen's face was a skull, with empty eye sockets and the fleshless grin of a corpse picked clean by ravens.

Marared let out a horrified cry, frantic to get Gerard and wake him before it was too late. Before he disappeared beneath the hills and was never seen again. But as hard as she struggled to go to him, she could not. She was tied down by ropes. Nay, not ropes, but fabric. The more she struggled, the tighter the layers of cloth bound her. She cried out again, tears of frustration seeping from her eyes.

"Hush, my love. 'Tis merely a dream. You are safe."

The world swam back into view. Gerard's dear face filled her vision as he leaned over her, his beautiful eyes moist with tears and stark with tenderness. She was in a bed. At home in Caer Brynfawr. Nay, not home. Her home was with Gerard. Wherever he went, she would follow. She took several deep breaths. There was no fairy queen, no mocking half-corpse trying to steal Gerard. He was safe, and so was she.

"How did I…?"

"You swooned. It worried us, but Hew reassured us that since you'd woken once, you were likely out of danger of being trapped in an unconscious state." He sighed softly. "But you were so pale and wan. So unlike yourself. I was almost relieved when you began to thrash and cry out. It meant you still had the strength to fight your way back to me."

Marared shuddered. "'Twas awful. I dreamed you were being stolen away by the fey. Except it wasn't one of the Fair Folk, but a demon garbed to look like one of them. I tried to help you escape, but I couldn't get to you." Another spasm of remembered dread swept through her.

Gerard stroked her arm. "You should not have been so afraid for me. I would never willingly leave you. The most stunning fey woman in the world couldn't tempt me."

She smiled at him as the terror receded. "The demon queen had enchanted you. You were riding your horse like a sleepwalker, following behind this monstrous being."

"Hearthfire would never have gone along with such a thing. And I'm certain horses are immune to fairy spells."

"Aye. The fey can't ensorcel animals. *They* always know the different between human and sidh."

"Sidh? What is that?"

"What the Irish call the fey. They believe there was once a race of enchanted beings who ruled Ireland and when they were defeated by the first humans, they retreated to beneath the hills. 'Tis very like the legends of the Fair Folk here. So much alike that that it seems there must be some truth to the tales."

Gerard shook his head. "I don't believe in such things. People want to blame evil events on supernatural beings, but I believe humans are responsible for the awful things that happen."

"Like Rhys. He was willing to kill me, if he thought my death would further his ends. He didn't care who suffered."

Gerard's voice was gentle. "He was willing to do anything he could try to free his beloved Cymru from the English. I know a young woman who once looked at things very much the same."

Marared met his gaze, hoping he would understand that she had changed. "That woman was a fool. With a child's view of the world. She has grown up now and understands how complicated things are. There are good people on both sides of any conflict. As well as many who have no say in the direction their lives take either way. To be a true leader means you must consider all your people and what would be best for them. I would love to see Cymru back under Cymric control. But not if it means most of my countrymen would suffer and have harsher lives because of the ceaseless conflict."

"Well said, my love." Gerard smoothed a lock of hair away from her face. "Now I should probably let you rest. You need true, healing rest, devoid of nightmares."

She grasped his hand. "I think I should eat first. My stomach is queasy, but some food might settle it."

"I'll fetch you something."

She squeezed his fingers tightly. "Hurry back. I can't go long without the sight of your handsome face. Simply gazing upon you seems to heal me."

"Whatever you wish, my love."

Gerard slipped his hand from her grasp and left the room. Marared stared after him wonderingly. What a journey she'd been on these past few months. This was the very bedchamber where she had shunned Gerard on their wedding night and made all sorts of silly vows never to acknowledge him as her husband. Now, here she was, feeling absolutely bereft whenever he left her. As if he filled the room with the air and sunshine she needed to live.

Her stomach growled. She touched it, feeling how flat, almost concave it was. How long had it been since she'd eaten? Another gurgle triggered a second thought. She counted backwards. Nearly six weeks had passed since she'd last had her courses. It was very early, and yet she suspected her nausea wasn't merely from her head injury.

She counted forward now, her hand on her belly. Early February meant a babe born around Imbolc, marking the beginning of lambing season. Delightful thoughts of a brown-haired, hazel-eyed babe filled her mind. She had wondered how she could ever feel any happier, and now she knew. There could be nothing more wonderful than having Gerard's baby.

IT TOOK SEVERAL days, but the headaches ceased, and Marared's nausea became manageable if she ate frequently. She felt well enough that her longing for Gerard had changed from a need for comfort to intense desire. But she didn't know how to broach the matter with him. He was so careful of her, as if she might be injured by the slightest touch. She'd finally convinced him to sleep with her, but it was as chaste as their early nights together at Tangwyl. How did she get him to respond to her as a *woman*?

She finally came up with a plan. After getting up and eating in the hall with everyone else, she excused herself. In the bedchamber, she stripped off all her clothes, unbraided her hair, smoothed it over her shoulders, and climbed into the bed.

Gerard came in a short while later. Seeing her in bed, a frown creased his brow. "Are you well? It's very early yet."

"Is it?" She gave him what she hoped was a provocative look and eased the bedcovers down to bare her shoulders and the tops of her breasts.

He gazed at her quizzically, until understanding dawned. "Are you certain? I don't want to hurt you."

"I vow if you don't come here this moment, I will be *very* hurt. Indeed, I might expire of frustration."

He still looked doubtful. She pulled the covers down to her waist and tossed her hair back. She felt bold and wanton. Fearless.

He let out a breath and moved toward the bed. "Should I undress?"

She nodded. "But hurry."

GERARD HAD NEVER disrobed so rapidly. He had to sit on the stool to remove his boots and unwrap the lacings holding up his braies. The rest of his clothing he shucked off.

Weeks of longing for his wife meant his erection was painfully intense. He took a deep breath and reminded himself of all the times he'd dreamed of this moment. In his fantasies, he took his time and savored every breath-taking moment of their lovemaking, leaving no part of her exquisite body unexplored. But how was he to make leisurely love to her when his whole being ached for immediate joining?

"What's wrong? Don't you want me?"

He let out a sharp bark of laughter. "Want you? Nay the problem is I want you far too badly. I fear I will not last. I don't want it to be like that."

She cocked her head and smiled teasingly. "You once told me there was nothing wrong with anything a man and a woman did in bed together, as long as it pleased both of them."

"That's exactly it. I want to please you, not mount you like some rutting stallion driven mad with lust."

She tossed her head like a restless pony. "Mayhaps that's what this mare wants. Mayhaps she doesn't want to wait."

Gerard almost said that mares were not women and the women he'd known preferred a little finesse. But then he realized this was Marared, wild, impulsive Marared. She was telling him exactly what she desired.

Even so, he hesitated. She didn't realize how close he was to losing all control. She was used to the cautious, restrained Gerard, who took no action without careful deliberation.

But he wasn't that man anymore, at least not when it came to her. She had taught him the pleasures of giving in to his feelings. Of letting the river of emotion and passion take him wherever it willed. He gave a swift nod and approached the bed.

Somehow, he still managed to kiss and caress her, even as his body trembled with the strain. To briefly delight in the sweetness of her lips and the pliant, silken magic of her body. But when she rubbed her body against his and moaned into his ear, he could stand no more. He slid his rock-hard shaft into her wet, eager sheath and gave into primal, pounding rhythms. He was a stallion or dog fox, driving into his mate as she keened her pleasure. They were joined, male and female, in the ancient dance of creation.

Afterward, he felt as if he had ascended to the heavens and then returned to earth as gently and easily as a cloud settling over the mountains. He curled against her and buried his face in the warm, fragrant hollow between her neck and shoulder. Never had he known such peace, such contentment.

Marared made a slow sound like a purr and stroked his hair. "See, was that not wonderful? Exactly as it should have been?"

"Aye, it was. For now."

She giggled. "There's more?"

"Oh, aye. Give me a moment or two and you will see."

"You're a veritable beast, my love."

"Only for you, *cariad*. With everyone else I am the most measured and careful and sane of men."

She giggled again and turned to face him. As her breasts brushed his arm, he knew it would not be long until he transformed into her mad, reckless lover once again.

EPILOGUE

Caer Brynfawr, December, 1204

GERARD GUIDED HEARTHFIRE down the trackway from the castle, with Marared riding pillion in front of him. "'Tis very cold. Are you certain you want to do this?"

"I'll be warm enough. I vow, the bigger the babe gets, the warmer I am." Marared's cape barely covered her stomach, but her swelling belly wasn't cold. "But I do feel sorry for Hearthfire, having to carry both of us."

"Even now, I'm certain you weigh less than my armor and weapons when I go into battle. The horse manages that well enough."

They left the valley and began to climb into the hills, Marared let out a sigh of satisfaction. Her breath immediately turned to frozen mist.

"'Tis definitely worth getting up so early to enjoy the dawn. Look how the light has turned everything pink and gold."

Gerard halted the horse. As far as the eye could see, everything was coated with frost, which was now tinted rose and apricot in the shimmering dawn light. Marared snuggled back against Gerard's broad chest. After all the activity of the past few weeks, it was wonderful to share this moment with him, just the two of them.

The sun rose and the magical hues gradually faded. Gerard urged the horse onward. Echoing her thoughts, he said, "'Tis a relief not to have to worry about politics or meetings."

"Or banquets and sleeping arrangements. Without Hilda and Aoife's help, I would never have managed it. It was challenging enough to host your liege lord and his wife, without also having Llywelyn ap Ioworth and his entourage arrive."

"At least Llywelyn didn't bring his wife, so you didn't have to worry about hosting an English princess. And you managed it all beautifully."

"As I said, I had lots of help. Even Lady Nicola offered advice and assistance. You are right, she is amazing. She looks like the epitome of refinement and elegance, yet she is the most practical and efficient person I've ever met. And she is beautiful, of course."

"Not as beautiful as you."

"That is a matter of opinion."

"Mayhaps."

She nudged Gerard with her shoulder. "Most men would prefer to be wed to someone like her, rather than a tempestuous and difficult woman like me. You said yourself you would have a preferred a more ordinary wife."

"Did I?"

"Aye. When we were having one of our early spats."

"Well, we both said some foolish things back then. I'd never met anyone like you, so I had no idea how to deal with you. And you weren't used to men like me, so you assumed the worst about everything I said and did."

"Well you were a *sais*, after all."

"Nay. I was a *filthy sais.*" He chuckled.

She swatted his arm. "Don't remind me. 'Twould seem Aoife and I were wrong on every count."

"I guess now she and Guy are wed, she has discovered that he is also not hung like a fieldmouse."

Marared giggled and swatted his arm again.

"Nor is he a bad dancer. I, on the other hand, have a way to go when it comes to partnering a light-footed sprite like you in a reel or jig."

"Sprite? I thought you said I was a fairy queen?"

"There is some of both in you." He used his free hand to stroke her cheek.

"What do you want our child to be like? You or me?"

"Whatever temperament they have, they will face challenges. If they are bold and passionate like you, they will have to learn to curb their emotions and consider the effect of their words and actions on other people. If they are like me, they will have to learn they cannot control everything in their lives, and the greatest joy sometimes comes from ignoring their thoughts and giving in to their feelings."

"You are wise, milord."

"It took you many months to decide that."

Once again, Marared swatted his arm. Then she shivered. "'Tis colder down here in the valley."

"And it will be colder still at the waterfall. Will it be worth it?"

"I vow, so far the view has been worth freezing over." She nodded to the scenery before them. As the sun rose, it transformed the silvery white terrain to a glittering realm. Oak and elm branches, gorse bushes and hawthorn bushes sparkled in the brilliant sunshine. Even though the frost was melting rapidly, at this moment they were surrounded by a glittering wonderland.

They savored the view a few moments, then Gerard urged the horse on again. "What do you think of Llywelyn's plan?"

"To try to unite all of Cymru? 'Tis what I've always believed we must do. We must stop fighting each other and work together to keep what is left of our country from being swallowed up by the English."

"Do you think it will work? Gwenwynwyn has been thwarted, and Rhys is dead."

"But there is still Maelgwn ap Rhys in the south to consider. Not to mention other men who think as my cousin did. Look at all of the warriors Rhys was able to convince to support him."

"Mostly young men, with no families to consider."

"Aye. There will always be those."

"Well, I am optimistic. Llywelyn is a shrewd and canny man, and he has powerful men on his side. Like the king and of course, Fawkes. And this day, I am in no mood to be gloomy or grim."

They rode on, down into the little glen. As they neared the waterfall, they saw it was frozen, the water turned to white ice, dripping softly as it melted.

"No water sprites today," Gerard said.

"Nor Fair Folk either. They are all safe and warm in their palace under the hills, feasting and making merry."

Gerard halted the horse, slid down and helped Marared dismount. He turned to her. "Ah, but they left their queen behind. The enchanting Marared."

Marared raised her face to kiss him. At this moment, heavily pregnant and garbed in bulky winter garments, she felt as far from being one of the lithe, carefree Fair Folk as she ever had. But all was well.

She was more than content to be mortal and to know the only magic she possessed was the love of a wonderful human man.

About the Author

I am fascinated by history, as well as Celtic myth and legend. These interests inspire and enrich most of my books, both historical romance and historical fantasy. Raised in the Midwest, I currently live in Wyoming with my husband, four cats and a dog. Besides writing and working (I'm employed in a public library) I enjoy gardening, travel and reading, of course!